The dream came as it always did. The enormous black bird turned its dirty, featherless head to regard Fordus curiously. *I name you Firesoul*, the creature pronounced, its words inaudible, yet strangely *felt* by the Plainsman.

"But I am Fordus."

Fordus is a Water Prophet, a nomad, a vagrant. But Fordus Firesoul . . .

Fordus smiled in his sleep. He loved this part of the dream.

Fordus Firesoul is the breaker of armies, the strong arm of the desert. The condor flapped its wings, and hot fetid air, heavy with the strong smell of creosote and sulfur and carrion, coursed over the young man. *Claim your own, Fordus Firesoul. Claim your inheritance.*

"My inheritance?"

Claim Istar.

® Saga

VILLAINS
Volume Six

The Dark Queen

Michael and Teri Williams

DRAGONLANCE®
Villains Series
Volume Six

THE DARK QUEEN
©1994 TSR, Inc.
All Rights Reserved.

Random House and its affiliate companies have worldwide distribution rights in the book trade for English language products of TSR, Inc.

Distributed to the book and hobby trade in the United Kingdom by TSR Ltd.

Distributed to the toy and hobby trade by regional distributors.

Cover art by Jeff Easley. Interior art by Karl Waller.

DRAGONLANCE is a registered trademark owned by TSR, Inc. The TSR logo is a trademark owned by TSR, Inc.

First Printing: December 1994
Printed in the United States of America.
Library of Congress Catalog Card Number: 94-60110

9 8 7 6 5 4 3 2 1

ISBN: 1-56076-925-4

TSR, Inc.
P.O. Box 756
Lake Geneva, WI 53147
U.S.A.

TSR Ltd.
120 Church End, Cherry Hinton
Cambridge CB1 3LB
United Kingdom

For all those who bring their visions to us through music, and most especially the singers of hope, faith, and love.

Many people have helped enrich the making of this book:

We would like to thank Mort Morss and David Kirchoff for valuable information regarding opals, and for their even more valuable friendships.

John and Annette Rice provided a wealth of horticultural knowledge, especially regarding desert and mountain foliage. We thank them for their expertise, and for Sunday afternoons in their home and greenhouse.

Sam and Debbie Vaughn shared their extensive knowledge of hawks and other birds of prey. Debbie's red-tailed hawk, Lucas, is the real-life character upon which Larken's hawk is based. Debbie is a Licensed General Falconer, skilled in an art that has adhered to rigorously defined rules and regulations since medieval times. Falconry is highly dangerous for the uninstructed: we strongly urge interested parties to consult the North American Falconers Association.

We thank our friend Carla V for her artist's skill and eye, and her wonderful photos.

Finally, we'd like to thank Jim DeLong for his support, prayers, and perspective during the long months of writing and revising. Jim, you're a happenin' guy, and it's a blessing to know you.

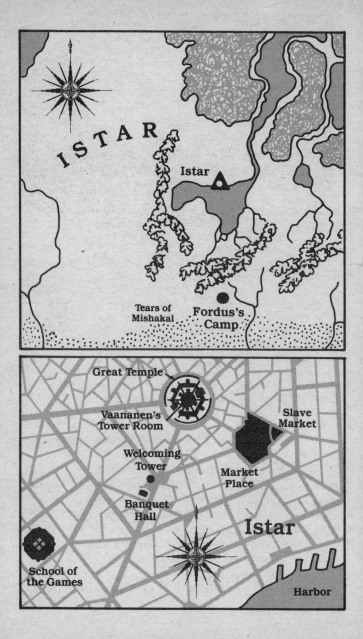

Prologue

Thunder rumbled through the tower's polished opal windows and rattled their thin frames like a Namer's medicine stick.

An answer of lightning flickered over the dry white plains north of the city. Already, sweeping rain fell upon the far port of Karthay and on the bay-side forests toward the harbors of Istar. Here in the city, above the Kingpriest's Tower, the afternoon sky grew sullen and tense, and the brilliant gemstone windowpanes darkened to a deep blue.

From his tower window, opened to the fresh and rising wind, the white-robed man could tell by the sharp scent and expectancy of moisture in the air and the racing, tumbling black clouds that the storm was moving swiftly. He turned to his lectern, to the frail ancient volume that lay open beneath an unlit, solitary green candle, and the new volume, half copied, beside it. The room dimmed suddenly, and a strong breeze threatened the lacy pages as they lifted violently under its force.

Furtively, he closed the window and lit the candle. His moss-green eyes sought the tilt of the door, and he assured himself that it was still bolted. The book was volatile: a collection of druidic prophecies that had been hidden by the most capable of the Lucanesti elves for over a millennium. It had been brought to Istar secretly during the collapse of northern Silvanesti, kept in the recesses of a vintner's private library for years.

The Kingpriest forbade possession of this old, crumbling book and others like it. Copying it promised certain imprisonment, or even worse, for these were the most forbidding of times.

The second year in the Edict of Thought Control.

Outside, the air crackled, and brown pigeons took sudden wing from the garden's pavement. The rainstorm drew closer. It soon would hover and crash over the city, washing the dusty stone streets and the brick alleys, drenching cart and pedestrian, awning and booth, from the sentries on the northern walls to the longshoremen at the southern piers.

Moving south, the man thought. To hover for some time over the lake, before the mountains would catch and stifle it. The plains and the desert beyond them would again be cheated of the soothing touch of water. No rain for them this time.

Perhaps not for months, or years.

Lightning flickered again over the northern sky,

tracing a final, ragged white line between the gray-blue clouds, like a deep flaw in a dark gem. The man shuddered and returned to the old book. In the shadowy room, he began to copy, translating the weblike, interlacing lines of the ancient elven alphabet into a more legible common text, re-forming the prophecy he had copied through the night, a text that had come down to alarming events, to an alarming passage.

He dipped his quill into the ink and cocked his hand. "In that time of the world," he wrote, "when the dark gods are still imprisoned in the vast emptiness of the Abyss, the legends of Istar will claim that all evil is banished forever—that a universal tide of goodness and light has swept across the continent at the coronation of the Kingpriest. All civilized Krynn, the legends will say, stands at the threshold of a silver age, an age of celebration and song, and the softer music of law and ritual.

"It will be the Age of Istar, they say, which a thousand years of histories will praise and exalt.

"The legends, of course, are wrong.

"Wrong about the law, the celebration, the ritual and song. Wrong about the age itself, which historians will remember as the Age of Darkness. . . ."

The man looked up from the book and massaged his temples. Half of the next page lay crumbled into bits, fallen away because of ill-treatment and the book's antiquity. Though he had reconstructed these very pages with care and skill and druidic magic, some passages were irretrievable, the pages on which they had been written either missing or deteriorated into glittering dust.

Dust. Like most of the Lucanesti themselves. The book was as mysterious as the elves who had penned it.

Holding his breath, he turned the fragmented page. Even so, scraps of vellum, light as dust motes, shook loose and hovered above the book, rising in the heat of the candle.

So as not to further disturb the fragile, precious pages, he raised his thick sleeve very slowly and exhaled into it, then read on: ". . . were wrong about the gods. True, the great lance of the hero Huma will strike a near-mortal blow against the Dark Queen . . ."

Silently, the reader marveled. Huma's heroism, a thousand years in the past, lay *in the future* for the ancient writer. This book was over a millennium old. And yet it now read like news of tomorrow.

"This queen, Takhisis of the Many Names, he will banish to the Abyss, where she and her barbarous minions will wait and brood in a sunless chasm, far from the warm and living world they desire to influence and rule.

"To reclaim her power, it would take . . ."

The man swore a mild, silent oath. The text broke off again, the sides of the ancient page lost forever, and words of the prophecy with them.

But perhaps a more powerful spell, he mused. Perhaps I can still reconstruct . . .

But that would have to wait until the others left for the service. Too noisy for now. With a shrug, he picked up where the text continued.

". . . that forms her body from the dust of the planet, restores her entry into the disheartened world. But until that time there will be other ways—faceted, more regular—to enter for a moment, for an hour, though the stay is brief and tantalizing in its brevity.

"Lightning is one way, and the powerful surge of flowing water another. For a time—sometimes a minute, sometimes an hour—the goddess will be able to channel her spark and spirit into a blinding flash in the western sky or the tumble of waters in the dark Thon-Thalas. For that brief and glorious breath, the world will spread before her, green and vulnerable in all its prospect . . .

"And then it will vanish, and what remains for her is Abthalom, her prison in the dark, shrieking swirls of the Abyss.

"Then, on one desert night, well into the reign of the last Kingpriest, the change will begin unexpectedly.

"Will begin like this.

"Reveling in a thunderstorm, riding the jagged lightning over the red mesa south of Istar, Takhisis will watch and exult as the black desert lies exposed to fire and power, and sudden torrential rains—the first in three years, the last ever in the Istarian desert—batter the desolate salt flats at the foot of the Red Plateau. When the lightning strikes the stand of black crystals she will scarcely notice, until the storm subsides and she finds herself hovering, a tiny spark in the heart of a glittering shard.

"How she will remain there, how she can linger, is a mystery unknown to druid or priest. And yet, by this peculiar accident, she will find a way back to the world.

"Oh, yes, the form she takes will be brittle. When she molds her new body into the shape of a snake, of a jackal—finally a woman—it will be a full year before she learns the art, before she can take shape without breaking or crumbling. Even after that, her stays will be short-lived, for without notice her crystalline flesh will crumble to salt, to sand, to dust, and she will be forced back to Abthalom again—back to the swirling darkness.

"To await a housing more amorphous. A home borne of water and slow time and the incantation of a powerful priest."

The man lifted his eyes from the book. Water and slow time? Incantations? Not enough to piece together the puzzle of this prophecy.

But the crystals. He could learn more of the crystals. He bent over the book, reading again.

"But after a dozen years, Takhisis will achieve a foothold of sorts in her old, accustomed haunts. She will dwell in the crystals for days, sometimes for weeks, a malign, animate spark that shapes the glittering stones to whatever form or guise takes her fancy.

"As a woman, as a warrior, as a viper or dragon, she can be all but indistinguishable from flesh and scale and blood. Beware her footprints. The massive weight of a waterless body will make them too deep for her size. And so, in those regions of Ansalon where sand and salt and crystal abound, the Dark Queen will begin to thrive and flourish.

"She will stop revolts and start them, depose a king and set a duke of her liking in his place. She will misdirect caravans across the Istarian desert so that all who travel with them die of exposure and thirst.

"She cannot remain, cannot establish herself, but her new presence will be stronger and remain longer than it ever has in lightning and dreams. Slowly she will regain her influence in Ergoth, in Thoradin, in the court of the Kingpriest at Istar."

The man's eyebrow raised. She would be coming here.

Why not? He had secretly expected it. Quickly he mined his memory—of rain, of the Istarian desert, of the last downpour by the Red Plateau.

Could it really have been twenty years?

She might already be here. With a rising apprehension, he turned the page.

"Takhisis will guard her newfound power jealously, but there will be other gods in the Abyss, just as eager to enter the world and turn the tide of history to their liking."

A sharp rap on the door startled the man. With a desperate, reflexive lurch he slammed the fragile book shut and hid it beneath his austere, blanketed cot.

"I am surprised," he marveled bleakly. "How remarkable."

Inwardly he cringed at the damage he had surely done to the delicate volume.

The lad at the door stood stooped and deferential, apologetic. After a barrage of the boy's tedious and lengthy explanations and many obeisant hand gestures, the man longed for the other servant—the voiceless one.

"The Kingpriest," the boy finally said, steepling his hands, his eyes cast to the floor, "requests the pleasure of your company."

The man nodded, snuffed the green candle, and followed the lad from the room. As they walked down the cool torchlit corridor, toward the Council Hall and the great and ever-pressing business of state, another roll of thunder sounded high above the city, the smell of ozone pressed into the man's nostrils, and the first wave of rain washed over the harbor.

Chapter 1

The Lady shrieked — a shriek that would echo for a century in the Abyss where she hovered on the dark airless currents of chaos. Takhisis furiously snapped her wings and shut her eyes against the vision unfolding before her.

Where had this warrior come from? How had he escaped her notice?

She had to know. And so, raging, she looked again at the man certain to thwart her plans to enter the world in a shape that was her own and would hold its boundaries amid the physics of Krynn.

He was a tall Plainsman, with unusual sky-blue, no, sea-blue eyes that stared past the flaming walls of her coveted Istar. His face was windburnt and ruddy, with a thick stubble of red beard unusual among his people. He wore a massive golden torc, inlaid with black glain opals, its ends knobbed and twisted at his throat.

The opals. So he was protected.

Takhisis guessed him to be about thirty by the faint lines on his handsome, tanned face, by the fine lacing of silver in his auburn hair.

He stood at the gates of a city in flames.

The Kingpriest's Tower burned gloriously, its sovereign dead, its swarm of clergy defeated and scattered like pigs . . .

Except for one. One white-robed figure held his hands aloft in exultation. She could not see the lone cleric's face, but for a moment a hot wind billowed back his sleeves and exposed the red oak leaf tattoo on his left wrist.

Druid. They were always there to vex her.

Then the vision wavered, brushed by the dark wings of another god.

Takhisis whirled in the blackness of the Abyss, her enemy a faint glimmer at the edge of sight.

Already too far away to follow, to punish.

Speed of a god.

But now all of them—the druid, the warrior, the Plainsmen army—faded from view as black fire washed over her vision.

Takhisis shook with another angry scream, but continued to watch as the Plainsman moved into her sight again, his eyes still cool and distant. Now he walked through the burning portals of Istar, to seize possession of all that lay before him. And beyond him.

From the way he moved, the sweep of his massive hand, Takhisis knew this man had never seen a defeat, never cried one tear in the humiliation of surrender.

And then, in the Dark Lady's vision, the shifting blue of those confident eyes turned and fastened on her, and for the first time since the Dragon Wars, since the Great Lance had banished her to this swirling nothingness, she felt the claws of fear rake her heart.

Locked in his stare as the scene dissolved, Takhisis spun in a slow circle, realizing that if she could not destroy him in time his rebel armies would lift her hard-wrought chains from all of Ansalon. This Plainsman would destroy her long and tedious work with the Kingpriest of Istar: her quiet, narcotic presence in the cleric's dreams, the controlled feeding of her plans into his sleeping mind.

The Kingpriest was more powerful than Takhisis had imagined. More learned in lore and godcraft than any mortal in the history of this world. He had barred all the gods from the face of Krynn—all of them, from high Paladine to low Hiddukel, from Zeboim of the seas to the three lunar children. They could return only fitfully, briefly—faint flickerings in rock crystal, in spindrift, at the blazing edge of meteors, or in the latticework of ice.

Then, when the light faded, the meteor cooled or the snow melted, their worldly stay was over, and they returned to Concordant Opposition, to the Ethereal Plane.

To Abthalom, the Abyss, where they shrieked and glided and waited to return.

But the Kingpriest was mortal. He could not last for long beneath the weight of his own momentous spellcraft.

To bind a god is exhausting work, Takhisis thought with a chuckle. They would find him, sooner or later, gibbering in his tower.

Then it would rain fire, and the gods would return.

But if Takhisis had her way, they would return to

find her already in power. They would find her fully enthroned amid her darkest minions, and even the gods would bow to her magnificence.

Already, through her insinuations, the Kingpriest had banished the magic-users, the elves, all bards, and every unorthodox scholar. Philanthropists and intellectuals had been stripped of power and riches, then sold into slavery to the mob of priests who swarmed through the Kingpriest's Tower, seeking favors, preferment, and bribes.

The Lucanesti elves, or what was left of them, the Kingpriest had imprisoned in the opal mines beneath the city, where they slaved to gather more of the fabled glain amid the rising rubble and dust of thirty years' labor.

Next to the Kingpriest, theirs was the most important service to her. For the black glain opals were the key to the goddess's intricate plot.

* * * * *

She had tried to enter the glain opal once.

The gem was filled with moisture, a stony blood that would nourish and sustain her indefinitely in hostile Krynn. *Godsblood*, the Lucanesti miners called it. She could only imagine the power, the havoc. She would be loose upon Krynn, were there a way to inhabit the stone . . .

So in a thunderstorm Takhisis had tried to enter the gem, but the flat black opacity blocked and scattered her energy and light. Shrieking in pain and anger, spread to the eight corners of the air in an explosion of fragmented light, the goddess regathered, tried again.

Was shattered again.

The stone was impermeable, proof against her

priest-bound energies.

But if the smooth, flawless stone were broken . . .

The moisture within it would house her a thousand years.

Godsblood indeed.

That, too, she would put into the hands of the pliable Kingpriest.

* * * * *

Thirty years in the forming had been Takhisis's plans. Three decades as she drew closer and painfully closer to the moment when disastrous, irretrievable events—*Cataclysmic* events, she thought, with a sinister smile—would rise amazingly out of the Kingpriest's droning, everyday policy. It had taken that long to push the city, the continent, the very matter of the world to the edge of a precipice lovely and sheer.

Now she was only five years away, six at most, from that moment when some regular rite or ceremony—a few words changed, along with a powerful magic, and most of all, a fostered, vaunting pride—would collapse the city, the government, the empire, and rend asunder the face of Krynn.

It would be a summoning ritual that would seem harmless and ordinary, perhaps even beneficent to all the clergy by then. But in it, the Kingpriest would chant words that, ten years earlier, he would have found blasphemous, abominable.

He would breathe into the dust of a thousand stones, seeking his dream, his shadow. So that her spirit might move freely in the world long denied her, he would shape her a body from the watery glain dust. And she would be home—on the throne of Krynn, as Istar fell and the world was renewed in chaos.

But all of this would fail, be grievously delayed at best, if the rebels prospered. There would be no compliant Kingpriest if this bearded Plainsman ever saw his campaign through.

Perhaps no Cataclysm.

How could she have missed him!

Her dark wings fanned the liquid void of the Abyss. Light rushed at her suddenly, as great gaps in the fabric of her prison plane opened briefly, tantalizingly on the bright world that Huma and the gods had denied her, and mountains, seas, and deserts rolled under her cold eye.

"There is great power in knowledge, great freedom," Takhisis whispered to herself. Her dark heart yet full of fear, she composed her vast mind to call forth the broken pieces of the Plainsman's history, for in his past, she thought, lay her best weapons against this horrifying future.

The black wind congealed and wavered, and Takhisis spread her wings and rested on its thrumming current. Scanning the past, searching for the key to this mystery, she saw . . .

Nothing. His past had been erased.

Sargonnas again.

Oh, she knew the power behind such veil and vanishment.

Quickly the goddess glanced around, her brilliant black eyes flickering over the gloom, the void. Scavenging wings circled at the edge of sight, and a mocking laughter rose from the darkness.

Sargonnas. *He* wanted to be first as well. But he was a buzzing insect to her, insidious vermin in the barren night.

Takhisis would treat with him later. This redbearded rebel was more immediate, perhaps more dangerous.

The Plainsman was a hunter, no doubt. They all were. And a fighter—else why the great threat to her plans? But there was more. There *had* to be more.

The past denied her, Takhisis rummaged the present of her new adversary. Scenes of a bright and relentless desert rushed at her. Twice more she brushed away the obscuring wings of Sargonnas. When she bellowed, the rebellious god drew back, tucked into the safety of the void.

She had not even discovered his name. Not yet.

She knew he had some kind of power with words. He spoke, and then the tribe moved, always finding the water they needed in their desert travels. She had watched him as he grew older and changed, his words taking on the colors of war, and his adoptive people gathering to make armies of men who respected him and women who not so secretly wanted him. His enemies—goblin and ogre, Solamnic and Istarian—fell before him by the thousands. At the end of every battle, there was a new song sung about this hero.

A small blond singer stood ever at his side, unkempt, her beauty masked by dry wind and miles of travel, a shallow flat drum in her hand and a hawk upon her thin arm. Her features were those of the Plainsmen—the high cheekbones, the deep brown eyes with their intelligent fire. Though she was lithe and long-limbed and gracefully formed, she was rough and awkward in movement, as though unaccustomed to the rule of her own body.

She was small, almost elven, and the white-blond hair was odd, freakish among the dark Que-Nara. She was the kind of child they would, during the Age of Dreams, have left exposed to the elements and fates. At their most merciful, they would have left a child such as she with sedentary villagers, where she would live life as a changeling, an oddity, in a humdrum farming hamlet where no one would ever look at her anyway.

But this one was different. *Imilus*, they called her kind—"gifted outlander." She traveled with the Que-Nara, singing the old songs of their legends, inventing new songs as the stories passed into myth.

There was power in her voice; she could be formidable . . .

Takhisis's laughter rumbled viciously in the dark void.

There was history between these two, the hero and the outlander, a subtle energy that surrounded them, creating a space, a distance. The Plainsman ignored the girl's worship and spoke to her seldomly, foregoing a place beside her at the nightly fires to watch and patrol with his warriors. Occasionally, he even took other women, indifferent to her obvious heartbreak.

More often he spoke to and fought alongside another: a small Lucanesti male, with the dark braided hair and mottled, opalescent skin of his kind.

This elf was ropy and flexible, a sinewy specimen who would never tend toward extra weight. He wore the leggings and tunic of the Que-Nara, yet his overshirt spoke of his own people—dark blue to match the height of the sky, or brown to match the depth of the desert, depending on how you looked at the garment, which way the light caught it.

Another outsider, this elf. And more interesting.

Takhisis chuckled, and the darkness shivered and tilted.

The elf fought without spear or throwing knife or kala. Hands and feet alone were his weaponry—all the protection he thought he would ever need.

Takhisis sighed in relief as the images of these

three continued to flicker and dance in the darkness of the Abyss. The opals protected them all, proof against her magic—the torc of the Plainsman, the skin of the elf.

Nonetheless, all of them were outlanders—all treading a very narrow path of acceptance and power in this tribe of clannish, superstitious people. An easy structure to alter, to invade, to break. The pieces of her plan were coming together.

Ah . . . my fragile, pretty singer, Takhisis cooed to the light-haired girl, your song of Istar's fall at your beloved's hand will never be sung. For he cannot outrun me, the little man cannot resist me, and you . . .

I will shatter your song like glass.

The elf would be easy. Revenge must be what he was after, revenge and freedom for his hostage people.

So it always was for the Lucanesti. In the intricate world of elves, oppression had made them simple, binding them, freeborn and slave alike. She could not destroy them herself—the opalescence of their skin and blood saw to that.

But again and again, the Kingpriest was useful. His mines were filled with the Lucanesti, digging and dying.

Takhisis turned in the great void and laughed low and sweetly. A slight echo of her uncertainty still rang in her ears. She rode the warm, swirling nightwinds of the Abyss through darkness on darkness, darkness layering darkness until those places where light had fled entirely seemed hazy, almost pale compared to the kind of darkness that surrounded them—a gloom of the spirit.

Arcing outward in the perpetual blackness, fluttering her pennons, she dropped straight down ten thousand fathoms, plummeting, falling, dreaming, until at length she floated amid a wild, universal hubbub of stunning sounds, a cloud of confused, disembodied voices, drifting through the hollow dark.

Through that negative plane of terror and chaos, borne on the nightwinds that whirled about her, buoying and buffeting her, indifferent to the continual whining and whirring of voices at the edge of nothingness, murmured the hysterical gnatsong of the damned.

She spread her wings and turned in a hot dry thermal, rising to the lip of the Abyss, to the glazed and dividing firmament beyond which she could not travel. It looked forbidding, mysterious, like thick ice on a bottomless pool.

Like the black face of the raw glain opal.

There, in the heart of nothing, Takhisis banked and glided, aloft on the current of her own dark strategies.

* * * * *

Behind her another shadow glided relentlessly at a safe distance, its own black wings extended like those of a giant scavenger, an enormous predatory bird.

Takhisis's consort, Sargonnas, banished into the Abyss along with his powerful mistress, had hidden in the deepest shadows to observe the same vision billowing out of the darkness. He saw the same burning city, the collapsing tower, and the elf and the girl and the blue-eyed man whom they followed.

And the armies—the irresistible armies—at the outskirts of Istar.

Oh, what Takhisis would not give to destroy this Plainsman hero and his few hundred followers! The upstart rebel was little more than a gifted escape artist now—eluding and fighting the slavers in a desert that his advisors, his oracles, and his own common sense told him not to leave.

But five years from now, when his strength and judgment had matured, when his numbers had increased by thousands and he stood at the gates of Istar, liberating the countless slaves and conquered peoples, his power would be grown so mighty that not even a goddess could stop him.

*   *   *   *   *

The salt flats of the southern desert lay a mile from the boundaries of the Que-Nara's firelight. Called the Tears of Mishakal since the Age of Light, it was an alien landscape to Plainsmen, to barbarians, even to the nomadic desert bandits who skirted its edges with muttered prayers to Sargonnas or Shinare.

Legends had it that those who strayed onto the salt flats rarely found their way back, but wandered the faceless landscape forever. Those same legends claimed that often the unwary traveler was drawn there by the song of the crystals, the contorted, glassy growths that rose from the heart of the flats, through which the desert wind chimed a faint, bizarre music.

None of the Plainsmen camped close to the salt flats, nor did the sentries patrol its borders. Its landscape extended to the blank horizon, as original and pure as it had lain during the Age of Dreams, and the eyes of the Que-Nara, turned north toward the grasslands and the distant Istarian threat, failed to notice a stirring in a nearby cluster of crystals, a twisted, sparkling tree of salt that began to sway and turn.

In the blended light of the three moons—the white, the red, and the unseen black moon, Nuitari—the crystals boiled and blackened, as though an unbearable heat passed through them, welding facet to adjoining facet until the branching facets melded and slowly took on a new shape.

As faceless as the salt flat, anonymous and half formed, it was nonetheless human . . .

Or humanlike.

For a moment it hovered between mineral and life, between salt and flesh, as though something in it warred between sleep and waking, stasis and movement. Then hands and fingers branched from the glossy arms, and the features of the face took sudden shape, as though an unseen sculptor had drawn them from the stone.

The woman moved, and the desert shuddered.

She was beautiful, dark and curiously angular, and naked in the black moonlight.

The woman knelt and scooped up a handful of salt. It poured black through her fingers, shimmering thin like silk, and she wrapped herself in the new, cascading cloth. Magically, her features softened, her skin grew supple and pale, and her amber eyes glittered under heavy, sensuous lashes.

But the hearts of those eyes were black, slitted vertically like a reptile's.

For a moment the woman stood still and practiced breathing as though it were a new and odd sensation. Then she stretched lazily, the silk riding soft and translucent up her pale, perfect legs.

"Oh, too long away," she murmured, and there was a chiming echo trapped in the depths of her voice. "Too long away from Ansalon and from the little world . . .

"If I cannot be opal yet, I shall be salt."

She walked out of the Abyss, out of the dead valley and into the pathless desert, the massive weight of her delicate feet crushing the sunbaked mosaic and parting the winds in her passage.

Chapter 2

Six hundred and more of the sack-robed rebels crossed the northern stretch of sand, the horizon shimmering purple and green in the midday heat.

Twice the scouts shouted forth a warning, sending a nervous flurry through their column. The miscalls were forgivable. After all, the lads were young, masterful on horseback but new to reconnaissance. Mirages they would have ignored a week ago boldly deceived them now.

Towers, they told Stormlight. Towers made of water at the northern edge of sight.

The elf smiled at their rashness, their excitability.

On horseback, hooded against the desert winds, he shielded his eyes and looked to the horizon, where the scouts beckoned and pointed.

"Illusion," he told them. "False light."

He sent them back in the column for refreshment, for shade.

They complied unwillingly, insisting that they had seen the great colored spires of Istar.

Stormlight knew better. The city was thirty miles away, across mountains and the expanse of Lake Istar. Furthermore, Fordus the Prophet had no plan to go there.

Not until he could walk through those gates in triumph.

That would be years and many followers in the future. For now, there was the Kingpriest's army to reckon with.

Stormlight stared across the tawny grassland, toward the north where the bright red star of Chislev rode low over the bunched backs of the mountains.

It was easy in the desert, where he and Fordus read the faceless terrain much like deep-sea navigators decoded the swell and tilt of the waves. It was Stormlight's nature to do so—the sympathy with water and rock that was his inheritance.

However, the fancy, soft generals of Istar had had little chance in the shifting sand and merciless heat.

Remembering it gave Stormlight a savage pleasure.

In late autumn, the Kingpriest had sent an irritated legion south into the desert, with orders to uproot the bandit, Fordus. That expedition had lasted two weeks in the blowing sand, with never a clear sighting of the quarry. Led by a few old fire pits and wisps of hope, the Istarians trudged south to the borders of Balifor where, short of water and exhausted by a dozen nights of fruitless searching, they were easy prey for Fordus's rebel force, which was half their size.

Twenty-seven Istarian soldiers were still missing—their helmets, shields, and bones scattered for miles among the dried, branching riverbeds the Lucanesti knew as the Tine. The rest of the unit had returned to the city with tales of a wolfish, wraith-like commander who could be in three places at once, who moved over sand like the wind and carried a thousand throwing axes on a belt at his waist, all designed by a mage who had vowed that never would a cast miss its target.

Twenty-seven Istarians and a mythology. Small payment for a hundred elves enslaved in the dark undercity, Stormlight thought bitterly. At least Istar would think twice before venturing into the desert again.

This, however, was a new place—the yellow grasslands south of the city itself, as promising as they were dangerous. It would take a full day of riding across their open expanse to reach the foothills, the mountains, and finally the outskirts of Istar. It was unknown country, treacherous and vague, and Fordus had been forced to leave behind more than two hundred of the Que-Nara, devout and basically peaceful Plainsmen whose gods had forbidden them to leave the desert in any act of aggression.

Still, close to four hundred Que-Nara remained with the rebels, proceeding against the warnings of their clerics, and the rest of the invading force was a ragged assembly of bandits and barbarians only lately come to the cause. Now, somewhere between these rebels and the dark foothills waited two proper legions—two thousand members of the crack

Istarian Guard: crossbow, spear, and sword units, along with a cavalry famous throughout Ansalon. Enemy enough to strike fear in the most daring commander.

Yet there was no fear, no hesitation in Fordus Firesoul, the pale-eyed Plainsman, Water Prophet and Lord of the Rebels.

Stormlight set his face in approval.

No fear was good.

After all, had not the Prophet routed the Istarians four, five times in the past?

Easy in the saddle, his translucent skin mottling with glittering green and orange flashes of an early opalescence, Stormlight watched the first shadows of the peaceful blue evening stretch across the level grasslands.

No fear was *very* good.

He cast aside his darker speculations.

* * * * *

In a small advance party not fifty yards away, Fordus the Prophet, on foot as usual, dropped to the ground in midstride. Behind him, two lieutenants and the bard paused and did likewise, Larken muffling the variegated head of her drum with the flat of her callused hand.

"Istar approaches," the commander whispered to them, with no more drama and moment than if he were observing the color of a horse or a strange cast of light in the clouds.

The tiny bard stared toward the foothills, straining to see what Fordus saw through the patch of knife-edged grass. Nothing.

But he knew. Fordus always knew about water and armies.

"If indeed it is two legions, we'll know it by nightfall," Fordus continued. "We'll count the lights of their campfires, like they want us to. Then I'll send Stormlight and six men to scout them closely and part the flesh from the shadows. If they've set enough fires for four legions, they're even more afraid of us than I've reckoned."

And tomorrow? the bard signed with one hand. Fordus lifted his eyes, anticipating her gesture, her question.

"They'll want to meet us in the open fields, Larken, to use their numbers and horse to advantage." The Prophet rose to a crouch, drawing a line with his finger along the sandy ground. "When they see our ragtag troops, only Que-Nara and bandits and a handful of Balifor crossbowmen, they'll think those are all who stand with me."

The lieutenants nodded, oblivious to the softly plodding hooves of Stormlight's horse some distance behind. Long ago they had learned to give their entire attention to their commander, to wait before they spoke.

Stormlight dismounted silently, bade the horse to lie down, and slipped through the circle of squatting rebels.

He knew well his old friend's ways. The plan would be simple, direct, and clean. Fordus was the type who'd take a sword to a knot rather than suffer a second more to untie it.

Yes, simple. And as always, successful. Fordus was no tactician, but in his hands, the most basic maneuvers blossomed to brilliance.

"The desert is with me, wherever I go," Fordus concluded quietly, his gaze focused on a distant place. "And we will bring them the desert, bring them sand and wind and mirrors of air, the deception of birds in the high grass."

One of the lieutenants, a young archer from Bali-for, shifted his weight and stifled a cough. It was always this way when the Prophet spoke in riddles.

But that was where Stormlight's task began. The elf let the Prophet's words settle on the assembled officers, then hooded his eyes with the white, translucent underlids of his people and stepped slightly away from the circle surrounding the chieftain.

"Second eyes," the Plainsmen called them—the white *lucerna* of the mining elves. Through that milky film, legacy of their race, the Lucanesti could see gems in dark tunnels, long veins of water in the heart of the sand . . .

Could see other things as well. The vein of truth in the subtle strata of words and images.

"The Prophet has spoken!" Stormlight proclaimed quietly, standing to survey the wave of mystified faces. The *lucerna* lifting, he raised hands that glittered purple with reflected light. It had come to him again, as it always did, in the midst of murmuring. Like lightning, the meaning of Fordus's cryptic poetry had struck his second in command.

"We'll hide half of you on the flanks," Stormlight continued, "and close around the Kingpriest's army when they charge. Gormion will command the southernmost troops, and when the Istarian lances contact her lines . . . the rest of us will spring out of the grass behind them. And may the axe of Jolith cleave through their ranks! There will be such a storm of sand and wind as never they have seen, and it will not touch us. The powers gather already." He pointed into the distance, where a rising cloud of dust marked the southern horizon. A hot breeze began to blow from the same direction.

The *sterim*. The wild desert storm that raced up into the Istarian mountains, gathering speed as it coursed over the plains, blinding and fierce in its fury. The elf's eyes glazed over, the brilliant *lucerna* closing once more, this time protectively against the anticipated wind.

Fordus's lieutenants nodded. These words they understood. As always, the plan was simple and elegant and practical—the poetry of war translated by the strange, exotic Stormlight.

It would work. They would "bring the desert to the Kingpriest," and his army would fall. It did not matter if they understood all of the words of the prophecy. They would win the battle.

Excitedly, brandishing their weapons and murmuring boasts and promises, the lieutenants dispersed into the ranks of the rebels. Only three remained: Fordus, Stormlight, and the bard.

"Where is the enemy now?" Stormlight asked, crouching by the commander. "What does the hawk say, Larken?"

The bard held his odd gaze for a moment and then motioned with her hands. *Three miles to the north, Stormlight. Lucas says they are three miles to the north. That's all you need to know.*

Stormlight and Fordus exchanged puzzled glances as the girl trotted away to join the receding column of troops.

"Larken hates me, doesn't she?" Stormlight asked, a crooked smile pleating his smooth and ageless face.

The commander shrugged. "Of course not, Stormlight. She's just poetic and high-strung. And you know she can only sing. It is a frustrating and sad thing when your hands must speak for you." He looked off over the northern plains.

"Temper or temperament, it's all the same," Stormlight concluded, following the commander's gaze into level, grassy nothingness. "But the Kingpriest is at hand. There's no time. The wind is rising."

* * * * *

The night passed in a haze of hot wind, and few of them found sleep in its discomfort.

But they were ready. Shortly before dawn, Stormlight crouched in the high rustling grass, watching as the Istarian commander signaled to raise his battle standards—the white tower on the red banner—in the weak morning light. The elf slowed his heartbeat, his breath shallowing until he stood motionless, his skin collecting sand and ash from the passing wind, crusting and knotting. Serenely, he sank into a stony quietude, indistinguishable from a thousand stones that littered the rubble-strewn edge of the desert.

When the Istarians had passed, he would slip from the stone disguise, appear in their midst with surprise and havoc.

The elf rises out of the ground . . .

His company of followers, the Que-Nara, hid in the high grass behind him, their faces painted brown, black, and yellow to match their flowing robes, the hard shadows, and the first slanting rays of the sun.

He was the rock amid the reeds. He was the stony heart of the army.

The left flank of the Istarian infantry passed not fifty feet from where Stormlight and his party lay hidden. The horsemen spread out before the advancing army, a dark-haired Solamnic Knight in the vanguard with three of his subordinates.

It was just as Fordus had predicted. The desert storm had gathered; a huge cloud of sand and hot blasting wind scoured the edge of the battlefield, seeming to await his command. The Kingpriest's army consisted of two thousand infantry, five hundred archers, and five hundred cavalry, among those a division of Solamnic Knights—the most formidable cavalry in the world. And yet the expected army looked curiously dwarfed, diminished, as though half its number had deserted in the night.

Stormlight stood serenely in the howling storm as the horsemen passed and the legion followed, heads lowered against the harsh, corrosive wind.

The *sterim* had allied itself with the rebels. Whenever an army arrayed itself against Fordus, it seemed that even the weather plotted to shape the fortunes of the day.

* * * * *

Fordus stood on a rise, in waving knee-high yellow grass, and faced the advancing Istarians. Brandishing a vicious-looking short axe, he shouted to his troops, challenged the approaching Solamnic cavalry . . .

Then he ducked and vanished.

The Solamnic outriders gaped and scanned the ranks, but Fordus was gone, true to his ghostly legend. Almost at once, a volley of arrows and stones rushed to meet them. Raising their shields against the onslaught, they forgot all about the rebel commander.

Meanwhile, Fordus slipped and dove through the high wind-driven grass. He moved swiftly, in a crouch, racing through the no-man's-land between the armies into the midst of the Solamnic horse. He weaved almost soundlessly amid churning legs and huge equine bodies, bound at unnatural speed for the western wing of his army—Larken's wing, waiting in hiding along the right Istarian flank, with the bard's hawk spiraling above like a solitary predator.

Running with uncanny, sure instinct, he sidestepped the first Istarian legionnaires, the blare of their trumpets canceling his soft footfalls on the dry ground. It was the moment of battle he loved, the first confusion in the enemy ranks, when he reveled in his fleetness of foot, his gift from the gods, his greatest deception, racing from one place on the field to another far-flung outpost with the speed of an antelope or the leopard that pursued it.

He ran so swiftly that survivors would claim that Fordus Firesoul was in two, three places at once. That he was not even human, but a phenomenon—a prince of the air and the shifting weather.

Crouching even lower, nearly tunneling through the rustling waves of grass, Fordus raced by the last of the cavalry so closely that his shoulder brushed against the white flank of a Solamnic mare. Into the far field he rushed, and suddenly two shadowy forms emerged from the nodding undergrowth.

Istarian infantry. Swordsmen.

In one immaculate movement, Fordus plucked a throwing axe from his belt and, scarcely rising from a crouch, launched it with a whirling sidearm motion at the head of the man on the right. The blade flashed neatly beneath the Istarian's chin, and, wheeling through the air in a bright red spray, embedded itself in the other man's back. Both soldiers gaped and fell to their knees, their arms jerking grotesquely at their sides.

As their eyes glazed over, the rebel passed between them and recovered his axe with no further resistance.

Just as Fordus reached his troops, he heard the Solamnic war cry from behind, answered by a whoop from the Que-Nara, the shrill trumpets of the charging Istarian infantry, and finally the sudden clash of metal against metal as the armies closed and the first serious combat began.

Rising to his full height, Fordus peered over the whipping grass as the rear guard of the Istarian army broke ranks and rushed to join the battle. He saw the enemy's battle standards dip and nod as the last of them breasted the tall grass, bound for the heart of the struggle. The cloud of wind-driven sand moved onto the field just as they reached it.

Fordus chuckled softly. It had all worked according to his plan. In five minutes, maybe less, the two flanks of his army would rise from hiding and attack the Istarian army from behind. Assaulted from all sides, blinded and coughing, the Istarian soldiers would battle surprise and chaos as well as his seasoned rebels.

The trap was baited, sprung, and closing. It was magnificent, clean and swift, like the tumble of a well-thrown axe through the air. And it was all too easy.

* * * * *

In a matter of minutes, the battle was decided, though the sandstorm raged through the whole afternoon.

When the Twelfth Istarian Legion hit the center of the rebel lines, Stormlight sprang from the rock-cloak and signaled his troops. The Que-Nara forces struck the reserves viciously with a flanking attack. Armed with the traditional weapons of the plains— bow and bola and hook-bladed kala—they tore fiercely into the unexpecting ranks. Reeling from the sudden onslaught, the Istarians panicked. The legionnaires dropped pike and sword, shield and broadaxe, and fled before the reckless barbarians, the fleet Plainsmen.

Fighting with no more weaponry than his hands and feet, Stormlight cut his way to the midst of the Istarian ranks, the stony crust of his skin slashing arm and leg and throat like a fierce, serrated blade. Spinning around a grizzled lancer, he felled a swordsman with a crisp stroke of his hand. Two mercenaries rushed to meet him. He dove between the baffled pair, and as they turned to strike, the elf drove his heels into their faces with a quick, power-ful handspring.

Bounding to his feet, Stormlight spun high in a circle, his right foot catching yet another Istarian lancer in the throat. The man's javelin broke as he fell, impaling him and finishing what Stormlight had begun.

With a deep breath, the elf looked around. There, on horseback, vainly trying to rally his troops, Gen-eral Josef Monoculus caught sight of the charging Stormlight and drew his ancient Solamnic sword to receive the rush of the enemy. With a cry and a cart-wheeling leap, Stormlight hurtled through the air, his heel crashing against the side of the general's helmet.

With a soft groan and unfocused eyes, the Istarian commander fell heavily from the saddle. Stormlight bounded onto the horse's back and, raising a broken Solamnic standard, rallied the rebels to this spot in

the center of the fight, laughing and singing an old
Abanasinian war song.

* * * * *

The men whooped when they saw Stormlight rise
in the fallen commander's saddle. Descending from
the grass-covered rise, they struck the leaderless
Istarians from the other flank, dealing quick death as
they slashed through the disorganized lines.

From the high ground, Fordus watched a little
absentmindedly as the rebels and the storm closed
like a vise around the floundering legions of Istar.

He saw the bird dive toward a distant cropping of
high grass, an Istarian archer level his bow at the
creature . . . And then, with a blinding magic that
still bedazzled the rebel leader, no matter how many
times he had seen it happen, Lucas vanished into a
fireball, into a nova of red and amber as though the
sun itself had opened and swallowed the bird.

The hawk would return later, from the high air. It
would bear stories to Larken of how the Istarians
had fled from the desert rout.

In the wake of the golden flame, a rider in Solamnic armor burst free of the chaos, galloping north
toward the foothills, toward safety.

Toward Istar and reinforcement, the bard's fingers
snapped out inches in front of Fordus's face. *There is
only one man who can outrun horses, outrun wind and
light and thought . . .*

Stirred by Larken, Fordus gathered himself again
and loped down the rise, gaining speed as he
reached the plain. He struck an angle to the path of
the rider, then broke into an all-out run, blazing
through the dry grass at astounding speed.

From the high ground, Larken watched and

marveled and chanted, her song weaving through the drum's swift cadence until word and rhythm were indistinguishable, seeming to drive the heartbeat of the racing man as he closed with the rider.

When the Solamnic horse refused to hurdle the banks of a dry creek bed, its rider had to rein the animal down the hard, sloping incline, losing valuable time in the process.

Fordus raced to the bank and stopped. Standing only fifty feet from the Solamnic, he drew his axe and sent it whistling through the air at the struggling rider.

The axe drove home between helmet and breastplate. Without another breath, the man slumped forward in the saddle, and the heavy Solamnic helmet toppled from his head.

This was no knight. All of fifteen, he was, if that old.

Larken, on the high ground a thousand yards away, saw the boy drop from the saddle, a shiny streak of red spreading from his throat onto the sand.

The drum head felt cold and alien beneath her fingers, and her hands trailed off into soft, mournful sounds.

* * * * *

The flanking attack of the rebels demolished the hapless Istarian infantry. By early evening, when the air had cleared and the sand resettled, General Josef Monoculus, his right eye heavily bandaged, stood propped between wounded Istarian regulars as he handed his sword to Fordus Firesoul. No more than two hundred of the Istarians survived; the prisoners would be taken to the desert's edge and set free, forced to travel the thirty miles to Istar unarmed and on foot. The sand from the storm had already covered the dead.

Stormlight thought of the harsh trek across the grasslands and looked toward the defeated soldiers. Some of the Istarians would not survive; hunger and thirst and exhaustion would dispatch a small number, and wild animals and bandits would seize a few more. But even a safe return to Istar did not mean that their ordeal was over. Many would fall prey to the *grashaunts*, the strange insanity that came from too long a stay in level and wide places. These wretches suffered from the delusion that the world around them was expanding, that if they strayed too long out of sight of home or friends, the distances would increase, and they might never find their way back. Such madmen would return to Istar, never again leaving the close confinements of barrack or cubicle or cell. They would waste away by their windows as they stared fearfully out into an uncertain world that was always receding.

It was true: Fordus treated his prisoners sternly. The road ahead of the defeated legionnaires was the most perilous one.

But not unfair. Indeed, the plains might treat them better than would the comrades and leaders who awaited their return to the city.

Istar brooked no failure, no weakness, and what was defeat but failure and weakness?

Rubbing his arm, bruised in dispatching a rather large and thickly armored Solamnic, a concerned Stormlight watched his commander.

Fordus stared beyond the sullen Solamnic, beyond the assembled, defeated Istarians . . . to a point on the horizon no man could see.

Stormlight shivered. Fordus had gone again to

that place where none of them—not even the bard Larken with her voice and drum—could reach him. When the sea-blue eyes fixed pale in the distance, sometimes all life would seem to flee from them. They glittered, then, like ice, like cut glass, like the salt crystals rising from the desert flats, and there was no warmth in their light, no heart behind the eyes' brilliance. What Fordus wanted, what he looked toward, Stormlight did not know.

"I accept the surrender of General Josef Monoculus," Fordus intoned by habit, the eyes of all resting rapt upon his windburnt, impassive face. "And I accept the surrender of his legions."

He waved his hand dramatically over the attendant rebels.

"And let those who lost dear friends," he pronounced, "console themselves that the losses were few and in my just and glorious cause."

For a moment his voice faded away, caught on a high northerly wind and carried into the mountains to lose itself in thin air and desolation.

Stormlight looked at his commander sharply. *Console themselves with few losses?*

His just and glorious cause?

Now Fordus rose to his full height above the wounded Josef Monoculus and his trembling Istarian supporters.

"And at this hour tomorrow," Fordus continued, "I shall grant these men unconditional freedom." The sea-blue eyes descended to the general, regarded him softly, warmly.

There! Stormlight thought with a strange and sudden relief. Fordus is back among us.

"Your arms will be . . . confiscated, sir," Fordus explained, quietly and kindly. "You will be allowed to keep your armor and your provisions. Steer by

Chislev and the sunrise."

"I *know* how to find my way across this damned wasteland!" the Solamnic growled.

"Then find it with my blessing," Fordus replied. He smiled absently, and Larken's drum began a slow, somber march. The Istarian troopers guided their commander back into the circle of his men, and mournfully, the defeated legion stacked its arms before the inconsolable general.

It would be the Games for him back in Istar. The doomed gladiatorial struggle against barbarian, dwarf, and Irda. The fortunes of Josef Monoculus had risen, had fallen.

There was some moral here, some fable for the devout, the scholarly. But being neither bard nor cleric, Stormlight climbed to the top of the rise and merely watched the sun set, his thoughts lulled by the warm light on his face and by the steady report of Larken's drum.

* * * * *

Fordus sat in the shadows as the sun descended.

A barbarian youth, schooled for a year as the commander's orderly, untied his boots, and Fordus reclined broodingly, his big hands interlaced behind his head.

A song to cheer you? Larken signed. There was a verse she had saved for this day, this victory, and she wanted the last of the sun for its singing.

"No cheerful songs this evening, Larken," Fordus murmured.

The melancholy had come upon him after the armored rider had fallen. He had watched the dead boy for a moment, the blood-matted blond hair waving forlornly in the whistling, hot wind, the horse wandering lazily off down the dry creek bed.

As Lunitari rose over the grasslands, purpling the waving grain with a slanted, bizarre light, Fordus brought himself back to the present. "I am tired of *too easy*," he said aloud, and the bard cocked her head alertly, reaching for the drum.

"No songs about Fordus Firesoul tonight," he said.

Larken nodded.

"Sing of Huma," Fordus urged. "He had someone to fight. Someone to test him, heart and wit and hand. Sing of Huma."

Her small hands tapping the rim of her precious drum, the bard began:

> *Out of the village, out of the thatched and clutching*
> *shires,*
> *Out of the grave and furrow, furrow and grave,*
> *Where his sword first tried the last cruel dances of*
> *childhood . . .*

Larken's was a soaring voice, a firm and powerful instrument that erased time and space. Fordus closed his eyes and settled into the old story, which ran its course under the bard's skillful rendering.

"Those were the times," he said, the song ended and the drum silent after a last, fading roll. "The times and the great adventures. When the shape of the story was larger than the lives of men.

"We have fallen on meaner times, Larken. The great villains are gone, and the great heroes. Who will stand against me now?"

They both fell silent as the rising red moon streaked the tents of the Plainsmen. Overhead, in a last circling flight before evening, Lucas called and banked in the light westering sun, amber rays still dancing over the tips of his wings like mastfire.

"Josef Monoculus was a fool," Fordus declared. "So are all the Istarian generals, all the fabled and fine Solamnic commanders. But perhaps the Kingpriest . . ."

He propped himself on his elbows, stared eagerly at Larken.

"Perhaps the Kingpriest!" he said again. "For he is a mystery who stands at the head of a great army. He is not only a man—he is a great and wondrous idea.

"And he speaks with the gods, as do I. Or so the Istarians say."

Fordus stroked his red beard thoughtfully.

"I pray that he is worthy of me. A man must have great enemies when his friends are small. If he has neither enemy nor friend to match his noble spirit, he is straitened, imprisoned. Forced to grow crooked in confinement.

"Without a worthy enemy, the world is a damnable wasteland."

For a long time he scanned the darkening camp below, and the sun sank from view, and only the red moon rode in the desert sky.

Chapter 3

By day Fordus's world was barren, sun-beaten, a country of exotic colors—of red and black rock and ochre earth and of hazy white salt flats, their crystals rising over the lifeless landscape like frozen, abstract trees. It was a country of extremes and sharp edges, of large sufferings and small deaths.

It was the desert night that Fordus loved most, especially when red Lunitari rode high overhead. In the darkness, the desert was transformed. The desolate landscape deepened with shadows, the salt flats glittered like discarded gems, and strange, nocturnal creatures ventured out of the dried arroyos. The air became temperate, almost cool, and sometimes a stray wind coursed over the dunes, bearing in its wake the faint whiff of cedar from Silvanesti or salt from the seas south of Balifor, snaking over the flats and the dry arroyos as though seeking water, or a body into which it could breathe its distant life.

The night sands were Fordus's refuge and his school, his peace and his nourishment. And so, after every victory, he returned to them.

But this time he returned in doubt and double-mindedness. His long robe wrapped around him, he dreamed. This night it was the lava dream—vivid and long known to him—the same dream that had first come to him at the edge of the Tears of Mishakal a year ago.

This dream had exalted him, lifted him from a destiny of water prophecy, a station of more importance than he'd ever dreamed or sought, and made him king of the desert.

The dream came as it always did—every detail the same as it had been the first time. And his response, as well, was the same, as though he acted in an ancient ritual play, performing an eternal seasonal role: Lord Winter, perhaps, or Branchala in the intricate elf-dramas Stormlight had told him about.

As always, the landscape grew red and took on a fiery quality. Molten, volcanic, it bubbled and boiled with a strange, unnatural vigor. In his dream, Fordus followed the narrow, arching bridge above the roiling lava flats, and at the other end of the bridge a dark cloud hovered, like an opening into the void.

Then the dark cloud unfolded. Black wings took shape in the shadows, and the cloud rolled and kneaded like the hot lake below.

Now the enormous black bird perched on the narrow bridge, turning its dirty, featherless head to regard him curiously, eagerly.

I name you Firesoul, the creature pronounced, its words inaudible, yet strangely *felt* along the muscle and tendon of Fordus's arm. He did not hear the voice as much as *touch* it.

"But I am Fordus," he said. He always said that.

Fordus is a Water Prophet, murmured the shadowy bird, steam rising from its matted pinions. *Fordus is a nomad, a vagrant.*

But Fordus Firesoul . . .

Fordus smiled in his sleep. He loved this part of the dream.

Fordus Firesoul is the breaker of armies, the strong arm of the desert. The rightful heir to marbled Istar.

The condor flapped its wings, and hot fetid air, heavy with the strong smell of creosote and sulfur and carrion, coursed over the bridge.

Claim your own, Fordus Firesoul, it murmured, and Fordus felt the words in the tips of his fingers.

Claim your inheritance.

My inheritance?

Claim Istar, commanded the bird. *There you will find the source of your being. You will find your origins. And you will discover who you really are.*

* * * * *

In the dark of early morning, Fordus awoke reassured, satisfied. He lay amid the rubble atop the Red Plateau, the highest point in the Istarian desert, as the eastern stars swam over him. He was alone except for a solitary guard, a Que-Nara spearman who drowsed, in untroubled oblivion, at his post.

Fordus let the man sleep in peace. The sentry had earned that much.

So had all the rebel army.

The short battle, despite the Istarian surrender, had exhausted them all, had claimed the lives of many. They had carried threescore from the fields, and for others, whose wounds were too great, they left blessings, full waterskins, and a death watch of loved ones.

Stormlight had come to him at sunset with the tidings. Two hundred and six rebels lay dead in the grasslands.

"Istar can lose three thousand," Stormlight warned him. "And three thousand again. What does the Kingpriest care for the wailing of widows? But two hundred is a grievous loss for us."

Fordus sat up, draping his long, powerful arms over his knees. The distant planets of fiery Sirrion and blue Reorx slowly converged over the tipped cup of Solinari, the white moon. He wished he could read the augury of stars, but the sky was opaque to him, for all its beauty.

Who knew the future from the shifting heavens? Not even Northstar, the tribe navigator.

And the mysterious glyphs Fordus had found in the kanaji, the ancient symbols that resonated in his thoughts and stirred him to the strange poetry . . . that stirred the armies in turn?

Well, the glyphs had not returned. The wind had passed over the fine, soft sand, and the kanaji's floor had remained faceless, unreadable once more.

Four hundred Que-Nara awaited his return from battle, pitching camp beneath the Red Plateau at the edge of the Tears of Mishakal. Though their gods had told them not to follow him out of the desert, that invasions and wars of aggression were iniquitous and wicked, they waited nonetheless. No one deserted Fordus Firesoul.

They would stand beside him in the sands when

the time came, braving Istar, Solamnia . . .
. . . the gods themselves . . .
. . . only if he, Fordus Firesoul, asked them to.

He thought of ungainly Larken, lovely beneath the grit and rawness, of her mute, unquestioning devotion. Then there was Stormlight, to whom he had given a measure of importance, and Northstar, whose confusion he had calmed.

He felt a strange emptiness as he stood above the rebel watchfires—the barbarian blazes interspersed amid the muted, efficient glow from the Plainsman camps like diffracted light on the face of a polished gemstone.

They would follow him, bandit and Plainsman both. But where would he lead, if the sands told him nothing?

* * * * *

Throughout her childhood, Larken had scavenged at the edge of the camps, companion to the dogs and birds of the Que-Nara hunters, able to imitate any sound she heard, outcast because of her freakish coloration and her constant vocal disturbances.

Again and again the Namers awoke to the sounds of dogs outside the tent, the dry hiss of the spring-jaw and the underground rumblings of the spirit naga. Arming themselves hastily and blearily with warding spells and the hook-bladed kala, they would emerge from the tents . . .

And find the little girl, singing all of these sounds uncannily into the night air, her matted, tangled hair an eerie white in the glow of the campfires.

Sending her away seemed the best thing to do, so that she could be among her own kind. As her unusual looks marked her as threateningly gifted, normal life in the tribe was an impossibility. Her parents could hardly contain their relief at her departure. It was, of course, for her own good.

Her gifts blossomed in a foreign country. She had come to Silvanesti natively superior to most of her instructors, intent and tireless at her songcraft. She rose through the great Bardic College of Silvanost too fast for everyone, until she was above them all.

Larken readily learned the first eight bardic modes, the traditional arrangements of note and rhythm that carried the bardic songs. She studied diligently and alone, as was her way, far from the flarings of temper and temperament displayed by her fellow students. As the bardic initiates, the high Silvanesti and the noble Solamnics, the Istarians and the western elves from Qualinesti, bickered and plotted in the tall towers of Silvanost, the girl sat by the waters of the Thon-Thalas, her knobby, callused feet submerged in the dark current, practicing the songs in her harsh, flexible soprano.

They had laughed at her, elf and highborn human alike. Called her "churl" and "guttersnipe." She ignored them serenely, mimicking the sound of floodwaters in the quarters of discomfited masters, the chitter of black squirrels in the vaults of the tower, which sent apprentice and novice alike up ladders with brooms. All the while, despite her echoes and pranks, Larken's thoughts remained serious, intent on the intricate bardic music.

By her second winter she had mastered all eight of the modes, mastered the drum and the nillean pipes, and most of all developed and strengthened a soprano voice that, though never melodious, never beautiful, left her teachers breathless, admiring its power and range.

Admiring, and fiercely resentful.

In the groves along the Thon-Thalas, where elf and human still mingled in green and quiet, the subject of her voice produced a jarring note of controversy. No student, the masters maintained from their green solitudes, especially no gritty slip of a girl from the plains, had ever learned the modes in only six seasons. There was foul play, no doubt—some hidden magic. It was not right.

Yet Larken learned *all* the modes, swiftly and readily and gracefully. Soon she tired of the traditional modes and began on the veiled ones, the intricate magical music that dwelt in the gap between audible notes. She learned the first four—the Kijonian for happiness, the Branchalan for growth, the Matherian for serenity, and then, alarmingly, the Solinian mode of visions and changes.

At a recital, when her mighty voice changed table water into snow, her teachers took the threat in hand.

In a ceremony usually saved for the seventh year, five green-robed bards—representing earth, air, fire, water, and memory—ended her brief apprenticeship. They all said it was for her own good, so that she could sooner return to her own kind.

She received the lorebook and her chosen companion, a young hawk she named Lucas—an outlandish bird whose bright green eyes, strikingly unusual for his species, promised that he could be schooled to magic.

The next decision rested with the college: the instrument, to be presented to the graduate by the resident bards of high Silvanost.

Larken had fully expected a drum, since that was the perfect musical complement for her voice, rough and rhythmical, the instrument of her people when they summoned the water or prepared for a distant battle. Yes, the drum would be most fitting.

But they gave her the lyre instead.

How appropriately taunting, they mused. A chamber musician's pretty little harp. A stringed dainty to be used to soothe some lord from his day's troubles. An instrument of peace, a fine thing if in the hand of one who cared not for battle and the rising of the blood and the clash of war.

They had chosen her trophy with a last, biting meanness in mind, and the message was clear: Be quiet, and be gone. To ensure this, they consulted a dark mage near Waylorn's Tower, a Master Calotte, who, with a curious smile, gave them the harp, and then loaned them his preoccupied apprentice to burden the young bard with a binding curse.

Larken could never compose an original melody, said the curse. A talented mimic, she was sentenced to mine her memory for songs recalled and half heard in a marginal childhood and in as marginal a stay at the bardic college.

But the apprentice botched the complicated spell. Nodding over the components, he mixed one moss with another, then reversed two words in the long incantation, so that although Larken was cursed to compose no original music, only her *spoken* words were affected, discredited. That seemed bad enough, for whenever Larken spoke, she spoke discordantly. Those around her thought they heard only the wind, or they forgot instantly what she said.

So her masters had promoted her and abused her at the same time. They set her on the road, far from Silvanost and the haunts of the Thon-Thalas, bound in a last tutelage to Arion Corvus, a master among traveling bards. When that was done, Larken was sent home, far more angry than when she'd left.

But old Corvus was wise, and knowing in the way

that a bard is knowing. At Larken's departure, he gave her the drum she carried now—a light, sturdy instrument with a head of sheer glain opal.

The drum was stone, and the sound from it was muffled, even ungainly. But Corvus insisted that it was the drum for her.

Muffled. Ungainly.

And *useful*, he added, a strange gleam in his ancient eyes. The drum is your companion. It will protect you.

Since that time Larken had wandered with the Que-Nara. Now she was Fordus's bard. She had come to sing the cause of the downtrodden, come to stand with him against the cold white rigors of Istar and its adamant righteousness, to free the thousands of Plainsmen who wore the collars of Istarian slavery.

She believed Fordus could eventually break any curse, even her misplaced one. She was the muse of sand and plateau and arroyo, taking the deeds of a rebel commander and breathing them full of poetry and legend and light. Through her song and the thousand cadences of her odd glain drum, Fordus the Water Prophet had become Fordus the Storm, Lord of the Rebels . . . Fordus the hero.

Still, the curse of Calotte's apprentice stayed with her, and when Larken spoke, her words fell into a great void. The result of this ludicrous situation was that she never spoke at all anymore, except to Lucas. The hawk seemed to understand her words, no matter how jumbled they sounded to human ears. Over the years she had invented a form of sign language nearly everyone could understand, and she had learned how to write in glyphs, runes, and common letters.

All the while, the magic of her music grew ever

more powerful. Her song remained loud and clear
and perpetually true, and sometimes it seemed to
border on prophecy when the marveling Plainsmen
heard it at the start of a hunt or a battle.

When her song rose to prophecy, it was as though
the desert blossomed, the arroyos filled with the
waters of the sung rivers, and the stars shifted in the
winter sky, Branchala's harp brilliant on the northern horizon. It was as though all prophecy
resounded in its ancient strings. They could not but
choose to listen, then, from the most wretched tone-
deaf bandit to Stormlight himself. Even Fordus
would turn to her and stare, with those sea-blue
desert eyes, and believe completely everything that
she sang about him.

And wonder if he could ever afford to set her free.

* * * * *

At the campsite the men were gathered—bandit
and barbarian and Plainsman, bound by wounds
and dirt and exhaustion, their eyes fixed restlessly
on the heights of the Red Plateau where the Lord of
the Rebels kept lonely vigil.

Larken slipped into the firelight, seating herself
between Stormlight and her cousin Northstar, the
slender young Plainsman who steered the Que-Nara
across the broad, featureless expanses of the Istarian
desert, guided by stars and prayers. Northstar
regarded her defiantly. At first he had refused to
accompany Fordus into the grasslands and had
matched words unsuccessfully against Larken's
battle song. Larken liked almost everything about
her cousin, from his quiet intelligence and resourcefulness to the hawk tattoo on his shoulder. And she
loved him in spite of his irritating piety, as strict and

somber as any Istarian's.

She shot him back a crooked smile. Northstar turned proudly away, and Stormlight's greeting, as usual, was little more than an uneasy nod. With a shrug, Larken settled in between the men and drew forth her drum. Lucas alit drowsily on her gloved arm, and she settled him on his ring perch, where he fluffed and fell quickly asleep, lulled by the warmth of the fire.

Across the circle, one of the bandit leaders, her long black hair glinting red from the firelight, was speaking loudly. Larken searched for memory. The woman's name was something harsh, unpleasant . . .

Gormion.

Yes. It fit her. The jumbled Tarsian name, taken when the woman had left the Que-Nara seven years ago. She was back now, at the head of a company of Thoradin bandits, momentarily allied with the rebels.

"He should never have been made Water Prophet, Stormlight," Gormion hissed. "You were there ten years ago. You know it's true."

"He prophesied," Stormlight declared, "and his words drew a map to the water. I would call that water prophecy. I would call *that* true."

"My grandfather should have been . . ." Gormion began. It was the same old story of strife and complaint. Old Racer had considered himself passed over by Fordus's father, and had voiced his complaints until his dying day. His sons, the oldest of whom was Gormion's father, had left the Que-Nara in anger, seeking residence among bandits in the Thoradin foothills.

Only in this discord did Gormion, granddaughter of Old Racer, acknowledge her Plainsman blood.

"Nor is he a better general," she spat, dark hands

waving in the glow of the firelight, a dozen stolen silver bracelets spangling her wrists. The bandits on either side of her, two rough men named Rann and Aeleth, could only nod in agreement since their mouths were stuffed with the bread Fordus had provided. "Retreat. What else do you call it," she continued, "when an army goes forward, fights, and falls back?"

"Repentance," Northstar replied, staring long into the fire.

"We obviously did not win," Gormion concluded with a sneer. "For we have retreated, and our commander repents."

The other bandits laughed and poked at one another.

"You're a fair-weather warrior, Gormion," Stormlight remarked. "Fordus feeds you, arms you. He provides your water in this dry and desolate place. You came to him when you were all nearly dead from the drought. He took you in. And today he gave you a *victory*. What else do you ask of him?"

"Gold," the bandit captain replied, flashing her bracelets in the firelight. "Gold and silver and the jewelry of Istar. I provide my followers, and he provides the gold. Victory? There is no victory without spoil. We retreated today because Fordus lost heart!"

"No fighter remembers all of the battle," Stormlight put forward. "How can we judge these things when we remember only in shards and slivers: the face of the man in front, a glint of light on a far hill, the brush of an arrow past our ear. Fragments. You can never claim full memory from them. So we must not speak of retreat, and who could know if or what Fordus repents? As for gold, other things are worth more. Every battle brings us closer to Istar. The last one will set my people free, and bring your gold as well. Be patient, Gormion."

Gormion acted as though she had not heard him. Her eyes shifted across the circle to Larken. "Let us ask the bard about the battle. Perhaps she remembers it all, since she fought none of it."

Larken returned the look with an icy stare. *No matter the fragment you remember,* she signed, *there was a full battle we won against the pride of Istar. This I will show you.*

She rattled the drumhammer across the stony head of the drum. Suddenly, Lucas fluttered awake on his perch, green-golden eyes wide and attentive. At a second drumroll, the hawk cried out in a long shriek that trailed away into a high, plaintive whistle.

It was all the bard needed to hear. Compressed in the cry was Lucas's full account of the entire battle, seen from the high vantage of his flight above the bloody plains. In a matter of seconds, Larken absorbed a vision of what had come to pass on the battlefield that day, and though the vision was barely formed and scarcely definable, she began to pick up its rhythm, and to hum around it, knowing she would discover the truth as she sang it, that it would surprise her as much as it did those who crouched around the fire, listening to their deeds take wing into history.

The hammer of Istar, the anvil of armies
Failed in the forge of Fordus's desert,
Failed on the plains when the sun passed over,
And the smoke rose up from a smithy of blood
While lost in the city the women lament,
> *Ash their companion,*
> *Fire is their father*
> *And the long war falls*
> *As the ravens gather.*

Gormion laughed wickedly and dismissed the song with a flick of her hand.

But Larken was only beginning. The drumbeat surged and galloped, and she found full voice.

Aeleth of Ergoth, harper of arrows,
Yours the first music the army remembers,
The arrow a bolt to the battle's thunder,
The string of the bow a song for Ilenus
Spearman of Istar struck in the vanguard:
> *The towers of Istar*
> *Mourn through the night,*
> *Bolt and harp*
> *And the arrow's flight.*

The drum beats faded to a long silence. Aeleth, somber and shaken, lifted his hands to the firelight. In the midst of Larken's singing, the entire experience had returned to him: the feel of the sunlight burning through the cloth sleeve pinned up on his right shoulder as he stood atop the rise in the grasslands, the army of Istar approaching, his arrow nocked and the bowstring taut. He remembered the thrum of the string, how it brushed against his cheek lightly, quivering as he brought down the bow . . .

How the spearman fell to his knees, dropping his weapon, his hands groping stupidly over the half-buried shaft of the arrow.

"Ilenus," Aeleth murmured. "The boy's name was Ilenus."

Then silently, as though all this knowledge struggled for a place in his mind and heart, Aeleth frowned and flexed his long, callused fingers.

Without prompting, Larken resumed the song. With crisp raps on the drum, she sang out other verses.

Rann of Balifor, Sword of the Bandits,
Rock of the army at Istar's coming,
The scar on your shoulder a glyph of the moon
As it shines on the dead in the damaged fields
As the night passes over the nation of Istar:
>*The long spear remembers*
>*The assembled flight*
>*The lodge of the arm*
>*In returning moonlight.*

This was obscure verse for a Baliforian thug. Rann shook his head in puzzlement, in disgust, but then, slowly, his attentions drifted to his shoulder, and a fresh wound throbbed with discovered pain. He remembered it all, now: sidestepping the charging mercenary, the sharp tug at his shoulder as he drove the hooked *kala* knife into a wide-eyed captain. He remembered wheeling about to face another assailant, a mist of blood encircling him.

His shoulder throbbed as each blow and parry rushed back to his blossoming memory.

"I remember it . . ." Rann breathed in wonder. "I remember it all."

Gormion rose and stalked from the firelight.

But the bard was not finished. As Larken continued, into the Song of Passing that named and heralded each of the fallen, the Plainsmen fell silent, remembering the battle in its swift and brutal entirety.

Stormlight, listening, recalled the fluttering high grass, the Istarian infantry passing so closely that he could smell the sweaty leather, read the elaborate gold insignia of the Istarian Guard. He recollected his troops, their painted faces and robes swathed with browns, blacks, and yellows, lying still until the sunlight and shadow and grass seemed to swallow them . . .

Northstar alone summoned to mind no earthly army, no array of spears or line of soldiers. Only the darkness of the sandstorm returned to him, abiding and deep, broken only by the unnatural movement of stars. Within that darkness dwelt the sound of inhuman voices, a clash of energy and movement he could not find the words to describe, and even the songs of Larken could not approach its menace and danger.

When the last note of the Passing sounded and the dead receded into their long, forgetful rest, something dark passed over and through the young scout.

He thought he saw a constellation, high in the vault of heaven, scatter and tumble onto the darkened plain.

Chapter 4

The dark woman crouched in the valley of crystal bones.

Overhead the red moon reeled crazily into the desert sky, but even that subdued light hurt her eyes.

She must learn to master this body. Learn its heaviness and inelegance in the short time before it dried and crumbled, in order to do the tasks she had set for herself. Already the blank, airless chaos of the Abyss seemed like a nightmare, like a harsh season in another age. Takhisis pushed that time to the back of her memory, breathing the night air, the faint smell of sage, the salt of the surrounding crystals.

Now was the time to scheme and countermine. Now, while the rebels divided and scattered, uncertain.

There is great power in knowledge, she told herself again.

Great freedom.

She groaned and practiced again the casual lifting of her incongruously heavy arm, the blinking of her eyes at proper intervals. The red-lit landscape glittered eerily, as though she watched the world from the heart of a gem. These eyes of crystal reflected an angular moonlight. Nearby, the salt flats, the pillars, seemed massive, disproportionately large. The plateau and arroyo, not a league away, seemed diminished, mysterious, as though glimpsed at the end of a thousand-mile tunnel.

The strange triad of Plainsman, bard, and elf seemed mysterious and distant as well, their thoughts and passions and motives still veiled to her.

Takhisis glanced up at the riding moon. Red Lunitari passed slowly over the eastern sky, over a gap in the heavens where the black moon rested, still unknown to the worldly astronomers.

A mask for Nuitari. A bright veil over the dark moon.

The girl would be the place to start, the goddess thought.

Slowly, the crystals that housed her spirit began to change, to restructure. To a passerby it would appear that one of the columns of salt—a large one, out in the middle of the flats—was melting, dissolving, reforming at the same time.

Takhisis's body hardened, became more angular. The shoulders broadened and the legs, once long and smooth and tapering, knotted as though an ancient wind had twisted and gnarled them.

It was a man now who walked the cooling sands of the desert. A man handsome and muscular and cold.

As he moved through the moonlight, his skin slowly grew translucent, then transparent. He was a ripple of darkness rising out of the desert night, no more visible than heat wavering over the cooling sands. Silently, he slipped by the outermost circle of Fordus's sentries.

Safe behind rebel lines, the warrior paused and listened, sinking slowly back into view, his skin darker, more opaque. Now the distant sound of a lyre chimed over his brittle hand, as the crystals in his fingers vibrated to the soft sound.

Good. The bard was playing. The music was uncomfortable, even disturbing, but it signaled her whereabouts.

Somewhere in the dry gulch, Takhisis—or rather the dark man who called himself Tamex—would find Larken. And the winnowing would begin.

* * * * *

Larken, too, had spent a sleepless night.

Alone in a weathered arroyo, at any time a place of danger, she waited for the inspiration of song and insight, she touched the three strings of the elven lyre, and she thought of Fordus.

"To the north he went," she began, her low, mellifluous voice unsteady as she searched for the melody in the darkness.

Lucas turned on his ring perch, head cocked alertly at the sound of the lyre.

"To the north came Fordus in the face of Istar . . ."

Larken fumbled with the lyre strings, striking a

quiet but dissonant chord. Lucas shrieked, raising the feathers on his head into a menacing crest.

"What? I know it was bad. Sorry," she replied to him, and his feathers smoothed over again. For an instant, a chill passed over her. Had she heard human words in the hawk's cry? Forgetting the moment, she dropped the lyre indifferently onto her lap.

Larken was glad her bardic instructors could not see her grope for words and flounder with strings. It would confirm what they had told her all along, about Plainsmen and the bardic calling, about her especially.

About this instrument they had hung upon her, useless and discordant in her hands.

Lucas cocked his head and stood very still on the round perch. His green eyes flashed with unearthly fire.

Larken looked at Lucas questioningly. "What?" she asked, this time wanting an answer.

Suddenly, a coldness overwhelmed her, as though the dry riverbed breathed the memory of violent water, of ice. A shadow passed between her and the moonlight—a cloud, a night bird . . .

The shadow paused above her.

Lucas covered his head with his wing and made a low, painful cry.

Slowly, Larken turned.

The dark man smiled handsomely, his face framed in moonlight. His tight-lidded amber eyes moved over her, and the black silk tunic rose rhythmically on his shoulders and chest. His legs were long and powerful, and he wore black leather boots—an odd choice for the desert, Larken thought somewhere at the edge of her mind.

He was a strange combination of beauty and eeriness, like a distorted reflection of the moon in water. Larken regarded him suspiciously, her hand drifting slowly and surely to the knife at her belt.

The dark man held her gaze, nodded.

"You are Larken the bard," he said, as though he named her for the first time with his words. With a movement lithe and graceful, he stepped toward her, wrested her hand from her knife . . . and kissed her fingers elegantly, his eyes never leaving hers.

Lucas shrieked from his perch, swelled with copper light, and tried to fly at the man, but his jesses tangled.

Larken swallowed hard and nodded, recovering her hand and soothing the hawk. "Hush, Lucas. It's all right."

The bird fluttered and hopped, but obediently kept to the perch.

"I am Tamex," the man said. "I come from the south, from the shining foothills."

Larken composed her face into neutrality. The man's hand had been very cold and hard. She started to sign a greeting, but something baffled her hands.

"While your army fought in the grasslands, I . . . crossed the desert. I searched for the Que-Nara camp, and awaited your return. Will you speak with me?"

I speak to no one but Lucas. I only sing, she motioned.

"I don't understand," said Tamex. "I know you can talk. I can hear what you say. Will you try?"

"You can hear me *speak*?" Larken's voice was husky, uncertain.

Tamex nodded. "I have come to serve your leader. I have come to undo the bondage of Istar. And I have come to listen to you."

Larken shook her head, deflecting his last offer. " 'Tis a tall order, to undo *that* city. Istar is the heart of the world." And then, after a moment, "How is it you hear my speech? It has been cursed."

"Does it matter?" Tamex dissembled, his reptilian eyes at last flickering away from hers. "Does any of that matter?"

He let his eyes play lazily across Larken's kneeling form, over her blond hair, her bronzed shoulders, and her slim thighs, bared to the evening's coolness.

His gaze flickered over the lyre and paused. The black diamonds in the heart of his eyes shuddered, narrowed, and vanished. Then, almost casually, his glance rested on the drum at Larken's side and the bone drumhammer.

"I have heard you play," he said. "Not the lyre. The drum. Your songs and words are worthy of heroes."

Flustered, the bard set down the lyre and reached for the drumhammer. It slipped from her hand and rattled noisily against the drum.

Tamex continued. "You are the one who exalts the Lord of the Rebels."

" 'Exalts'?"

"You magnify him beyond his deeds."

For a moment, brief as the gap between lightning and thunder, the bard's eyes widened. She felt exposed, uncovered by a sudden, surprising welling in her heart, as if she swirled in dark airlessness. Then the world tilted back into focus—the arroyo, the twining moonlight, the tall handsome warrior standing above her.

"Tell me about him," the dark man whispered.

She rose unsteadily and took a deep breath. Again she was Larken; the words stumbled back to her.

"About his gifts? His prophecies?" She turned the drumhammer in her hand.

"Tell me."

"Twenty-five years ago," Larken began, "the Que-Nara found a child nestled against a dune.

"We never knew who left him there, who had abandoned him to the harsh desert elements. It was great fortune, almost a miracle, that anyone noticed the baby. Fordus had not cried or called out, not even then, and the man who found him, a Plainsman chief named Kestrel, feared that the child was damaged, addled . . .

" 'Touched by Sirrion,' the Namer had said, as Kestrel held the silent infant before him on the Naming Night. 'The Firemaster is in his eyes.'

"It was the call of the poet, the madman."

"Then he was touched . . . by the gods?" Tamex asked, a brief, enigmatic smile passing over his pale face.

"So the Namer said," Larken replied, her eyes downcast, looking at the lyre on the ground. "But none of the Plainsmen understood or even wanted to.

"In each generation, only a few are touched by the fire god. Sirrion's mark comes double-edged: For each child who is blessed with inspiration, with insight and poetry, a thousand others become babblers, lunatics who dance at the red moon's rising, the responsibility for their complete care falling to their families, their people."

" 'Tis a hard life for those bearing the gods' touch," Tamex observed dryly. "But how did the Plainsmen . . . *receive* him?"

"The chief took the news . . . well, like a chieftain," Larken began. "After all, he had found the child and chosen to rescue it. Kestrel was a widower; no woman's hand graced his tents. He tended the child himself, awkwardly but well enough. He handed Fordus over to an attentive wet nurse, carried him in a pouch sewn into his shirt lining.

"The blue-eyed baby was hale enough, and grew tough, thin, and sinewy—like any Plainsman child.

But always the tribe watched for the sign of Sirrion's touch, for vision or madness.

"It was fifteen years before they knew for sure."

Tamex started to speak, to interrupt, to ask a question, but Larken had begun the first great story, the one she had sung a hundred times around the rebel campfires when morale was low, when faith in Fordus ebbed or wavered.

It felt strange to *say* the words again. It felt strange not to sign or sing them.

"To the eye of the warrior and the eye of the outrunner, young Fordus seemed normal enough— hunting with the other children, helping with the fire, and the catching of lizards for the cook pot. He sat watch when he was old enough to hold a spear and wait out the night.

"Yet when he first began to speak, at the late age of five or six, his talk was veiled and bizarre, a peculiar poetry of riddle and paradox.

"He spoke of moons and of black sand, of crystal and hawk, and sailing, ominous planets. Kestrel was afraid of no man, but the touch of the gods unnerved him. He continued to feed and shelter the boy, but he could not bring himself to love him.

"The other boys welcomed Fordus on the hunt; after all, he was the chief's adopted son, fleetest of foot and stronger than any. His was the axe that felled boar and leopard, goblin and giant scorpion. But in the Telling Time, when the hunt was relived around fire and tent, when the smallest deed staggered beneath the largest boasts, he spoke not at all. Stormlight spoke for him, telling his stories to the listening tribe.

"*Fordus* they called him on his naming night— when he took on his name and passed from boyhood. *Fordus*. The old Kharolian word for the desert storm, the high wind racing out of nowhere and the blinding deluge of rain. The force that fills the arroyos, that drowns the entire world in its hour."

"What about *before* the naming?" Tamex asked, leaning toward the girl intently, almost hungrily.

"Before?" It was as though the idea was alien to her.

"Nothing of . . . *opals*, then?" he asked.

"Opals?" Larken frowned. "Nothing more than the torc found beside him as a child—the necklace that grew in size as Fordus grew to maturity."

"How intriguing," Tamex observed, lightly, almost casually. "What else do you know of this . . . torc?"

Larken knew nothing. And something within her told her it was dangerous to guess.

"I know what I am telling you," she said, her eyes fixed on the dark interloper. "Nothing more."

Tamex's eyes fell suddenly flat and cold.

"Tell me of the prophecy, then," he whispered. "Tell me."

Larken shifted, wiped her hands on the front of her tunic as she met the dark man's odd stare. Had one eye blinked more slowly than the other?

"At fifteen," she continued, "Fordus was faster than the tribal outrunners, faster than the leopards and able to pace the gazelle at the desert's edge. Nor would he use that speed in cowardice or caution; he was brave to the borders of recklessness, and yet he calmed and sustained the boys who followed him.

"Then the rains failed, for the first time after the death of the old Water Prophet.

"And the chieftain called council.

"The Namers had searched the sky for months. They tried the old methods of insight and augury—what the old Prophet had done to serve the tribe for fifty years. They augured by star, by stone, by the twining moons, but no rain was promised and no rain came.

"It was a dark time, they tell me, and soon augury passed into grumbling, and grumbling into the silence of growing despair. Then Kestrel called them all together—boy and man, warrior and outrunner, and sentry and firekeeper.

"He told them he was sending them for water."

Larken paused, tilted her head as though she listened to the air.

"The desert abounds with hidden springs," she said. "Sometimes there are oases, unexpected or suddenly, mysteriously newborn from the desert's lack and dryness. Sometimes there are springs under rocks, a thin brown trickle in a muddy arroyo. But without a Prophet, the chances of finding water are thin.

"When the chief ordered the water search, he ordered it in desperation. And after a week, even the oldest and wisest of the Namers had given up.

"Racer pressed to be named the tribe's Water Prophet; the title was his by right and age. He pleaded for the ceremony—the vow to be said before his blood kin, acknowledged on sacred ground, and beneath the shining north star. Then he would fast, and meditate, and perhaps find water, perhaps not. It was a hard and thankless task, water prophecy, and yet Old Racer desired it with all his might. But while Racer sued and cajoled and threatened, the water-skins dried and the youngest children took on the parched, haunted eyes of the drought-stricken.

"At fifteen, for the first time, Fordus spoke for himself at the Telling.

"In the midst of the boasts and dreary bravado he stood, as the firelight mocked the false cheer of the thirsty men around him. He stood, and at his standing, the camp fell silent.

"With the kala, Kestrel pointed to his adopted son.

All eyes turned to the lean, muscular youth, who stood resolutely, confidently, flanked by his friends Stormlight the elf and Northstar, almost still a child.

" 'What do I care of your little hunts,' Fordus asked, 'of your spears and your bola, your journey of leagues and nights?'

"He took the old language of the hunter's boast and returned it to them, scalding and unforgiving.

"Racer spat, and his company of Namers nodded their beaded locks in support.

"A murmur rushed through the assembled hunters, but Fordus only smiled. 'Save your water, Racer,' he cautioned. 'With *your* prophecies, you will need it. Boast and brood and despair of water. As for me, I shall find the water we need.'

"Then Fordus turned and stalked from the camp, with two of his friends at his side. The older men talked of it all night, but by morning they had forgotten, departing on their own search for the legendary god-given spot from which the water would rise.

"Meanwhile, the three young men hunted on their own."

"A rebel even then," Tamex observed, his voice cold and insinuating.

"But a rebel then for the good of all," Larken replied. She reddened and avoided the dark man's stare.

"Then? And not now?" This Tamex was no fool. He had heard the wound in her voice, the regret and resentment.

"Judge for yourself," Larken answered blandly, and resumed the story.

"The lads combed the desert within sight of the camp, keeping the low fires of the Que-Nara constantly to their left as they circled the settlement. Fordus loped ahead of them, not even winded, as I have seen him do many times since in the vanguard of armies. And I am sure he paid no more attention to his two companions than to the missing red moon or the slow clouds straddling the western sky.

"When he reached the rise," she continued, absently stroking the glowing drumhead, "Fordus stopped and leaned against a smooth, upright stone. Stormlight and Northstar were a step behind him, as always.

"Overhead the white moon sailed serenely out of the clouds, and suddenly the entire desert stretched before them, desolate and featureless as the face of that moon. Salt crystals dotted the arid landscape, catching the moonlight like blades, like slivers of glass.

"Salt and stone, but no water.

"This was south of here, in old country indeed. The ground they stood on once formed the northernmost borders of Silvanesti, back in the Age of Light. 'Twas woodland until the Second Dragon War, when Lady Chaos laid waste to the Elflands. Now it is rubble and salt, salt and rubble."

Tamex said nothing. The two of them sat in silence, there in the bed of the dried-up river.

"Elf country," Larken continued, her thoughts haunted by the prospect of such devastation. "Druid's country. And then . . ."

Tamex stirred restlessly. "I know. I know. The Dragon Wars. But what of Fordus?"

"Fordus? Oh, yes. That was the night he found the kanaji."

"Kanaji?"

"A druidic oracle pit. I first saw them near Silvanost, on the banks of the Thon-Thalas. Wide declivities, covered with netting and leaves. The druids descend into them to meditate, to . . . find enlightenment."

"How? How do they work, these . . ."

"Kanaji? Druidic magic," the bard answered elusively. Something in her shrank from the ardent questioning. "Fordus found the pit that evening. He stood upon it, as though it had summoned him there.

"Dig they did, hoping beyond their wildest hopes for water. Then the three of them knelt together, pulling the heavy stone away.

"They found a hollow chamber, round, of limestone block, just large enough for two good-sized people to sit in. The floor was nothing but fine white sand, which looked as if it had gone undisturbed by wind and water for a thousand years.

"Fordus hopped into the circular chamber, Stormlight close behind. They examined the gray, gritty walls, the shadowed circumference, while the youngest, little Northstar, stood above them in an impatient watch.

"Fordus and Stormlight sat in the fine sand. They joked—the nervous, blustering jests of young men in holy places. But the ancientness and reverence of the place soon stilled their laughter, and they sat in silence as, over the dry expanse of the desert, the chanting of the elders drifted to the rise and down into the kanaji pit.

"The lads went still. In the reverence they had been taught since infancy, Stormlight and Northstar looked up toward the heavens, toward the mobius of Mishakal and the harp of Branchala.

"Fordus, on the other hand, looked toward the floor of the kanaji. Then, suddenly, as the sand began to ripple and eddy beneath him, he glanced up at Stormlight, motioned his friend's gaze to the changing sand, to the strange glyphs forming in the pristine whiteness.

" 'Druidic,' my cousin Northstar told them. 'The picture language of a thousand years past.'

"With a whoop, Fordus raced across the level expanse toward the fires of the men, leaving his companions agape at the emerging symbols.

"Curious, not a little irritated at being disturbed at their ritual, the elders were led to the kanaji. Staring down into the pit, all of them noticed the change in Fordus—the sea-blue eyes suddenly bright and focused, as though his earlier addling had been lifted, the pupils dilated until a core of fathomless dark seemed to rise out of that blue sea.

"His lips moved slowly. With great effort, as though he were translating the hidden language of the gods, he breathed a single syllable, then another.

"Crouched by the lip of the kanaji, Racer made the warding sign, protection against the Lady, and the destruction that follows her."

"A foolish sign," Tamex observed. "A foolish superstition."

"Whatever its wisdom, he did not complete it. With a firm grip Kestrel grasped the old conniver's wrist. 'There will be no warding of my son,' he decreed. 'Let him speak, Racer. Unless *you* can read glyph and symbol.'

"Silenced, Racer glared at Fordus, who knelt now above the signs fully formed.

" 'Axe,' Fordus muttered. 'Tower and Lightning. The rain is hewn of light and memory.'

"The elders glanced at each other uncertainly. Surely some of them thought of Sirrion's touch, of the flame of poetry or madness.

"Then Stormlight, his white eyes staring into the whirling depths of Fordus's blue, translated for them all.

" 'Halfway between the Red Plateau and the Tears of Mishakal,' he pronounced. 'Seven feet below the surface. Water enough for a month of travel.'

"They had to confirm Fordus's prophecy. Later that night they would dig to the water and their thirst would end. But now, in a starlit cluster, Kestrel set his hands on the head of his adopted son and began the chieftain's chant that would name the lad Water Prophet.

" 'It cannot be!' Racer shouted, bargaining for time, for delay, for anything that would keep the title out of the grasp of the upstart. 'The gods honor only the Prophet who stands beneath the North Star. It has not yet risen! You know this, Kestrel, and yet you wrest the robes from me and confer them on your firestruck son. It is not according to tradition, not fitting, not permitted, not . . . not . . .'

"Silently, triumphantly, Kestrel pointed at the lad who stood over his son. 'Who stands above Fordus, Racer?' he asked. 'What is the name of that lad?'

"Northstar, in his place by design or accident, knelt by the lip of the kanaji and, reaching down into the pit, gently and reverently touched the top of Fordus's head."

Larken smiled and stretched, rising from the bed of the old river and dusting the sand from her tunic.

"That is the story, Tamex. That is the way it is told at the Telling."

"But never so splendidly," Tamex soothed. "Never by the fabled bard, the Breath of the Gods herself."

Suddenly, as though she were awakening from a trance, an enchantment, Larken looked at her solitary audience in a new, harsh light.

He seemed much shorter than when he had first appeared, scarcely an hour ago.

Chapter 5

Every morning, despite several floors of stone under his
room, Vaananen awoke to the sound of rending rock
beneath the city. Sometimes it infiltrated his dawn
dreams and he thought he, too, labored in the dank,
musty tunnels to blast and hammer and drag forth
the glain opals for the Kingpriest. This morning, the
dreams had become especially vivid, and the constant pounding of the city's secret heart lingered in
his ears even now as he strode rapidly down a
higher passage to keep a regular appointment with
his sparring partner.

Down the spiral staircase he ran, his high-necked

practice shirt already damp from the rising heat of the day, his arms covered past the wrists in padded sleeves to turn the blows of long sword and dagger. When he reached the ground floor, he drew forth a bronze key, wrought in the shape of a sidewinding serpent, inserted it into the elaborate lock on the heavy oaken door, and took the last easy breath he would get for the next two hours.

"You are almost late," said the Kingpriest, tossing a rough-hewn pole at the druid.

Vaananen deftly caught both the weapon and the malice. He bowed in silent reply, his eyes never leaving the sea-blue stare of his opponent. This is the last time, he thought, stepping inside the walled garden.

For eight years, Vaananen had fought the Kingpriest in these small battles, never winning, never telling, and always leaving the sovereign with the suspicion that Vaananen used magic rather than martial skill to survive.

It was all for Vincus, these weekly combats and humiliations. The lad could not help that his father had been an unfaithful weapons-master to an unfaithful ruler, that instead of teaching the Kingpriest the form of the broadsword prohibited to clerical orders, old Hannakus had tried to skip town, taking with him a hundred of the Kingpriest's treasured glain opals.

The Istarian Guard had caught Vincus's father before he reached the walls. They had arrested old Hannakus, tried him, and executed him. But they had never found the opals. The Kingpriest had maintained that the son, at the time a mere boy of twelve, should work off the father's debt in the opal mines beneath the city.

It was a death sentence. Vaananen intervened, promising his services in Hannakus's old role. And promising his silence as the Kingpriest, in a sacrilege older than the faith, took up the edged blade that was forbidden to all who served the gods in holy orders.

Now, that service, that silence, was almost over.

The Kingpriest turned his head at last and paced to the farthest point in the practice circle, examined the blade of his sword, and placed a booted foot against one of the smooth white shells that marked fair ground for the fight.

Vaananen dropped to a crouch and balanced in his right hand the light pole, which was actually a living tree, its roots bundled tightly and its branches pruned away. The Kingpriest never played by the rules; there would be no salutation. Vaananen drew a long breath, loosened his legs, and waited.

The Kingpriest pretended to adjust his grip for a moment, then charged the druid on the right. Vaananen stood his ground until his attacker's blade whistled through the air in a long, deadly downstroke, then pivoted exactly six inches aside to catch the Kingpriest lightly in the back of the head with the pole and knock him to his knees.

Before the Kingpriest could regain sight, breath, and footing, Vaananen threw himself to the ground and lay still. Long ago, he had learned that never a blow was dealt to this sovereign that was not repaid tenfold outside the arena; it was best to ungracefully sprawl in the appearance of one cut down by the mighty swipe of the monarch's blade.

The Kingpriest rose, furious and wild, only to find his fighting partner in seemingly worse condition after the clash. He laughed smugly and kicked the druid until he "regained consciousness."

And so it went for an hour and more, Vaananen spinning, dodging, rolling, and feinting, always adjusting cooly to the attack, and only occasionally dealing the Kingpriest a gentle tap with the length of the bound tree. Vaananen kept it interesting, but never, to the Kingpriest's utter frustration, did he seem to become angry or lose control.

"You willow-heart!" the Kingpriest taunted. "It is our last round—have you no more spirit left than this? Did you leave your manhood in a grove of rotten oak?"

It is not my fight, Vaananen would say to himself. This is for Vincus's freedom, so that he will never inhabit the darkness of the mines. Then Vaananen would smile and think of another way to turn the Kingpriest's forbidden blade, never allowing it to touch him.

At last, just before the round was meant to be over, the Kingpriest, seething with anger, stopped the exchange.

"Come over here," he panted. "Stand exactly here." He pointed to the outside of the ring of shells. The sea-blue eyes shone with rage and cunning.

Vaananen knew if he left the sparring ground before the round was over that it would be a foul, and would give the Kingpriest an opportunity to deliver an undefended blow. The blade glistened in the noonday sun, its edge razor-sharp and lethal. The Kingpriest did not care for blunted weapons.

Vaananen moved to the center of the ring and stood his ground. It was a show of truce—the most vulnerable place in the arena.

"Do you decline my order, noble Vaananen?" the Kingpriest said smoothly. "I think there is a penalty for that. . . . I think you will do five more years of this game, this time with no padded shirt, eh?"

For the first time, Vaananen spoke. "I have paid the debt of Vincus's blood. He *will* go free. And you cannot coerce me. You violate your Order by using this broadsword. The game is over."

The Kingpriest smiled, his sea-blue eyes flickering coldly. "You will stay in my service," he said. "You are bound to me by oath. Many others who are unworthy serve me—from the thief's son to peasants . . ."

He eyed Vaananen cagily.

"Perhaps even druids. Cast out from their own Order for the gods know . . . what crimes?"

Vaananen's face betrayed no emotion.

"Now, willow-heart, we will arrange to pay *your* debt," the Kingpriest said with a low chuckle.

Slowly, he stirred the border of shells with his booted foot, walking around the ring, narrowing the circle around the silent druid.

* * * * *

Lazily the goddess walked through the Tears of Mishakal, the crystal structures rising in bizarre angles, catching the red moonlight until they seemed like blades dripping with blood.

The crystals that housed her changed as well. No longer was she Tamex, the menacing, mysterious warrior that would trouble Larken's dreams for yet a dozen nights.

She was Tanila now—a lithe and lovely woman, a creature of darkness to be feared and desired by man and elf alike. Casting her black eyes toward the heavens, the goddess breathed a summoning word . . .

And in the far sky, somewhere over Istar on the northern horizon, a star winked out and the long line of dune and mountain darkened ever so slightly.

Good. Her powers were growing. She could again subvert the deep heavens with an old spell or a quiet incantation. Somewhere in the far void of space, as dark and lifeless as her prison in the abyss, a black star cooled and died, collapsing on itself, and ten planets—ten worlds—felt the first glazing of a final ice.

Who knew what civilizations now lay chilled and silent, abandoned by warmth and light and life?

Indeed, who cared? What was important was that she could *do* it—could leave the world desolate with a breath, a thought. Oh, her powers were mighty, and though Krynn was held against her, safe for now in the shelter of a bright wing, she would govern it soon. She knew it.

It was a matter of months—of a few years at the most—and this was the place to begin.

Takhisis knew how the salt flats had received their name. Profane ground, where healing failed and revelation faded.

No wonder Mishakal wept.

But the goddess who now passed through the latticework of crystal thought little of healing, less of revelation. On her mind were the rebel leaders, the close-knit triad of bard, elf, and . . .

She had no word for Fordus. Not yet. She knew him only through repute and legend, through his victories and through the song of his bard.

The bard was easy. Larken did not know her own power—the hidden magic of the lyre she resented and discarded, the awesome potential of her voice if she could free it of her own fear and anger.

Takhisis smiled. Fear and anger were her favorite lieutenants.

Fear and anger followed the elf as well.

Neither of them knew themselves, much less their commander.

The sand stirred, marking the wake of the goddess, a sinuous, twisting path like the trail left by a snake.

The next time she would come to them as Tanila, and the elf would be probed and sounded. He was Lucanesti, friend to the opals.

And oh, the opals would be important soon.

But first, there was small business to attend to at the edge of the grasslands.

* * * * *

The grasslands rose out of sleep to embrace him, the long grain swaying in the windless fields.

Fordus knew he was dreaming because what he saw did not match what he felt.

He did not like unexpected dreams. But so be it.

Would the battle come, or the light? One or the other always appeared in his dreams, and he learned from them both, from what the battle showed him or the light told him to say.

A purple rise, dotted with fir trees and blasted vallenwoods, rushed to meet him. Above them, a dozen birds wheeled slowly.

Hawks? Was Larken's hawk Lucas among them? He called to the birds in his mind; they approached, descended.

Not hawks. Scavengers.

Then it is a battle dream, he thought. I shall feel my dreaming in the morning run, in new soreness and stretching. But I shall win this battle as I win them all. Larken will finally sing of how I defeated Istar in desert, in grasslands . . .

Even in dreams.

He had no time to savor the prospects. Suddenly the rise fell away, as though the earth itself had collapsed beneath him. Fordus leapt over a spinning, white-hot void and landed stiffly and unsteadily at the crumbling edge of a bluff. A solitary Istarian warrior instantly appeared before him—a golden man, hooded and helmed, his shield adorned with seven alabaster spires, his broad shoulders draped with a black tunic.

Well, then, Fordus thought. He reached for the axe at his belt.

It was not there.

For a moment, fear surged through him, dream-like and obscure, then he brushed it aside with a laugh.

After all, it is a dream. What is the worst that can happen?

Across the arid, level ground, in the wail of a hot wind, the warrior beckoned slowly, trumpeting a challenge in an inhuman tongue. His seven-spired shield glittered ever more brightly until the dream was swallowed by its light. Then shadow returned, and the man stood closer, alone and unarmed, as though he had cast aside his weaponry out of con-tempt. Now he assumed a wrestler's stance: a low, feline crouch, fingers spread like claws.

With long strides, moving so slowly it seemed that he waded through waist-high sand, Fordus closed with the warrior.

They collided to the sound of distant thunder. The arms of the enemy were cold and metallic, hard and heavy as bronze. The Istarian warrior spun about with a roar, hurling Fordus over his head. Whooping in delight, Fordus released his grip at the height of the violent arc, and somersaulting through the air, landed lightly on the sun-scorched ledge some dis-tance away. Behind him, rocks and dust toppled into a bottomless crevasse.

It is *my* dream. I can master it.

The warrior now bristled with six waving arms like an angry burnished insect, like a living statue of some barbarian harvest god. The sunlight danced like flame on his helmet.

It is my dream . . .

Fordus hurtled toward the warrior, who cried out and braced himself for the impact.

This collision was totally silent, as though all sound had fled at the force of the impact. The golden warrior rocked on his heels but kept his balance, lifting the struggling Fordus off the ground, four of the arms drawing him closer . . .

Fordus heard the hissing, smelled the fetid breath of his adversary. Fascinated, distracted, he gazed into the warrior's eyes.

Lidless and lifeless. Reptilian, the vertical slits in the heart of the eyes opening like a parted curtain, to reveal a dark nothingness, a deep and abiding void . . .

Fordus shook his head, wrestled the enemy's multiple grasp, his own sudden drowsiness and lack of resistance, the growing trust that it would not be so bad, this defeat, that it would all go for the better if he gave up the struggling . . . if he gave in . . . and looked into the curtained eyes that opened to perpetual blackness.

* * * * *

Fordus bolted upright, stifling a cry. His head rang with pain, and his skin felt raw and tender. His arms ached, the muscles cramping like they'd been gripped in the jaws of some monstrous, relentless creature.

But he was safe atop the Red Plateau. Not twenty yards away, the young sentry still snored at his post. Fordus leapt to his feet, intent on throttling the lad, but his legs shook with the dream's exertion, and a cold sweat rushed over him like a desert downpour.

Leave the lad alone. No sentry could protect him

from his dreams.

Angrily, he looked up into the spacious desert sky, where the starry horns of Kiri-Jolith menaced the Dark Queen's constellation.

"Where were you in all of this, old bison? Old grandfather?" Fordus asked sullenly. He stood up slowly. The heavy gold torc at his neck felt tight. With a last look at the sleeping sentry, Fordus began to run.

Since his early childhood, running had carried him away from deceptions, from confinement and complexities. When he sprinted over desert or plain, when the wind took him up and carried him over dune and moon-dappled rise, when in the power of his stride he seemed to *become* the wind—only then could Fordus think clearly. He could cleanse his mind of the mystery of glyph and sand, of the prophecies that passed through him. When he ran, his blood pounding in his ears, he was purely, completely free.

Tonight Fordus outran the wind itself. Suddenly, with a dreamlike swiftness, he found himself crossing the dunes. The Red Plateau appeared on the far horizon, and from the rebel camp arose a faint array of lights.

He crowed with delight and ran even harder toward the widest expanse of the desert. The red moonlight bathed the landscape ahead, and soon he passed altogether from sight of the plateau, to a point in the desert where the hard red ground stretched in all directions, uninterrupted to the edge of the horizon.

All the while, Fordus had the strangest sense that something was running beside him. From the corner of his eye, he saw it, a black spot coursing over the moonlit desert floor. It stayed at the margins of his vision like a specter, like the dark moon rumored by astronomers and mages.

No matter how quickly he moved, the darkness kept precise pace.

Something in Fordus's fears told him that it was his dream in pursuit, that somehow the golden warrior on the sunbaked ledge had ridden his thoughts into the waking world to follow him, to run him down.

He would not have that. His strides lengthened.

Across the desert they ranged, runner and shadow, their swift path turning toward the sunrise. Suddenly, as the full sun breasted the horizon, the shadow lurched toward Fordus. With a cry, he wheeled to meet it, throwing axe ready in his hand. The shadow loomed above him, transparent and faintly faceted, no more visible than heat wavering over the cooling sands. He saw, in its swirling depths, a pair of amber eyes.

Lidless and lifeless. Reptilian.

Never breaking stride, Fordus charged at the enemy. The shadow closed around him, blinding him, then suddenly it was sunlight and sand again, he was sailing in midair over a dune, the shadow was gone, and the ground had fallen away beneath him, just like in his dream.

Softer sand cushioned his fall, but it began to swirl beneath him as he tried to scramble to his feet. Clumsily, helplessly, he spiraled lower and lower into a funnel of slick sand, a whirlpool delivering him into a dark hole, a central pit.

In the heart of that pit, the morning sunlight glinted on a bulbous green eye, several sets of clicking antennae, and a huge set of widely opened mandibles.

Springjaw! Fordus thought frantically, groping for another axe as the creature scuttled toward him hungrily.

Chapter 6

From his vantage point in the lofty tower, the Kingpriest watched a meteor plummet through the distant sky above the Tower of High Sorcery, dropping out over Lake Istar, where it crumbled and collapsed into the water like dust sprinkled from the heavens.

Like dust.

The ruler of Istar turned from the window.

His private chambers were as spare as a novice monk's. So he insisted, despite the flattery of the attendant clergy and the growing temptation to surround himself with beautiful things. A single cot and a threadbare rug lay in the center of a vast and vaulted room.

By day, the chamber was austere, but lovely in the subtle light that shone through the opalescent windows.

But it was night now in Istar, and by night the Kingpriest saw shadows. At night, if he gazed too long into the graceful garden below the tower window, he saw the trees as things with daggers, and the streams and fountains blackened and thickened under the silent moons.

No. He would not look into darkness, would not think on his . . . transgressions. Better to sit here by a cheery fire, to sift the dust—the *opal* dust—that would eventually bring his joy.

The windows had told him about the opals long ago as he walked in private meditation along the outer passageway, the huge, encircling hall of the tower.

Alone, his white hood raised above immaculate white robes, the Kingpriest had been praying, but the prayer passed into a curious reverie in which he remembered his early days of priesthood, a candlelit chamber in the novices' quarters . . .

A girl. An auburn-haired chambermaid.

His hands trembled at the memory. So lost was he in a dream of ancient lust that he did not hear the windows speak at first. But the words intruded at last on his thoughts, and, startled, he looked toward the sun-struck clerestory, where the surface of the pink, opalescent windows whirled with unnatural light.

Like calls to like, they told him, each window speaking in a voice of different pitch and timbre, until it seemed as though a choir sang the words into his baffled hearing.

"Like calls to like, indeed," he whispered in reply, when the corridor had settled into expectant silence.

"Water to water, and stone to stone."

He did not know why he had thought of water and stone.

Furtively, he glanced up and down the hall. Perhaps someone was weaving deceptive and illegal magic to make him seem the fool . . .

Seem unsuitable.

Two windows at the bend of the hall widened and darkened, as though the corridor itself were watching.

Like calls to like, they repeated, strangely and absurdly, as the great scholar ransacked his memory of ancient scroll and codex for any mention of speaking windows, of omen and sign and portent.

His memory returned to the girl, to the candlelight pale on her bare skin. In the corridor, the windows promised him that auburn-haired girl. Her, or another just like her.

It was time, they urged him, to take a bride.

She was approaching, the windows told him. The Kingpriest's bride. Soon the time would come, in ceremony and ritual, when he could call her forth, anchor her errant spirit in a new, lithe body.

When the time was right, they would teach him the chant, the arcane somatic movements. But for now, he should gather the material components.

The dust of a thousand glain opals.

It seemed an obscure command, and yet, lulled by the prospects of the young girl, he vowed to comply, to gather. There in opalescent light he took a firm, unbreakable oath, and twenty years later, when he ascended the throne of the Kingpriest, he set about fulfilling his duty to the swirling, disembodied voices.

The stones would house his approaching bride, some god had promised him, through the translucency of opals.

The sounds of the city faded into the darkness and the approaching morning. Sleepless and eager, the Kingpriest sat on the edge of his cot, black dust sifting and tumbling through his pale, anticipatory fingers.

* * * * *

The young man slipped through the dark Istarian alleys, his movements silent and veiled.

Twice he lurched into shadowy doorways, standing breathlessly still until a squadron of soldiers rattled by on the moonlit street, Lunitari spangling their bronze armor with a blood-red light. Winding his way through the intricate streets of the city like a burglar, he passed the School of the Games.

Silently, anonymously, he continued past the Banquet Hall and the Welcoming Tower, once festive buildings now muted with night and the recent news of an Istarian defeat. He stepped into the moonlight here, and the red glow tumbled onto his dark skin, his green-gold eyes, the short, well-kept beard. His hair was cut in the dark roach of Istarian servitude—the topknot extending from nape to widow's peak. His wide mouth fell into a secret mocking smile.

They said Fordus had put it to the Kingpriest. Put it to him well in the grasslands to the south. Whoever Fordus was.

Now those vaunted legions, decimated and leaderless, camped by Istar's outer walls with their backs to the cold stone, their garbage piling up around them, had orders to defend the city at all costs.

It was ludicrous. They heard the march of rebels in the wind and confused the low stars on the northern horizon with a thousand rebel campfires on the plains. They saw Fordus's face under every lackey's hood.

Still, Istar was far from beaten. The army that this Fordus had crushed, though formidable, was not a tenth of the Kingpriest's power. Already the city echoed with new tidings, with the rumor of military movement in high places, of counterattack and reprisal.

When the young man was halfway across the Central Court, a third patrol approached—slowly, with a clatter of gruff voices and new, ill-fitting armor. The young man crawled catlike beneath a broken wagon abandoned not a hundred feet from the main entrance to the Great Temple. He held his breath again until the last of the soldiers passed, muting his thoughts in case a cleric traveled with them. When the courtyard was once again clear, he peered through the cracked spokes of the wagon wheel at the dome of the Great Temple glittering in moonlight, red as the helmets and breastplates of the patrolling soldiers.

As he watched, the bell in the lofty tower swayed and tolled the fourth hour since the turn of night— the last hour of darkness.

Vincus was somewhat early; the call to First Prayer was not for several minutes. He would have to wait until the clerics began their silent, ritual movement toward chamber and candlelit chapel. Then, when most of the residents' thoughts woolgathered in peasant rite and pretty ceremony, he could cross the open courtyard undetected.

Vincus crawled up into the tilted bed of the wagon and, lying back in the sour straw, lifted and then settled his seamless silver collar so that it did not clank against the wood. The bright heavy circle was marked only by the common lettering of his name.

Vincus was a temple slave, and not a contented one.

For a year now, he had served as silent go-between in the usual tower intrigues, and in one case, he abetted the out-and-out treason of an eccentric, superstitious priest from the west—a man strangely attuned to weather and seasons and growing things, more pleasant to him than any of those mush-faced, white-robed sycophants.

But in the end, all sides were the same to Vincus. All sides but his own. Daily, patiently, he awaited an opportunity either to steal enough to pay off his father's debts or somehow to break the silver collar, the sign of Temple slavery that neither smith nor armorer would dare loosen. If he were free of that collar, he could flee into the city shadows, let his hair grow back and lose himself among the narrow side streets and alleys and winding sewers he knew so well.

His chance would come. Not tonight, but soon, he knew.

Meanwhile, this hiding place was odorous, but at least it was comfortable. He had waited in far worse surroundings: in the dark rat-infested cellar of an ale-house, in the cobwebbed rafters of a foul-smelling tannery, once even neck-deep in oily harbor water, clinging for his life to the treacherously barnacled side of a moored ship.

The ship had been the worst, for Vincus was no swimmer, and the barnacles had cut and savaged his hands.

With that memory in mind, the wagon bed seemed suddenly more than sufficient.

Scarcely an hour from now, while the clergy droned and murmured in the first foolish rite of the day and the hard-hatted soldiers drowsed at their assigned guard posts, he could cross the courtyard virtually unnoticed. Slipping from shadow to shadow, he could scale the outer wall, stroll through the garden to the braided green silk rope dangling from the high window that would be left open for him, and there, in the shadow of vallenwood branches, scramble up the tower wall like a burglar.

For wasn't that what he was? A thief of secret thoughts?

Vincus laughed silently and closed his eyes, rustling into the soft, makeshift mattress. He could drowse now, for his days on the streets of Istar had taught him to sleep with a strange vigilance. Soft sounds three blocks away tumbled like dreams through the edge of his senses, and Vincus took note of each of them: the low chuckling of a pigeon stirring in sleep, the scuttling of a rat amid the offal in an alley.

The sound of a dagger drawn from a gilded sheath.

Instantly, Vincus's golden eyes popped open. His right hand slowly reached to a fold in his tunic, where he kept his homemade leather sling and six stones. Once again motionless, assured his weapon was there, he turned his head with agonizing slowness to the slit in the wagon's side, where the boards had long ago shrunk and parted. From there he watched the mouths of the alleys, listening for metal on metal again, for a clue to the sound's direction in the directionless dark.

He fought down his fearful imaginings. Perhaps it was another patrol, this time with dogs or Irda or minotaur. Or a ghost. After all, the city was said to be deep with the roving dead.

Maybe an evil god, set on a cruel and arbitrary hunt. Hiddukel of the broken scales. Chemosh of the undead, his yellowed skull agleam in torchlight.

Vincus closed his eyes, banished all the fears. Had the kindly Vaananen not taught him that such gods could not prosper against him?

Kick them in the backside, I will, he thought. And send them packing to the Abyss.

You are safe, Vincus, he reminded himself. You have not come this far to be abandoned. Your chance will come.

Finally, he heard the dagger replaced, the sound scarcely in range and nearly lost in the clatter of hoofbeats from a passing rider.

Traveling away, Vincus thought. Whoever it is. Traveling toward the School of the Games.

He relaxed, staring past the foul straw up into the city sky. Faintly, through the ash and smoke and torchlight, he caught a glimmer of stars in the northern sky. Bright Sirrion floated through the constellated harp of Branchala, as though the old planet played accompaniment to this sly nocturnal business.

It was curious tidings Vincus had gathered tonight for Vaananen at the Temple. Dissent in the ranks. First threat to the rebels. Try as he might—and Vincus was shrewd and inventive—he could not piece together a story out of the fragments he had heard. An Istarian mercenary captain, an augurer, and a seller of salt in the Marketplace—three conversations had spawned three versions of a rumor. Each story seemed somehow linked with the others, sharing a common substance like the facets of a crystal, but again like facets, each shed diverging and fractured truth.

But it was not Vincus's job to piece together the evidence. Calmly and silently he waited to deliver it, while the fiery old planet passed through the starry harp and the last hour of the night turned into the first of the morning.

* * * * *

The tower bells tolled that first hour, and the city of Istar wakened slowly in the early morning darkness.

In the corridors of the great marble temple, dozens of white-robed figures filed down the shining steps from the Outer Tower toward the Sacred Chamber, the underground sanctuary in which the Kingpriest and the principal clerics of Istar greeted every new day with First Prayer. The torches that lined the stairwell and the corridors smoked and sputtered, and among the clergy were many who nodded or shuffled sleepily, wrested from hard sleep and comfortable beds by ritual demand.

At other places in the temple and in the city, more clergy gathered in similar ceremony, but those in the Sacred Chamber were the chosen, the elite whose service to Istar had spanned years, decades—in some cases, even the reigns of several Kingpriests.

At an hour more daylit or in a place less secure, the guards might have counted the white robes that entered the chamber that morning. Had they done so, they would have found that four of the number were missing, and that the infirmaries of the temple accounted for only three of the absent clergy.

But the hour was early, the guards as drowsy as the celebrants. The bronze-armored sentries nodded and blinked and closed the doors to the chamber at the appointed time, never knowing that one whose presence was expected—the cleric Vaananen of Near Qualinesti—had chosen not to attend the morning's ceremonies.

Instead, Brother Vaananen remained in his meditation chamber, stirring the fine white sand in his rena garden.

Vaananen was a westerner, and therefore seemed quite austere to some of the others in the brotherhood—mainly the Istarians who were spoiled by the city's soft ways and easy living. He was a tall, spare man, with long black-and-silver hair, which he kept clubbed neatly at his neck. His eyes were moss green and seemed to fill his entire face.

Vaananen smiled frequently, but always in secret, under his ample hood. He was a disguised druid working among the clerics, a man whose solitary pursuits made for few friends.

All the better.

His druidic masters had set him in Istar with the purpose of salvaging any ancient texts from the Kingpriest's destructive edicts. Secretly, painstakingly, Vaananen copied what he could find, translating from rune and glyph into the common alphabet, and smuggling the new-made books out by silent courier and under other covers and titles.

Of late, he had found new things to do as well.

Vaananen's chamber was sparely and beautifully appointed: a small carved cot, a handmade teak table and copy desk, an exquisite stained glass lamp, and the rena garden—a simple, ten-foot-square recession in the floor, filled with sharp-grained white sand and punctuated with cacti and three large but movable stones, each of which represented one of the moons.

The secret of the garden was an old sylvan magic, perfected among the elves who, in the Age of Dreams, brought the sand into the forest to build the first of the renas. These elves had also known the true meaning of the stones: that the black stone was augury, foretelling with the fractured, fitful light of divination, while the red stone told the past, its vision warped by the many versions of history. The white stone showed the present, showed what was happening someplace, usually unknown, a hundred feet or a thousand miles from the reader.

Moving slowly, carefully over the bright sand, Vaananen stirred circles with one foot. He bent, hoisted the red stone, and set it beside the white. Then, seating himself on the black stone, he stared across the broken expanse of sand, reading the fresh geometry of dune and ripple, the violet shadows cast by the stones.

The rena garden was now only a relaxation tool among the human clergy of Qualinesti. Absorbed and tamed into the Istarian theocracy, it was little more than a sedative, its true ancient powers forgotten. Now the sand and the abstract positioning of the stones were supposed to calm the mind for contemplation, create a serenity in much the same way as, say, growing flowers or watching a waterfall.

Vaananen stared intently at the red, lava-pocked stone.

Sedative, indeed. The Istarian brothers did not know the half of it.

He passed a hand over the large, squat cactus in the center of the sand, feeling its aura of moisture and expectancy.

Rain. Rain within the hour.

But still no rain in the desert.

Slowly he stood, pacing softly about the garden, his eyes on the center of the square, where the combed dunes spiraled tightly like a whirlpool around the three glyphs he had drawn in the sand.

Rolling up the white sleeves of his robe, Vaananen rubbed off a patch of concealing potion on the inside of his left wrist and focused on the red oak leaf tattooed there. He had hidden this mark from his comrades for the six years he had served with the Kingpriest's clergy.

The red oak leaf. The druid's hand.

Vaananen focused, and the glyphs glowed and shimmered and then disappeared. Now, miles away, they would rest in the floor of the kanaji.

The rebels would find water now. They would also learn of the Istarian withdrawals.

Briskly, without ceremony, he crouched and raked over the smooth sand where the glyphs had been. The area once again matched the rest of the garden's surface.

From the rumors that swirled about the temple, through the corridors, towers, and the roseate Audience Hall of the Kingpriest, Vaananen was certain that all his meticulously drawn symbols had done their distant work.

So it had been for years.

His heart had gone out to the eccentric, alien Plainsman lad who had found the ancient kanaji, the boy who searched for water. And so, through the first years of Fordus's Water Prophecy, Vaananen had guided the young man, and with druidic augury located the underground sources of water for the Que-Nara, informing Fordus through glyph and kanaji.

When, after the inexplicable dream a year ago, the Water Prophet became the War Prophet, and the rebellion against Istar began, the druid had begun to shroud even more information in the ancient symbols: the location of Istarian troops and their movements.

He also kept a constant warding spell upon the golden torc around Fordus's neck. This, too, was magic at a distance, and the druid's sleep was fitful and unsettled as his incantations protected the wandering Plainsman from the elements, the Istarians . . .

And from something else, far more grim and dark and powerful. Vaananen was not sure exactly what this larger menace was, but he had his suspicions.

Zeboim, perhaps. Or Hiddukel. Or an evil god even more powerful. Of one thing Vaananen was certain. He was safe, and so were the rebels he protected, only as long as he was beneath Istarian notice.

So he stayed obscure and low, and helped Fordus quietly.

Obviously, the lad had a gift. He could discover both weather and tactics in the shimmering lines on the sand. And then the elf would translate Fordus's reverie, and the Plainsmen would travel, and Istar would fall to another desert defeat.

So it had been, and so it was.

With his finger he traced the next of the spirals inward, then sat back on his heels. Slowly, the sand began to boil and turn about the white stone.

Good, the druid thought. A sign from the present.

Suddenly, the white stone dulled and grayed, its brilliance transformed to a sick, fish-belly white, and the whirling sand sent out ripple after ripple, the white stone sinking slowly into the garden until it rested at the bottom of a widening coil of sand.

Then the stone itself began to bristle and swell. Vaananen watched in horrified fascination as the thing sprouted eight white, rootlike legs, which suddenly began to twitch and wave . . .

Like the funnel trap of a springjaw, the druid thought, and felt the hair on his arms rise. Peace. 'Tis but a vision.

Yet despite himself, Vaananen shrank from the image. A human form appeared at the edge of the whirlpool, a wavering translucent shape like a mirage on the desert horizon. The apparition scrambled vainly toward the top of the sandy whirlpool, the springjaw clambering after it, its smaller set of fangs clacking hungrily.

"Fordus!" Vaananen whispered, stepping forward in alarm. He knew that somewhere this was actually happening. The rebel was fighting with a monster. Here in his chamber, powerless to help, the druid could only watch and hope.

And breathe the warding over the distant torc.

At the edge of the eddying sand, the ghostly man clutched, grappled, slid back. The springjaw scrambled toward him, a dull light shining in its great green eye. Huge, sand-colored, and insectlike, it scrabbled at the bottom of a funneling pit, its ragged jaws opening like a crab's claw, like a Nerakan mantrap.

Fordus lurched toward the lip of the pit and safety as the creature reared and plunged, its huge mandibles encircling his ankle, widening, arching . . .

"Watch the other eyes . . ." Vaananen muttered, staring at the dull black orbs resting behind the false, brilliant eyes of the springjaw. The black eyes, the true ones, would signal the attack.

He breathed a prayer that Fordus would know this as well.

The great jaws hinged and wavered over the Plainsman's leg. Sliding down the sandy incline, Fordus snatched an axe from his belt, pivoted, and hurled the weapon solidly into the thorax of the attacking monster. The springjaw roared, staggered back, its black eyes rolling swiftly beneath the chitinous exoskeleton of the head.

"Now!" the druid cried, and thirty miles away, in the heart of the desert, the Prophet felt the torc at his neck quiver and draw him up. With a last burst of furious energy, Fordus set his other foot on the springjaw's head and pushed. Crying out as the swiftly closing jaw flayed the skin of his ankle, the Plainsman rolled clear of the trap, pulling himself onto level ground as the springjaw slid back into crumbling darkness. He sat on the edge of the sand funnel, thankful to be alive, clutching his wounded foot.

Which already was beginning to swell with the monster's poison.

Vaananen leaned forward, trying vainly to judge the severity of the wound. But the white sand whirled in the other direction, and slowly the stone rose to the surface of the garden. Innocent and mute, it lay where the druid had placed it, next to the red stone, where its shadow formed a soothing pattern on the manicured sand.

Vaananen exhaled. The vision was over. The sand was smooth, featureless again. He was alone and safe in his sparely appointed room, the shadows on the walls lengthening and deepening as the colored lamplight dwindled.

Vaananen raised his head at the soft sound on the windowsill. Vincus gracefully lowered himself into the room.

"What did you bring me?" the druid asked, smiling and turning to face his visitor.

The young man's dark hands flashed quickly, racing through an array of ancient hand-signs.

"Of course you may sit," Vaananen said, chuckling as he detected the smell of sour hay. "And the pitcher of lemon-water on the table is for you."

Vincus drank eagerly, then seated himself on the druid's cot. Swiftly his hands moved from sign to sign, like a mage's gestures before some momentous conjury.

"So they all mention this dissent among the rebels," Vaananen mused. "Mercenary, augurer, salt seller—same story."

Vincus nodded.

Vaananen turned slowly back to the sand. "But no more than a passing word?"

Vincus shook his head, then noticed the druid's back was to him. He shrugged and took another drink of the water.

"And what do *you* make of it, Vincus?" Vaananen asked, glancing over his shoulder.

The young man flashed three quick, dramatic signs in the lamplit air, and the druid laughed softly.

"Nor do I. But you have done your job. Now I must do mine."

Vincus gestured at the water pitcher.

"Of course," the druid replied. "Have all you like. Then you should leave quickly, the same way, I think. Prayers are short in these times, and your master will expect you in his quarters."

A scowl passed over the open face of the young man. Balandar, Vincus's master, was not unkind, and his library boasted the best collections among the Istarian clergy. But servitude was servitude, and it went hard to trade the freedom of the streets and the night for confinement and the slave collar—even if the collar was made of shining silver.

Vaananen turned away uncomfortably. In a moment Vincus would climb back through the window and into the garden. He would reach Balandar's quarters in plenty of time to make the fire, pour wine from a rare and valuable stock for the ancient cleric, then set out his robes for the next morning. In an hour, old Balandar would be snoring, and Vincus would recover the time—for reading, for sleeping or eating.

For anything but freedom. Vaananen did not like to think about it.

Vincus's father had died in servitude, and the Kingpriest had visited the man's punishment on the next generation, but unlike the elves miles below them, digging into rock and oblivion, Vincus could have his freedom eventually. Someday, he vowed silently, Vincus will go free.

Carefully, the druid traced the glyphs once more in the pristine sand. Fordus would live. He *had* to.

And he would need water and tactics at once.

The Tine. The sign that would take him to the ancient dried fork of the river. There was water underground. Easy enough.

Third day of Solinari was more complex. The compressed, multiple meaning of the glyph. Water three feet below the surface, Istarian forces three days away . . .

Blanking his mind, Vaananen looked at the third symbol.

No Wind. Favorable weather, favorable strategy. The principal Istarian force lay miles and miles away, regrouped in defensive positions.

Good news on all fronts—news to be sent to Fordus over the miles.

But there was also this unsettling news Vincus had brought to him.

Rocking back on his heels, the druid inspected his handiwork. He needed a fourth glyph, to show warning.

He drew the chitinous exoskeleton, the antennae, the wide, hinged mandibles.

Springjaw. It would be fresh in Fordus's mind.

Beware. The ground is unsteady.

Chapter 7

Three days into Fordus's absence, the rebel camp grew more and more uneasy. They were nomads, and three days in one place was too long. The livestock had grazed the scrub completely to the cracked and stony ground, and the last water was nearly gone. All the while, the camp was abuzz with new arrivals, as Plainsmen from all over the region came and went in Fordus's itinerant quarters.

It was not unusual for Fordus to be gone a day, perhaps even overnight. The rebels were accustomed to their commander's retreats into the desert fastness: Fordus leaving Stormlight in charge and departing for the kanaji, to the level lands beyond, in search of water or, sometimes, enlightenment. Frequently, after a night alone in the wasteland, fasting and meditating, he returned to the encampment exhausted but strangely alert, speaking cryptically of his desert visions.

The elf would give them words of direction, settle poetry into policy, oracle into tactics. Then the battles would follow, and the victories. It had been that way since Fordus became the War Prophet.

It was the way things worked when they needed water. But this time they were three nights waiting, in the wake of their most costly victory.

Even Larken began to watch the horizons with more than a little fear.

* * * * *

Apprehension spread like poison through the rebel camp, and Stormlight gathered scouts and outrunners to search for the missing commander. However, a different sort of gathering took place where the plains tumbled down into desert, not a mile from the site of the recent bloody battle.

Just north of the grassy rise where Fordus had watched the battle unfold, scarcely an hour before sunrise on the second day of his absence, two Istarian cavalrymen rode south toward the Tine, cloaked in black against the fitful white moonlight. They were lean veterans of a dozen campaigns, hard and cynical and almost impossible to fool, borne by a mysterious summons to a moonlit council with the enemy.

They had come to this spot in the boulder-strewn rubble, awaiting the man who approached them now on foot and alone, trudging across a wide expanse of packed sand and sawgrass.

"No place for 'em to hide an escort, sir," the older of the cavalrymen observed. Absently, he stroked the sergeant's bar on the shoulder of his breastplate. "There's a mile between him and the cover of shadow."

The younger man nodded. He was the officer, the one in charge. By reflex, he rested a gloved hand on the hilt of his sword and traced the cold carving on it.

There was something very odd about this walking stranger. He moved heavily through the uneven terrain, never once dodging briar or gully. He did not break stride—not until he was within hailing distance. Then, in a low, conversational voice, he greeted the Istarians.

"The time is now, gentlemen," he declared. His amber, slitted eyes narrowed, and he drew the black silk tunic close around him as cover against the desert night. "The time is now, if you're men enough to seize it."

"Come with us," the officer demanded curtly. "Tell me what you know."

The man stood his ground and turned stiffly to his left, his black hair cascading over his face, and pointed to a mesa low and dark on the horizon.

"The rebels are there," he announced, ignoring the circling horses. "Camped at the base of Red Plateau. It's been three days since they've seen Fordus Firesoul, and in his absence a dozen warring factions have sprung up in the camp. The old guard, the ones with Fordus since he became the Prophet, they all follow Stormlight and Larken. But some of the Que-Nara and many of the barbarians are looking to Northstar, while the bandits go with Gormion. And then . . ." the informer concluded, pausing meaningfully, "there are those of us . . . secretly loyal to Istar. Those whose future is tied intimately to the fortunes of the Kingpriest."

The Istarians exchanged a skeptical glance and a curled smile.

"I tell you, their commander is missing," the informer insisted. " 'Tis now, or 'tis a long and bloody war, I tell you. I offer you a great gift!"

The officer considered this ultimatum. A dozen miles to the north, the defeated Istarian army huddled against the outer walls of the city, awaiting reinforcements recalled posthaste from their stations along the Thoradin border. Until relief arrived, the decimated remnants of Istar's pride crouched nervously at their campsites, imagining rebels in the shadows of rocks, in the moonlit tilt of the grass.

No. Though something about the informer's words edged on the truth, the time to attack was *not* now.

And yet . . .

Accustomed to quick, uncompromised decision, the young Istarian officer resolved the issue at once. He would send this veiled informer packing, then follow at a distance.

"What you advise is impossible," he said.

The man scowled. "And why?"

"I owe you no explanation."

"You already regret your decision," the informer growled, pointing a pale, almost translucent finger at the two men on horseback.

The officer did not reply, his gaze on the distant plateau. Out there, if the informer spoke the truth, hundreds of rebels camped by fires carefully banked and concealed so that their collected light would not lift the purple shadows on the horizon. "After all," he finally said, "how do we know that you are not sent to lure us into even greater troubles? Perhaps you are Fordus himself!" He laughed mockingly.

Angrily, the informer turned away, casting a last venomous glance over his shoulder. He moved quickly and silently back into the desert, a dark shape passing over the moonlit sands. The cavalrymen sat silently atop their horses until, on a dune at the farthest reaches of sight, the informer stopped and lifted his arms to the cloudy heavens.

"Dramatic sort, ain't he, sir?" the sergeant asked with a chuckle.

There was no answer.

For a long, idle moment, the sergeant watched the horizon. "Shall we follow him, sir?" he asked, turning slowly toward the younger man.

Who had vanished entirely.

The officer's mare stood wide-eyed and trembling, black powder tumbling from her saddle, pooling on the ground in a murky pyramid, rising with a horrifying symmetry as though it lay in the bottom of a bewitched hourglass.

A bronze Istarian breastplate rocked pitifully on the hard ground, a helmet and a pair of white gloves not a dozen feet away.

Inanely, the sergeant reached for his sword.

A lone nightbird wheeled above, the moonlight silver on its extended wings.

* * * * *

Poison. Delicious poison.

The venom of ten thousand years flowed through the Dark Queen as, in her faceted, crystalline body, she stalked across the desert's edge toward the distant fires of the Plainsmen.

She thought of the dead cavalryman with glee and

relish.

Such to all, Plainsman or Istarian, who crossed her purposes. Especially the one who escaped her springjaw minion.

Such to the gods themselves who stood in her way.

In the starlit dome of the desert sky, the son of the goddess tilted into view, still invisible to the mundane eye—to human and elf, to dwarf and kender. Even the most powerful sorceries would strain to locate the black moon, for Nuitari awaited his time, eluding eye and glass and augury, the deluded forecasts of Istarian astrologers.

But Takhisis could see him, of course, as he glided high overhead, obscuring bright Sirrion and Shinare in his passage.

Her son. Her dark pride.

From his birth, Nuitari had been the wedge between her and her consort, the black incident in the Age of Starbirth that drove apart Takhisis and Sargonnas before the world began.

Oh, I won that battle at the waking of time, Takhisis thought. And I shall win all battles hence.

The dark moon had been her oath, her promise to the other gods. To seal their agreement to never again make war on the face of the planet, each family of gods had agreed to create a child who would become blood-brother to the children created by the other families. Bound in kinship and in covenant, they would bless the world of Krynn with magic.

The silver child of Paladine and Mishakal, bright Solinari, was the first to ascend into the heavens. This eldest child showered forth a warm, beneficent magic, and the people of Paladine, the highborn elves, had lifted their arms to the descending moonlight. And the humans, the Youngest Born, had lifted their arms as well to the red light of Lunitari, the child born of Gilean the Book, chief god of the neutral pantheon.

Both of them sailed through the heavens now, aloft in an egg of silver and an egg of scarlet. When they hatched, the moons—husks of the gods, the ancient philosophers would call them—sailed through the skies of Krynn as refuge and home for the godlings . . .

And, in the binding age of the Kingpriest, their prisons.

But this was long before Istar, long before the Age of Might.

In the void above the whirling planet, Takhisis and Sargonnas had created the child. Their coupling was joyless, loveless, for already both gods had fallen away from one another into the dark abyss of themselves. In a dark cloud above the swelling Courrain, the goddess had overwhelmed her consort with a powerful magic, and forced Sargonnas to bear the child.

For a day and a night, the great scavenging god had lingered in the cloud of steam and volcanic ash, the miasma hovering sullenly over the ocean surface. Takhisis, watchful in her strange motherhood, circled the cloud and waited, as deafening cries of labor and rage burst forth from the eddying darkness.

For a day and a night and another day, she circled and waited, her hidden consort bellowing and vowing vengeance.

"Let it come," Takhisis taunted. "Oh, let your worst return to me, Sargonnas. I shall forego the pain and the labor, and when you have fulfilled your part . . .

"The spirit of the child will be mine alone."

At sunset on the second day, as the ocean waters flamed with the setting sun, the golden egg of the Condor sailed from the cloud.

The third moon. Nuitari the gold.

She remembered it well. How the great Condor, steaming and reeking with volcanic fire, had circled over the golden egg, menacing and boding.

"No, Takhisis!" Sargonnas had challenged, for the first time defying her, setting his contemptible, smoldering form against her will and desire. "I have borne this thing through magic and darkness and searing pain! I shall foster it, and it will be my emissary in the night sky of Krynn."

She had not expected the rage that rose up and nearly choked her. The eastern sands of the Ansalon coastline, those rocky beaches that would in time become Mithas and Kothas, islands of minotaurs, blackened in the heat of her passing wings as she swooped and circled the despicable rebel, the traitorous god and his bright, golden trophy.

"Nuitari is mine!" she shrieked in reply, and the Worldscap Mountains erupted with the first volcanoes. "Mine, do you hear?" Lightning riddled the evening sky, and for the first time the forest crackled, struck by the kindling heat from the heavens. "Or I shall destroy the thing. Shell and godling and all!"

The two gods circled the golden oval, the black batwings of Takhisis whirling in narrowing circles about the matted, smoking feathers of the scavenger, who fanned the ocean air with the stench of carrion.

"You would not destroy the godling," Sargonnas croaked, fire and sunlight brindling over his mottled apterium. "Not when you could *master* him!"

"You contemptible parasite!" spat the goddess. "You gem-hoarding *adjunct*! You sniveling, emulous, dunghill *fowl*!"

Fire raced through the salty air and scattered, and Sargonnas perched atop the sailing golden egg, mantling his wings above the bright treasure.

" 'Would not destroy the godling,' you say?" Takhisis rumbled. "I will show you all my compassion, Sargonnas. I will show you the abundance of my heart."

Arching in the sky, her black wings shadowing the older moons, Takhisis drew the ocean wind into her lungs and belched forth a column of black fire. For a moment the condor and his glittering prize vanished in the dark blaze, and the heavens fluttered and extinguished. Deprived of sunlight and star, the planet cooled and frosted, and the deepest winter settled on Ansalon, unnatural in the month of Summer Run. But slowly, because the goddess was not the only force on Krynn, the stars returned one by one, the first ones rising in the constellation of the Dragon, then the surrounding luminaries and, finally, the planets and the moons.

A dark shape hung in the heavens, its burnt wings still brooding above the egg, above the blackened shell and the seared godling within.

Nuitari was never the same after that. Dark-haired and sickly, suffering a fiery malady in the depths of his lungs and throat, he spoke in hoarse whispers from the first days, from his hatching time.

So Takhisis remembered as she passed over the unsettled sands. Above her the dark moon drifted furtively between the stars, and she looked up approvingly at the twisted path of her son.

Sargonnas had been right.

Why destroy the child you can bend to your will completely?

She thought of the Kingpriest in his high tower,

counting the opals that would bring her to the surface of Krynn.

She glided toward the lights of campfires, and a solitary bird, circling over her cautiously, called softly and sped away.

* * * * *

The same bird shrieked again as it sailed over Fordus, who knelt on the floor of the kanaji.

Exhausted and much the worse for his struggle with the springjaw, his grazed ankle swelling with a trace of the creature's poison, Fordus had struggled to the edge of the Tears of Mishakal. There he found the kanaji, and there he waited for the glyphs amid the strange, chiming music of the wind over the salt crystals, the lights of the camp a mile away glowing on the other side of the Tears.

Fordus closed his eyes. Clutching his ankle, he stared at the windswept sand in the open, circular chamber. For a terrifying moment, he confused it with the springjaw's lair and then remembered where he was. But his ankle had been touched by a plume of the acid that was the clumsy springjaw's other defense.

"Come forth," he muttered finally, teeth clenched.

And then, the new glyphs formed in the eddying sand.

The Tine. The sign for water. Of that he was sure.

Third day of Solinari.

That was more puzzling. But when he gave it voice in the midst of his people, when Stormlight heard the prophecy and interpreted it in the common language, his mind would know what his heart now sensed here in the kanaji.

No Wind.

It was a mystery to him, an obscure arrangement of shape and line and half-resemblance. And then, emerging from the pristine, level sand, came a fourth, extraordinary glyph.

Springjaw.

Fordus blinked in confusion. But it had already happened! The funnel, the ground giving way beneath him . . .

This fiery sting in his ankle and the rising fever.

Slowly he set his thoughts aside—this time with more difficulty, as the pain in his foot and his leg thrust him again and again into the labyrinth of his mind, into doubts and fears that the words would not come, that Stormlight and Larken would not find him, that the gods themselves had turned away.

Instead, he stared at the symbols, closed his eyes. There. He had it. The four glyphs were committed to memory, and then as always, they vanished immediately, leaving the floor of the pit clean and unruffled.

Fordus tightened the neck of his robe, his opal collar hot and constricting. He could not remove the torc. Long ago the glyphs had warned of dire consequence if he did so. But he was pained and uncomfortable. His fever made the desert chill almost unbearable.

Fordus tried to stand, and suddenly the kanaji rocked with a red light, throwing him back to his knees. He closed his eyes and saw the acid spurt again, eating relentlessly into the flesh of his booted ankle.

Leaning against the limestone wall, he pulled himself up on his feet again.

Have to get out of here, he thought. Into the light. Into the air.

Get home. Get warm.

Painfully, his skin hurting with every touch of his

robe, he crawled out of the pit and rested—for a minute, ten minutes, an hour?—on the baked earth at its rim. Dimly his fevered mind registered the faint music of the salt crystals, and for a while, he slept or tried to sleep.

Again the dream came to him. The lake of fire. The spindle bridge. The dark, winged form, the flattery and coaxing . . . the promise of finding out who he was.

Briefly, in the flitting fashion of delirium, it seemed like Racer stepped into his dream. Grizzled and venomous, his wrinkled face a sinkhole of malice, Racer shuffled onto the narrow bridge and into the winged shadow, his spindly ancient form commingling with the strange, birdlike cloud until Racer became the condor, the condor Racer.

No. No unexpected dreams.

Fordus woke and stood, drunkenly lurching toward the shimmering stones and the camp and safety. Not a hundred yards into his desperate effort, the cracked earth seemed to rise, to trip him, and he fell to his hands and knees, clambering over the ground like a scorpion, like a monstrous crab.

He reached the level top of the small rise. Ahead, the Tears of Mishakal seemed hazy, even more distant, as though in trying to run toward them he had in fact run in the opposite direction.

Fordus looked back, toward the kanaji.

A wide expanse of desert land lay between him and the standing rock and baked, cracked earth, its red-brown surface scored with an intricate webbing of lines.

For a moment, on the horizon, Fordus thought he saw Kestrel. He raised his hand, shouted or thought he shouted . . .

Then he remembered that his foster father was

two years dead, buried at the ancient dry fork of the Tine.

Then who . . . ?

Kestrel's form wavered at the edge of his sight, like a rain cloud. Slowly another form took shape inside it—another man, dressed in brilliant white, his robes dispelling the shadow like smoke in the wind.

Fordus stared at the man until his eyes hurt. A midsized man, balding, with sky-blue . . .

No, *sea-blue* eyes . . .

Then, as suddenly as it had appeared, the image was gone, leaving the bare desert bathed in the eerie moonlight, a desolate flatland that stretched for as far as Fordus could see.

His fever still torrid, the Water Prophet stared absently at the cracked earth until the cracks themselves began to take shape.

A glyph. Then another.

The whole desert has become my kanaji, Fordus thought incoherently, triumphantly. He began to read the wavering lines on the earth.

One resembled a tower. The other a chair.

In swift hallucinatory fashion, Fordus put a meaning together.

"I shall sit on the throne of Istar," he breathed. "I have waited for this summons.

"The rule of empire awaits me. The world has become my kanaji, my ground of visions. I shall lift the tyranny of the Kingpriest . . .

"And I shall rule in his stead. I know who I am. I am the Kingpriest."

All messages of water forgotten, Fordus rolled exultantly onto his back, staring up at the reeling heavens. The earth had spoken, naming him rightful Kingpriest of Istar.

It was glorious news.

What he had found was better than water.

He was the Prophet and he was the prophecy.

Above him, the hawk banked and rushed on a high wind back to the rebel camp. At his mistress's orders, Lucas was searching for the commander, guided by faint, barely comprehensible voices on the edge of the wind. The hawk heard a dozen languages breathed into the air: the sleepy muttering of an elf-child somewhere in the darkness beneath Istar, the last gurgled sigh of a merchant murdered on the edge of the desert, the quiet sermons of the high grass and the ancient vallenwoods far, far to the south in Silvanost.

Among these sounds arose at last the murmur of the Water Prophet, strange, distracted talk of runes and water and the fall of cities.

Lucas found him on a flat stretch of desert south of the Tears. Sharp-eyed and vigilant, the hawk saw Fordus crawling and babbling, coming to rest at last on a rise midway between the salt flats and the standing stone from which he had been returning.

He seemed to be talking to someone, but there was nobody there.

Chapter 8

The hawk swooped through the firelight, and the smoke and rising cinders scattered in his path.

With a shrill, whistling cry, glowing red and amber in the midst of his nightfire, Lucas swept over the rebel campsite like a meteor, startling sentries, rousing the bandits from talk of discontent and sullen conspiracy. Gormion, crouched at dice in a circle of her followers, looked up sullenly and made a warding sign with a flash of silver bracelets, while Rann and Aeleth reached instinctively for their weapons.

Larken was standing by Northstar and Stormlight

at the arroyo's edge. She heard Lucas's cry, lifted her padded glove, and braced to receive the bird. With a sudden, graceful dive and an upsweep, the hawk struck hard on the underside of the glove, bells jingling while his talons fastened in the layered wool and leather. Then he murmured and pulled himself upright, Larken adjusting his jesses until he perched comfortably on her arm.

Despite her strength and preparation, Larken had staggered this time when the hawk landed. Her arm still shocked a bit, Larken began to look the bird over, spreading his feathers with her ashy fingers, making sure Lucas had not been attacked by a larger raptor. Northstar and Stormlight stepped back apprehensively.

The hawk leaned against his mistress, crying softly like a waking child into her coarse, matted hair. Larken stopped her inspection and listened.

Fordus is approaching, she signed, translating Lucas's cry. *He is near, but there is a cloud above him. Lucas saw no more of the Prophet.*

"But he saw other things."

The bird's eyes glittered greenly.

"Then sing us *that* sight, Larken," Northstar urged.

The bard glanced uncomfortably at her younger cousin. For Northstar, the solutions were easy: he read the stars, the paths of the desert, and his destination was mapped. He did not understand the wild moment in which the singer gives her heart to the bird, when the light expands, when the hawk's cry becomes words and the words become song.

When you sing because you cannot choose otherwise.

Almost unwillingly, in a soft voice unaccompanied by her drum, Larken began the hawk's song.

The music was an old sea chantey from Balifor—
somehow she remembered the music—but the
words, as always, were new and fresh, gaining
power as they came to her in the firelit dark of the
campsite.

The dark man in the desert
The dark man on the plain
The dark man in the gap of the sky
Is no dark man.

His home is not in moonlight
His home is not in sun
The dark man on the grassy hill
Is no dark man.

O his arms are stone and water
O his blood is stone and sand
The dark man in the circled camp
Is no dark man.

As swiftly as they had come, the words ceased.
Lucas fluffed contentedly, the last of his ruddy light
sprinkling onto the desert floor, and the fires themselves seemed to contract once more around the
huddled campsites. Larken placed the bird on his
perch and sat down, resting her face in her hands.
Already she could barely remember what she had
sung, for the words had risen unbidden, had passed
through her like light through a faceted glass.

The eyes of the listeners turned to Stormlight, who
stared silently into the fire.

This time the elf was not sure of the meanings.
This was an exotic musing of bard and bird. It was
like a foreign language he almost knew.

Stormlight cleared his throat, the white *lucerna* lifting from his golden eyes. "There is a spy come in the midst of us," he declared. "Someone who is not what he seems. That's what the hawk was saying, as I follow it. Yes. That is what the bird said."

Larken and Northstar exchanged an uncomfortable glance.

"A spy," Stormlight repeated, this time with more certainty.

Tamex stepped into the firelight.

The hawk cried out, and raised his wings high, his hooked beak open and threatening.

At one moment, the firelit margins of air seemed to waver and glimmer, and then Tamex was among them, visible, tangible. Silently he moved into full view, his black silk tunic shimmering. He shook the dust from the tops of his boots and scanned the circle of rebels indifferently. The firelight glowed through his skin, and for a moment, the sharp-eyed Northstar thought that the warrior's fingers seemed crooked and arched, like talons.

Who was this man, born of the midnight desert?

"The dark man," Stormlight breathed. "Who is not what he seems."

Larken shot him a sullen look. And then she flushed, uncertain why she wanted to defend this man.

Tamex turned to meet them, black eyes angry and glittering like polished onyx. Gormion, Rann, and Aeleth, never true loyalists to Fordus or his officers, rose to stand beside Tamex, their hands already on the hilts of their weapons.

"Where have you been, warrior?" Stormlight asked, his voice cold and low.

Tamex shrugged. The bandits closed behind him.

At a nearby campfire, three Plainsmen rose and, clutching their spears, walked slowly, menacingly, toward Gormion, casting wavering shadows over the warring lights.

Something brushed Stormlight's shoulder. Northstar had appeared beside him. Though more scout than warrior, the young man was ready to do his part—knife drawn and keen eyes shifting alertly over the dark man and his bandit following.

Larken watched with rising alarm, and Lucas whistled uneasily.

The two warriors—the elf and the pale, mysterious Tamex—were locked in a stare that could end only in combat.

Then the cry of a sentry fractured the tense silence, and nearly all eyes whipped toward the sound. The young Plainsman atop the Red Plateau pointed north and shouted.

"Cavalry! Two hundred from the north!"

Tamex broke off the stare with Stormlight and smiled wickedly. So they *had* come, after all.

* * * * *

Trained by the Solamnics over the three centuries of their alliance, the Istarian cavalry were almost as brilliant, as swift and effective as their teachers. Accomplished swordsmen and deadly bowmen, they fought from horseback, frequently tied to the saddle to keep them astride their mounts in close combat. They were also much more ruthless than the Solamnics. A Solamnic Knight stayed his hand in occasional mercy against the enemy, whether man or elf or dwarf or even ogre, for his Oath told him "Est Sularus oth Mithas"—"My Honor is My Life."

Istarians, on the other hand, followed neither Oath nor Measure. The stories of their raids were horrible.

Stormlight's heart sank at the sentry's alarm. For a brief moment he struggled for a plan, for the words to express it.

When Tamex seized that moment to begin shouting, the rebels jumped at his words.

"Smother the campfires!" the black-cloaked man ordered. Quickly Rann kicked sand over Gormion's banked fire, and throughout the campsite, the smoke disappeared from the night air.

"To the Plateau!" Stormlight ordered, but his words were lost in Tamex's bellowing cry—a voice inhumanly loud.

"Back to the Tears!" the dark man ordered. "We'll fight them from the rocks!" The old and the young abandoned their campfires and did what they were told, hurrying to the safe maze of standing crystal.

Stormlight called to the surrounding Plainsmen, but they were already moving, following Tamex and Gormion toward the eerie field. It was five hundred yards from the campsite to the rocks, over level and open ground, but Tamex led the way, gathering barbarians and bandits as he skirted the edge of the salt flats. More campfires winked out to darkness, and then, at the edge of the camp, a column of Istarian torches wavered and bobbed and advanced.

"Plume! Stardancer!" Stormlight shouted, but the two young men lingered foolishly, ardent to shed Istarian blood. Desperately Stormlight grabbed for Stardancer, but the lad was too quick as he brushed past. A group of young Plainsmen and younger bandits, whooping and beckoning to the approaching torches, girded themselves for battle.

"You fools!" Stormlight shouted.

Then the sound of hoofbeats, distant at first, became deafening, inevitable. The first horse breasted into view, the bronze Istarian armor glistening in the torchlight. With a cry, Northstar wrestled the rider from his saddle, but the ropes that tied the Istarian in place tightened and held, and the startled horse galloped through the ashes of a smothered fire, dragging both men over the hard ground.

Stormlight crouched in his fighting stance as a dozen cavalry took shape in the darkness. Bursting into the camp, swords drawn and spears readied, the riders tore into their quarry like leopards into a helpless herd of sheep. Young Plume fell with a scream, impaled on an Istarian spear, and an even younger boy, an orphan named Lightfoot, fell beside him. Indifferent as a storm or a desert wind, the horsemen hurdled the dying bodies on their way toward a handful of bandits clustered around Aeleth at the edge of the Tears of Mishakal.

"No!" Stormlight shouted, as the rebel resistance broke into rout and panic. Plainsman and barbarian—women, old men, and children, exposed in the open country between the campsite and the salt flats—fell before the swords of the Istarians as they scrambled through ash and sand and rubble.

Their swords blooded with threescore innocents, the cavalry closed with Aeleth's bandits in a racket of war cries and clashing metal. The Tears echoed dolefully with the screams of the wounded and dying.

Where are you, Fordus? Stormlight thought, racing toward Mishakal's Tears. You would know what to . . . what to . . .

He stopped in horror as a dark wind passed over him.

Tamex appeared and, hook-bladed kala raised aloft, rallied the rebels against the circling Istarians. The mysterious warrior, whose bravery and inventiveness had rescued two hundred noncombatants from the merciless cavalry, had apparently returned to avenge the deaths of those he could not save.

As veiled and unsavory as the black-robed man might seem, at least he fought like a hero. The first strong sweep of his weapon drove an Istarian lancer from horseback, the saddle cords snapping with the force of the blow. Tamex wheeled like a ritual dancer, slowly and confidently blocking two spear thrusts and the downward swipe of a sword that seemed to pass through his arm but obviously did not, the blade shimmering bloodless and ineffectual in the firelight.

With a laugh that rang through the crystals, Tamex hooked his blade into the chest of the attacking swordsman, through shield and bronze and leather and bone. The Istarian fell, and the cavalry scattered before the strange and formidable champion.

Like a mythic figure from the Age of Huma, Tamex pivoted amid the horsemen, pulling one, two, a third from their saddles. Aeleth's bow felled another two, and Rann, his battle-rage enkindled by Tamex's valor, leapt up behind the saddle and slit the throat of a hapless officer.

Suddenly, the brazen call of a trumpet rose from the chaos of battlesound and resounding laughter. The Istarian commander rose in his stirrups, signaling frantically at his disorganized troops. One of Gormion's black-feathered arrows flashed through the moonlight and lodged in his shoulder, and the officer cried out and wheeled his horse back into the darkness.

Nor was Stormlight idle, as Tamex and the bandits turned the tide of the battle. Breathing a prayer to Branchala, the wiry elf raced between galloping horses and, with a powerful, high kick, drove his heel soundly into the helmet of an Istarian spearman, shattering bronze and skull. The man toppled dead from the horse, and wrestling the animal under control, Stormlight mounted and galloped off after the escaping Istarian commander.

And then it was all over, leaving an eerie silence, punctuated by only a few distant shouts and the soft cries of the dying.

Northstar and Larken cautiously waded through the grisly campsite, where the dark, clean sands of the Istarian desert had become a shambles, a slaughterhouse. Over a hundred rebels lay dead or dying among the extinguished fires. Over half of them were the very young and very old, unable to move with the quickness that the situation had demanded. The others, forty or so, were the young braves of the company—the blustering youths who had thrown themselves recklessly at the attacking enemy. Sprawled amid sand and ash, run through by short sword and cavalry spear, they were mute testimony to the fate of a leaderless army. The survivors—those the dark man had led into the Tears of Mishakal—returned to the camp slowly, soberly.

It could have been even worse, Larken signed to her cousin. *Had not Tamex saved those he could, then rallied the bandits and come to our aid . . .*

Northstar turned to argue, but the sight of the black-robed man stopped his words.

Framed in torchlight, Tamex stood haughtily before a mound of Istarian dead. Under his supervision, the bandits had spread through the battleground, gathering bodies for a huge, midnight pyre. Roughly, indifferently, they threw the last of the Istarian corpses on the heap, and Tamex signaled to the torchbearers, who crouched and ignited the kindling beneath the bodies.

In the new, fitful light, the black-robed warrior

watched the flames rise with a look that Northstar could only describe as *exultant*. His broad arms folded across his chest, Tamex laughed softly. The fire touched the first of the dead, and the dark man's amber eyes flickered with their burning reflections.

With an eye accustomed to reading the constellations, Northstar followed the flames to the heavens.

Gilean was there, the starry Book in the height of the sky. Half encircling it, spread along the western sky, was Paladine's constellation, a huge and brilliant arc almost obscured by the clouds and the smoke.

Northstar strained to see the eastern sky. There would be the sign of the Dark Lady, the stars in a dim and sinuous pattern always facing those of Paladine, as if in perpetual war . . .

But the smoke was now too thick.

And yet something had changed up there.

As he gazed into the shrouded sky, Northstar shuddered with a cold and dark sensation. Something passed over him and through him. He was afraid again, afraid and weary. Suddenly he was dizzy; he lowered his gaze.

Tamex was staring at him, his eyes burning like distant, hostile stars. The shadow he cast in the fierce light of the fire was enormous, spreading.

For a moment, it seemed to have wings.

* * * * *

Fordus saw the first fires in the crystals.

He woke from another fevered dream, from a reverie of glyph and symbol, to desperate shouts on the wind. Somehow he had circled the rebel camp in his wandering, had strayed into the Tears of Mishakal. Through the gemlike landscape the cries and screams intermingled with the chiming, then echoed off the facets of the farthest glassy growths.

For a moment he did not know where he was. Blearily he scrambled to his feet, drank the last from his water flask, and looked for Larken, for Stormlight. His swollen foot gave beneath him, and he fell, clutching at the nearest crystal, which broke cleanly in his iron fever grip, its top flat and level like a plateau. The wind rushed from him, and he lay on his back in the dark sand, cursing bad circumstance, the rotten luck of springjaws and falls and poison.

Slowly, amid chime and echo, he recognized the distant cries as the clamor of battle. Shapes milled at the edge of his vision. There were people in the salt flats, cowering, hiding.

Steadying himself against the largest crystal, Fordus regained his footing and hobbled toward the sound, toward the people. On all sides the red moonlight glittered, reflected off the crystals until the rebel chieftain was dazzled and confused, turned about like a wanderer in a house of mirrors.

Through the maze of light and sound Fordus stumbled, his apprehension growing. He recalled the stories about the Tears—the vanished travelers even in this new age of might, the deadly serenades of crystal and wind and evil magic. On the faces of the crystals he saw towering fires, the glint of bronze armor, the flash of steel.

And the soft, ominous sheen of black silk, as a solitary warrior paced through the shifting light.

He heard the sound of Istarian trumpets, the signaled retreat. For a moment he rejoiced, shifting his weight from his swollen foot and listening for cheers, for the victory cry of the rebel troops.

Instead, it was the smell of smoke that reached him on the wind—of burning wood and straw, and an acrid, unsettling smell he remembered from his youth, when once a raiding band of Irda had ransacked the camp where he lived.

The burning dead. The smell of pyres and the old, barbaric funerals of the Age of Dreams.

And also on the wind, beneath the crackle of fires, the keening of women, the wailing of men and the moans of the wounded, a solitary voice, no louder than a whisper, came to him as though borne from the crystals themselves.

A whisper on the wind, so soft that he was never sure whether he really had heard it, or if it was only that his thoughts and fears had prompted the words.

Without you, the voice insinuated, dark and seductive and denying. *They have defeated Istar without you, Fordus.*

Dismayed, the rebel lowered himself to the salty sand.

Chapter 9

Stormlight lost the Istarian rider in the pitch black of the night.

At one moment, the man was a shape ahead of him, flitting in and out of the gloom like a wraith. Stormlight tried valiantly to keep pace, but the Istarian was a seasoned rider, as at home in the night as in the saddle.

Finally, the Istarian vanished entirely. At one moment he was the wraith, the shadow, and then . . . he was nothing, not even sand. The desolate, scrubby landscape stretched into darkness all around the pursuing elf. Stormlight found himself in an unknown, bleak terrain, where forked black tree trunks sprouted starkly out of the crusty earth.

"I have followed him too far," he told himself, wrestling with a rising alarm. "I can see the foothills to the north, the mouth of the Central Pass. We're out on the plains somewhere, too close to Istar and its armies . . ."

Then the horse brushed by one of the dark trees, which crumbled into powder, streaking the animal's flank with a long, black stain.

Not trees. Crystals.

A light wind chimed through the glittering forest.

"The salt flats," Stormlight whispered. "The Tears of Mishakal."

At once he turned his horse about, intent on riding out of the perilous region, out to the safety of the desert, out to the plains. Even the prospect of Istarian armies no longer daunted him, faced as he was with night and magic and the dangerous illusions of this crystalline maze.

Slowly the horse weaved between the crystals, and Stormlight scanned the opaque horizon for signs of torchlight, of campfires, of a moon or a fortunate star. He refused to think on the old legends of his people, on how the salt flats would open to swallow the traveler, how they drew you toward their heart and toward your destruction by the serenade of the wind over the crystals—a cruel, cold wind that tumbled suddenly into song and language, against which, the legends said, the listener was powerless.

Amid the mist and the high chiming, amid the shifting dark shapes and the crunch of his horse's hooves through the crusted layers of sand and salt, Stormlight rode in widening circles, looking for light, for clear ground. He breathed a string of memorized prayers—to Shinare and to his patron Branchala, to Gilean the Book for knowledge, and of course to Mishakal herself, the goddess of healing whose tears, it was said, had created these flats.

All of his efforts—both strategy and prayer—seemed for naught. As the night wore on, Stormlight found himself moving into a deeper and deeper darkness. Now, though the stars and planets scattered the flats with a mysterious half-light, the elf could see no more than ten feet ahead of his horse. The pocked and hoof-churned ground told him he had passed this way before.

Instead of widening circles, his path had spiraled inward, turning toward the center of the salt flats, where the darkness was most dense, the country most confusing.

"Stop," he whispered, and reined in the horse. With a rising sense of unease, he scanned the maze around him for some clue, some glimmering—some definable light to guide him anywhere.

In seven hundred years of roaming the desert, it was as close as he had ever come to being lost.

When he reached what appeared to be the center of the salt flats he dismounted slowly, testing the ground beneath his feet and carefully leading his horse toward the centermost crystals.

It would be a long time—four, maybe five hours—until dawn. If the Tears of Mishakal were the legendary death trap, why, he was already dead. And yet, if they were only confusing and impassable terrain . . .

If nothing else, the sunrise would show him reliable east.

Stormlight sat at the foot of the crystal, leaning

back against the dark surface, which crumbled slightly against his weight. He sat, and waited, and watched for light.

After a while—Stormlight was unsure whether it was an hour, three hours, five hours—the darkness began to lift, and the wind chiming through the crystals calmed in the anticipation of approaching dawn. Now he could make out his face reflected on the facets of crystal.

It was distorted. In the nearest crystal, one eye was magnified, outsized, while in another not three feet away, his face was grotesquely narrowed, as though he had passed through a crack in a wall.

Yet another facet showed him as squat, shorter than he ever remembered. Always sensitive about his height, Stormlight turned quickly away.

And saw yet another, and another, each one bending, twisting, or otherwise translating his form into something bizarre and grotesque, some even reflecting those other reflections in an infinity of confusion.

Like the visions and prophecies that milled through the rebel camp, he thought. Each was a way of looking at the world, of holding the light so that it reflected the beholder as much as what he beheld.

"It is all too confusing," Stormlight murmured.

He closed his eyes and prayed again to Mishakal, for insight and healing wisdom. After all, this land was named for her, and hers as well was the power of healing, to restore the fractured and distorted body to its natural health.

No voice of the goddess did he hear, whistling through the crystal fields with revelation. And yet . . .

The solution came to him softly and slowly—it

was so simple that his laughter rang through the Tears in recognition.

He would need eyes, of course, to guide him out of the salt flats. And his own eyes were subject to the mirror maze of the crystals, the distraction and distortion and misdirection.

Still chuckling to himself, Stormlight mounted and, leaning back in the saddle, laid the reins gently over the animal's withers. He closed his eyes, brought down the *lucerna*, and surrendered to the horse. The animal serenely wandered through the crystals, bent toward the edge of the salt flats, toward open country, and toward his breakfast.

Stormlight let himself be carried homeward, his thoughts on cool water—if water indeed had been found—and the morning's quith-pa and bread. A sudden lurch from the horse snapped him back to alertness. Instantly wary, Stormlight opened his eyes and sat upright.

Dark shapes lay ahead of him, gray lines and imprints on the surface of the black salt. Stormlight took up the reins and guided the horse toward them.

One of the crystals—once a very large one, he guessed—lay in powder and rubble, a forlorn heap in the middle of a wasteland. Half out of idleness, half out of curiosity, Stormlight dismounted to examine it more closely.

The facets of the crystals caught the first pink light, and for a moment they shone softly, warmly, like freshly mined gems. Was it this that had prompted his people to go underground years ago? Had they mistaken something like this black glimmering for the stone more rare, for the glain opals their priests and Namers had told them lay deep beneath the Khalkist and Vingaard Mountains?

It was a story older than his own memories—how,

adopted, he had come to reside with the Que-Nara.

Stormlight had little recollection of his people. He recalled a face half-revealed by firelight, the smell of buckskin and pine, the touch of a soft hand . . .

Memories from childhood, or from a hundred years of wandering. He could not distinguish which.

But he remembered well the ambush at the desert's edge. The red armor and white banners of Istar, the knives of the slavers and the white-hot pain in his side.

He shrugged, pushing away the memory. Alone then, he was even more alone now in the Tears of Mishakal. That was the past, and to dwell on it was foolish, especially here in the deceptive salt flats, where a despairing thought could be your last.

Idly, the elf shifted his foot through the odd rubble.

Then the new light shone on a track—a single deep footprint in the black salt.

Stormlight crouched in the rubble, peering more closely.

A woman's print. Two days old, maybe three. Narrow and graceful, and incredibly deep.

As though she had sunk to her knees in the packed sand.

Yet the print was strangely delicate. The soft whorls of the heel marked the fine-grained, compressed salt, and the foot was clearly defined and free of callus and scar.

She did not walk much. At least not barefoot. Even a child among trackers would know that.

With a rough, leathery finger, Stormlight traced the graceful instep of the print.

He should know something more. The footprint taunted him with a mystery, with a secret in its spirals and simple, deep lines . . .

Lines. Like the foot of an infant.

Stormlight rested on his heels. Slowly, with a judicious sweep of his hand, he blew the drifted black salt from another print, and another. Then rising to his feet, he mounted the horse and followed the trail of the woman out of the Tears—a trail that seemed to rise out of nothingness, out of the blank center of the flats.

It could be a trap, he cautioned himself. The gods know there is danger in this . . . there is danger . . .

Yet he followed with a strange fascination as the path weaved sinuously through the standing crystals. Leaning low, face pressed against the horse's withers, he read the dark sand with a skill born of centuries in the hunt. When the slowly rising sun gave him direction, it revealed the footprints again, a thin path stalking over the salt flats, the steps wider and wider apart.

Had he looked up from this close, intent scrutiny, he might have seen the Plainsman's form reflected in the mirroring crystal—the wounded man lying in the salt flats, his ruddy beard matted with the last swallow from his now-empty waterskin.

He might have found Fordus, helped the Prophet to safety.

But in his oblivion, Stormlight passed near the wounded commander, who stared at him blearily, resentfully, through the maze of crystals.

She's running now, Stormlight thought, rising in the saddle, his thoughts focused on the strange, feminine tracks.

But running to what? Or from what?

Now it seemed that the woman's foot had expanded, widened, kept changing, the toes fusing and splaying.

Stormlight leaned against the warm neck of the

horse and let forth a slow, uneasy breath. It was a clawed creature he followed now, an enormous thing that had trampled a path over the salt flats, crushing rock and crystal in its heedless journey. All of his instincts told him to leave well enough alone, that the danger he had only suspected when he took up the trail was close to him now, a rumbling just at the edge of his hearing, an acrid smell beneath the smoke of a distant campfire.

The fires of the rebels. The monster was headed toward the Red Plateau, toward his drowsing, battle-dazed people.

With a click of his tongue and a shrill whistle, Stormlight spurred his horse through the black flats, longing for Fordus's speed, for the speed of the wind or a comet.

You are too late, a deep, denying voice told him, its cold, resonant words mingling with his thoughts until Stormlight could not tell whether it was the voice he heard or the bleak suggestions of his own worst imaginings.

"No!" Stormlight shouted. Suddenly the trail ended before him, the monstrous tracks vanished into unruffled black salt. Alarmed, confused, the elf wheeled the horse in a wide frantic circle and retraced his path. In the heart of the last track, in the very center of the enormous, splayed claw, a man's booted footprint lay in the dark sand as though he had stepped in that spot only, dropped from the sky or born from the swirling earth.

Stormlight reined in his horse. The human print was like a deep embedded thought of the clawed thing, like a glyph drawn in a time of dreams and dragons. Out of the monstrous print, boot prints led—the heavy steps of a man walking resolutely toward the rebel camps.

Cautiously, with his horse slowed to a walk, the Plainsman followed.

* * * * *

Tired and dirty, Larken watched the last of the flames lick the black rubble of the pyre.

Children, the old, and the flower of Plainsmen manhood had been put to the Istarian swords. Innocent and defenseless or ill-prepared and rash, they had fallen before the enemy like sacrificial offerings. Their deaths were even more monstrous because of the dishonor involved—the cavalry ambush that savaged graybeard and infant alike.

In the brilliant dawn, there was no way to mask the night's slaughter. The Istarian cavalry had left over a hundred rebels dead. Now, as the funeral fires themselves died and smoldered, it was the bard's duty to sing the Song of Passing, a farewell to all the departed, from the youngest to the wizened old. Each of the dead would be remembered in a verse, a line, a phrase of the song, so that none left the world unheralded. Larken's song would probably continue through the next night.

And longer still, if the augurers found no water.

Already miserably fatigued, Larken struck the drum once, twice, and waited for words and music to come to mind. The drumhead mottled and darkened in her hand, as though it, too, was mourning.

When no song came, Northstar sat down beside Larken, draping his arm consolingly over his cousin's shoulders.

Tamex approached them, smoke curling over the black silk of his robe.

Larken gave the dark stranger a sidelong glance. Though she had nothing for the dead, words that would attend Tamex's deeds and the music that would exalt his glory suddenly flooded her mind.

The bard felt unsettled, troubled by the strange, unbidden music. The melody was simple—a Plainsman ballad from her deepest childhood—with the first lines about the dark man and the mystery and the desert night. Still, some part of her refused to give voice to them.

Her drumming was soft and tentative as she hovered like a hawk between singing and silence.

Then a cry arose from the Plainsmen, and a dozen or so ragged children rushed toward a solitary rider emerging from the Tears of Mishakal.

It took Larken a moment to realize that the rider was Stormlight.

The elf leapt from the saddle and, with a swift and relentless stride, made his way through the group of children and past the smoldering campfires, brushing by Gormion and Aeleth as though the bandits were mist or high grass. Taking Larken's drum hand firmly and gently in his grasp, he guided her away from the fireside, away from her startled listeners, and when the two of them had passed out of earshot from the rest of the rebels, he spoke to her fervently, whispering through clenched teeth.

"Whatever you do, singer, whatever the magic you wield by drum and song, I command your silence now!"

Command? Larken signed, bristling at the elf's rough words. *Take your hand from me, Stormlight!*

Her gestures snapped sharp and final in the air between them. Slipping his grasp, the bard stalked off toward the Red Plateau.

Stormlight caught up with her. Overhead, Lucas soared out of the black salt flats.

"I know the power of your song," the elf insisted.

"How it raises up and it casts down . . ."

"Stop!" Larken shouted, but Stormlight continued, never hearing her.

"You were set to sing the glories of Tamex—this new and sudden hero. I could see it. But think of this before you sing. Whose bard have you been through the long months of exile and wandering and rebellion? And who is it you love?"

I know, Larken admitted, this time signing more evenly. *Fordus is still our commander.*

"And Tamex," Stormlight added, "is *not* who he seems to be!"

Larken shot the elf a searching glance. Something deeper than knowing, deeper even than song, told her that Stormlight spoke the truth, and that she knew it too well.

Tell me who he is, Stormlight, she gestured.

Then the hawk screamed above her, and all eyes lifted to the Red Plateau.

Fordus stood on the great height, overlooking the campsite and the ruin it had become.

* * * * *

He had climbed out of the salt flats and made the arduous ascent of the Red Plateau, his swollen foot still throbbing and aflame with the springjaw's poison. Twice more he had stumbled, his strong fingers scrabbling on the plateau's heights, as the desert reeled below him, a breathtaking distance into a black, crystalline void.

Let it go . . . let it go . . . you are weary, the desert seemed to say. The hard rock and the razored crystal beckoned to him—and for a brief, dizzy moment he listened, leaning out into the silent air, his iron grip slackening.

But he thought he heard a drum, distant and faint in the blurred encampment, and despite his grogginess and the deafening pulse of his blood, he had kept his balance.

Now he raised his arms to the heavens and shouted to the sunstruck sky, to the solitary reeling hawk, to the sea of uplifted faces now gathered in the black rubble below.

"I have returned from the desert. From the heart of the desert I have returned."

A dark man—someone new to the camp, and menacing—sneered at him. "Where were you when *Istar* returned?"

An approving murmur rose from the assembled rebels, loudest among the milling bandits.

Heedless of the noise and growing strife, Larken rushed by Tamex toward the staggering Fordus, humming a quick healing song.

"Your departure was . . . singularly convenient, Water Prophet," Tamex continued, folding his pale arms and glaring at Fordus with cold, reptilian eyes. "I trust that you at least have water to show for such a costly absence?"

Climbing the slow incline to the top of the plateau, Larken sang more loudly, her ragged voice transformed by concern for the wounded man. The tune was an ancient one, but in her voice it renewed and empowered, gaining depth and strength. Even the battle-wounded, lying on the blankets about the campfires, felt some stirrings of healing.

Suddenly Fordus's fever broke, and as the sweat rushed over his body, the glyphs returned to his shocked and dazzled memory.

"I have brought you this," he shouted, pointing at the pooling liquid on his skin, "as a foretaste of the water we shall find elsewhere. For the glyphs are the sign of the Tine, the Third Day of Solinari, and No Wind."

Though exhausted and bleary, he knew to keep the sign of the Springjaw from them—the ominous glyph that foretold danger—at least for now.

And he hid the other glyphs, too—the Tower and Chair. The signs that Fordus Firesoul was the King-priest of Istar.

He hid much and said little, but Stormlight listened intently to what he said. Suddenly, as it always did, the interpretation came to him.

"At the Tine!" he shouted. "Water three feet, four feet under! Hail the Water Prophet!"

"Who brings us the water!" Northstar chimed exultantly. He spun about, looking for Tamex.

But Tamex was nowhere to be found. On the bit of rock where he had stood only moments before, between Gormion and Rann, a dark dust wavered and dispelled.

For a moment Northstar wondered again who this man was. From where had he come? To where had he vanished? The question unresolved, the young guide stepped into the shadowy vacancy and lifted his eyes loyally to the rebel commander, who staggered a little in the full sunlight.

Larken began a second song of healing, of reconciliation and celebration—the song just as powerful, designed to drive away the darkness that had brushed against her people, that had dwelt among them for a while.

This healing song was as ancient as Krynn itself—so ancient that, according to the legend, the larkenvales themselves had taught the words to the first elven bards. And again in this late and fallen time, the old words worked. Tough, wiry grass suddenly bristled in the sands and the salt. A soft mist gathered and rose from the watery sand, bathing the Plainsmen and the bandits, rising up the sheer face of the Red Plateau until Fordus himself felt the cooling balm, felt the soothing mist wash over him and the poison slow in his hectic blood.

He looked down. The swelling in his foot had subsided.

The rebel leader raised his hands to the heavens once more, triumphantly and defiantly. He had mastered the darkness and the old death; he had returned from the desert with visions.

At the foot of the blossoming mesa, the Plainsmen danced.

Chapter 10

Takhisis stormed into the fastness of the salt flats. The warrior's body she inhabited had stiffened and dried, almost to the point of crumbling and dissolving, so the goddess moved heavily, clumsily.

Muttering a dark oath, she hastened between the droning crystals, over the level black sand, silk robe and translucent, faceted legs blurred with unnatural speed. The crystals themselves bent at her passing, like trees in a strong wind.

Takhisis crossed the flats to an upturned spot among the crystals, a black whorl of churned salt and crossing tracks. She had wandered this spot upon other nights, clad in the crystal flesh of the dark woman, her other avatar.

Now, preparing for yet another change, the goddess crouched amid the black rubble, her glinting hands dry and fragile from her long stay in the invented body. Her brittle finger traced the outline of new tracks in the salt.

A fresh trail. A horse. Its path encircled this centermost spot . . .

And headed for the rebel camp, weaving through the barren landscape of crystals.

Takhisis glanced up warily, the features of her face suddenly crumbling, hardened and angular. Sunlight caught in her eyes and vanished, the warrior's body she inhabited glittered like polished onyx.

Somehow, she would get to that elf, Takhisis thought, as her assumed form of Tamex crumbled into black powder. She would eliminate that slight, wiry shadow with the desert eyes and the grand suspicions.

He must know of the opals. Of the watery black stones and their secrets. After all, he was Lucanesti, the opalescence of his own skin protecting him from her energies.

But he was vulnerable . . . on other counts.

The goddess hovered, a dark, incandescent cloud over the pooled salt.

Slowly, the salt and rubble began to whirl, as if borne on an unearthly wind. The spinning, unnatural cloud took on another shape—that of a huge creature, its leathery, angular batwings fanning the chaos of the hurtling debris. For a moment the cloud dwarfed the surrounding crystals, then suddenly it began to diminish toward a smaller, more solid form—that of the beautiful dark-haired woman, the temptress of all mythologies.

* * * * *

The woman emerged secretly from the Tears of Mishakal, at the southernmost edge of the salt flats after sunset. She came when the watches changed and the sentries, caught in the last business of the day before their long night vigil, turned their attentions briefly and idly elsewhere.

Nobody saw the whirling black sand, borne on a cold night wind, as it descended and coalesced at the border of the salt flats. Nobody saw the woman it formed, saw her slip into the camp. She blended in at once and well, her black silk robe discarded for a deerskin Plainsman tunic Tamex had taken from one of the newly dead. Nobody saw the woman take a place by the fires of the Que-Nara, her long dark hair tangled and covered with sand as though she had been grieving.

But it was not long until they noticed her, Plainsman and bandit and barbarian alike. They could not help but notice.

The woman was splendidly beautiful, her skin pale and luminous and her amber eyes glittering under heavy, sensuous lashes. But those eyes were red-rimmed and that pale face tearstained, and though her face was cold and impassive, it was easy to see that she had lost someone—someone dear—in the raids of the morning. And though all the men of the encampment looked upon her admiringly, longingly, they kept the mourner's distance out of decency.

Even Gormion's bandits were respectfully silent in her presence.

Stormlight noticed the woman as well, as he stood alone by his fire near the foot of the Red Plateau. Above, like a soft accompaniment to her arrival, the bard's singing tumbled from the height of the mesa, where Larken kept watch over Fordus as he drowsed and waked and wandered and continued to heal.

* * * * *

The woman's amber eyes followed the elf intently as he walked across the littered campground. Stormlight approached slowly, drawn to stand silently beside her fire, the opalescence in his skin playing from blues to golds in the flickering light.

Stormlight wished then that Larken had come with him, to fable *his* deeds into wonders and miracles for this enchanting woman. His face flushed at the foolish prospect. He needed no glamour or go-betweens. He would show her who he was, without embellishment or ornament. He . . .

But what was he thinking? She was likely a new widow.

"You're too close to the fire, sir," a soft, echoing voice observed, breaking through the tangle of his confused thoughts.

"I . . . I beg . . ."

He stepped back as small sparks scattered on his lower legs, spangling his boots for a brief, uncomfortable moment. He thought the woman laughed, but her expression was unchanged, nor had she moved from her spot by the dwindling fire.

"Here," Stormlight muttered, clumsily tossing kindling onto the blaze. "It will be cold tonight, and your fire is failing."

"Thank you," the woman said, her voice chilly and somber. She lifted her amber eyes to him for a moment, then lowered them demurely.

Stormlight hovered above the fire, more dried twigs in his hand. He started to turn, started to slip into the shadows back to his lonely post, but her presence held him in unwilling fascination—the firelight shimmering on her dark hair, the pale, almost translucent skin.

When she spoke again, it was like precious rain in the expectant desert.

"I am Tanila," she pronounced. "From the south. From Abanasinia."

"Que-Shu?" he asked hopefully. Larken's father was of the Que-Shu tribe. He knew something of those Plainsmen.

The woman shook her head slowly. "Que-Kiri. From the foothills near Xak Tsaroth."

Stormlight nodded, but they were names only, these distant tribes and places. The strange woman remained a mystery.

"You are Stormlight," she said, her voice still strangely vacant. "And you command these armies."

"No," Stormlight began, crouching by the fire, his gemlike hands radiating purples and reds as he extended them to the warming glow. "Fordus commands the armies. I am his lieutenant."

"You *are* Stormlight the elf, are you not?" Tanila asked skeptically. "I have heard that Stormlight commands these armies."

For a moment his heart cried *Yes! Yes, I command these armies, in the field and in encampment. Fordus is only foxfire, a brilliant spark, and I am the substance, I am the guide through the wilderness of his words . . .*

But he stopped before he voiced the cry, amazed at his own vehemence and dishonor.

"My husband . . ." Tanila continued, her gaze shifting toward the fire, "my husband fought in your legions. Moccasin was his name."

Still shaken by his own vaulting thoughts, Stormlight plumbed his memory for the face of the man, for the name itself.

Nothing. It was as though Tanila's husband had vanished in the depths of the desert, and the sands had settled over him for a thousand years.

"I . . . I am sure he was a brave man, Tanila," he offered, knowing his answer was not enough.

In the distance, by the foot of the Red Plateau, the campfires waxed with a brighter light, and for the first time on that somber evening, the sounds of music and storytelling arose from the encampment. As is often the case in a warrior's camp, the rebels were putting the ambush behind them. Having mourned the dead for a brief space, they had set about to bolster their hearts for the coming day.

For if the Istarian cavalry had struck once . . .

Stormlight glanced toward the fires, which seemed to glow across a gap of miles and years. Part of him longed to be in the midst of the councils. There his cool presence was encouragement.

"Go ahead and join the others, if it please you," Tanila urged. "You have been most kind."

She sat by the fire, her dark hair covered in ash and sand, but oddly, almost unnaturally, beautiful.

Larken's drum sounded, and her sinewy voice carried over the campfires. They were too far away for Stormlight to make out her words, but he no longer listened to them.

For the first time, as he sat beside her near the fire, Tanila smiled at him. He banished his awareness of the camp at once, his thoughts transfixed by her depthless amber eyes.

He remembered little of what he said to her that night, but he was surprised that he said it.

Long tales he told, ranging across hundreds of years, of his wandering days with the Lucanesti, and finally of the ambush, the slavers, and his hostage people in the caverns below Istar. The telling drained him, sapping his strength as his story unwound. And Tanila changed as he spoke, the mourning lifting from her until Stormlight could see only the devastating, almost haughty beauty that had no doubt imprisoned . . .

Moccasin. Yes, that had been his name.

Tanila listened intently as Stormlight told her of the night among the crystals when, for the first time, Fordus read the mysterious glyphs of the gods. Tanila was most curious about that night, her questions soft at first, encouraging the story, then more subtle, more detailed. When he turned to other stories—of their exploits in Fordus's youth, of the hunts and the battles, and of this great venture against the rule of the Kingpriest—her interest seemed to waver. Yet he persisted, story after story as the night passed toward morning.

She asked him most often about the opals, leaning toward him hungrily as he explained the stones his people had hunted for since the early times: the white and the black, the water and fire.

And of course the opal darker than black—the glain, which the Lucanesti called the godsblood, for obscure reasons lost in the Age of Light. Her questions tunneled and probed, her eyes urged and tempted and haunted.

The eyes. The elf felt swallowed by their loveliness.

The dawn came before he expected or even imagined, the eastern horizon rising from the darkness and the night's fires fading into the sunlight. Slowly, with the barking of dogs and the cry of Larken's hawk hunting overhead, the camp awakened. Now Stormlight could make out shapes moving from tent to tent, and he realized to his dismay that he had been thoughtless and rude, filling Tanila's mourning night with his boastful stories.

"And all of this . . . from that single night in the salt flats," Tanila remarked, her amber eyes brilliant and alert.

Stormlight shifted uncomfortably and rose to his feet. The eyes again. Where had he seen them before? His memory was tired and scattered.

She was just a girl. Dark-haired and very beautiful.

But she had noticed him—*preferred* him—to Fordus.

As he was turning back to her, to those glorious amber eyes, as he thought of another story and a story to follow that one, suddenly a call rose up from the encampment. Fordus approached, hobbling, leaning on Larken for support.

"So this is where the night has kept you!" Fordus exclaimed, a strange laughter in his voice.

Now Tanila rose to her feet, brushing back her hair with a graceful wave of her translucent hand. Modestly, she lowered her gaze at the approach of the commander.

Fordus's sea-blue gaze darted from Stormlight to Tanila as though he read a glyph in the morning sand. He smiled fiercely, and the bright blue of his eyes grew suddenly flat and cold.

"Who is your friend, Stormlight?" he asked quietly, gently pushing away Larken and standing unsteadily on his own. "Lady, I do not recall your presence in this camp, and I would remember those eyes and the long temptation of this raven hair."

Larken stepped away, a look of familiar hurt and anger passing over her face.

Fordus took two wobbly steps toward Tanila and extended his hand, his fingers playing softly with a braided strand of her hair. "I know I would remember *you*," he murmured lazily.

"Her name is Tanila," Stormlight replied icily, glaring at the commander. Fordus was like this—had always been like this—the joy of the chase and the conquest impelling him in the hunt, in battle, and in more tender matters. He meant no harm, no injury, but when he set forth, he was cold and indifferent to the hearts of all around him.

"Tanila?" Fordus replied, blue eyes locked with amber in a fervent, stormy exchange.

"The widow of Moccasin," Stormlight continued. "One of your followers, who fell yesterday in the *ambush*." His own voice annoyed him with its thin, weak self-righteousness.

"I am sorry to hear of your loss, Tanila," Fordus said, his expression never changing. "In such a sorrowful time, it is the commander's duty to see . . . that all your needs are met."

"Great Branchala!" Larken spat, turning from the fire and stalking back toward the camp, whistling to the hawk as she broke into a run.

Of course, Fordus's gaze never wavered.

"I shall study to be deserving of your kindness," Tanila replied, almost formally and yet with a subtle and sinuous heat.

It was Stormlight's turn to mutter.

Then, overhead, Larken's hawk screamed in alarm.

All eyes shifted to the bird, the moment forgotten in the outcry and the approaching tumult of his wings. Lucas swooped out of the pale morning sky and, gliding low across the shadowy sand, struck the gloved hand of his mistress and frantically pulled himself upright. His shrieks and whistles were shrill, almost deafening, and a strange green light flashed over his pinions. Larken soothed the creature, her fingers stroking his feathers like harp strings.

Stormlight rushed to the side of the bard. Fordus was not far behind, the pain in his foot forgotten.

Larken stared at them, her brown eyes wide with alarm.

"Istarians?" Fordus asked, his right hand reaching instinctively for the throwing axe at his belt. Still the bird screeched and yammered. Larken raised her hand to the two men, motioning for their silence.

Not Istarians, she signed with one hand, inclining her ear toward the loud, insistent bird. *Not sandlings nor ankheg, not panther . . .*

"Then *what?*" Fordus exclaimed impatiently.

Larken shook her head, her fingers slow and deliberate.

Their fresh hostility forgotten for the moment, Fordus and Stormlight exchanged troubled glances.

It is nothing he knows, Larken concluded, as the bird whistled once more and fell silent. *Nothing he has ever seen. There is no word for it in Hawk.*

"Then we shall find the words for it," Stormlight declared.

Fordus nodded and drew forth his axe.

By the cooling ashes of the fire, Tanila regarded them impassively. The black pupils of her amber eyes slitted and closed.

Chapter 11

There was no word in Hawk for what happened next, either.

Though Fordus's scouts were sharp-eyed, skilled in reading trail and terrain, the subtle change in the nearby sands raised no alarm at first. By morning the dunes had shifted to encircle a huge, undulating mass of sand. The men were curious. A dozen of them, veterans of a hundred journeys and a score of battles, crouched around the disturbance, regarding it cautiously, intently.

It was a springjaw at worst, they told themselves, setting its funneled trap for unwary travelers. More likely a sandling, or the simple change of an overnight wind.

So the scouts kept their posts and turned their sights to the far horizons, to the edge of the salt flats—to anything, in short, except the whorling, lifting sands at their feet.

Indeed, they had almost forgotten this strange movement when the first rumbling shook the ground around them. The youngest of the scouts, standing not twenty yards from the disturbance, pointed and screamed . . .

And was swallowed by the first spray of molten sand that surged from the ruptured heart of the desert.

Dumbstruck, two other scouts fell seconds later, as the sands all around them erupted and, like an eerie, hidden volcano, rained glowing glass upon Plainsman and bandit alike. Overhead, the bard's hawk soared to a great height, the heat on his wings unbearable even at a thousand feet above this sudden holocaust.

The bird cried out, again and again.

*　*　*　*　*

It was less than an hour before Fordus reached the site of the eruptions. Larken and Stormlight followed him, and Northstar and the woman Tanila. Gormion and a dozen of her bandits were not far behind.

What they saw was a desert scarred unnaturally by fissures and craters and chasms, glazed over with a steaming, muddy caul. It looked like a country imagined from heat and light and attendant fire. Shadows of indignant desert birds reeled far overhead, and at the edges of the spreading lava the sand crackled, melted, and added to the rising flood.

For a moment, the handful of rebels fell silent. Fordus, his injury forgotten, took one firm step toward the smoldering landscape. Stormlight walked to his side, took his arm, and held him back.

Slowly, the sand at the center of the great wound hardened to dark crystal.

"What is it?" Gormion hissed, her hand slipping absurdly to the hilt of her dagger.

She received no answer. Neither Plainsman nor Prophet nor bard could decipher this mystery.

Yet one among them knew. One who veiled her knowledge behind expressionless amber eyes.

There were other gods in the Abyss, just as eager as Takhisis to enter the world and turn the tide of history to their liking. Zeboim had followed Takhisis once, and Morgion—the tempests in coastal waters and the plagues borne out of the marshes were testament to their ingenuity—but they lacked the power to stay more than minutes, more than an hour at most.

But when the sand glazed and melted that day in the Istarian desert, spreading slowly toward the Plainsman encampment beneath the Red Plateau and destroying everything in its path, it was prelude to something far greater, far more disruptive. Takhisis recognized that at once. Another of her kind—a strong one with powers to rival her own—had discovered her secret and followed her through the crystalline gap between worlds.

And she knew who he was.

* * * * *

"What is it?" Gormion asked again, more insistently this time as the molten sand slowly swallowed the dunes.

"Volcano," Stormlight replied tersely, his eyes never leaving the glowing swirl of glass. "I've seen them before. Long ago, from the foothills of Thoradin. We had best move the camp, and quickly."

Gormion was more than ready to comply. Her silver jewelry rattled as she waved wildly at her bandit followers, whistling and motioning them back toward the camp. Fordus and Stormlight made ready to follow, but suddenly, as they turned toward the Red Plateau, they were startled by a loud, unearthly screech.

Tanila lay in the path of the flowing slag, writhing and clutching her ankle.

Without thinking, Stormlight raced toward the fallen woman. In the sand his footing was unsteady, and once, nightmarishly, he stumbled and fell, bracing himself on his hands not a foot from the glowing, blistering pool.

He felt the heat like a hundred suns, and his eyes blinked and smarted.

With a cry, he closed the milky *lucerna*, pushed himself away from the slag, and staggered to Tanila, slipping his arm about her waist and dragging her blindly toward the safer crest of the nearest dune. She felt incredibly heavy, resistant in his grasp. With a desperate heave, he drew her to safety, toppled over the far side of the dune, and lay breathless, facedown in the sand. Around him a chaos of sounds eddied and swirled—the cries of the bandits, Northstar's voice carried on a white-hot wind.

He could not believe Tanila's heaviness, how hard and brittle her body had felt in his hands. It was as though the slag had covered her and cooled, turning her to stone, to glass. He turned toward her, incredulous, longing to touch her again.

Her foot was missing, the ankle snapped and

severed like hewn stone, no blood flowing from the wound. Stormlight gaped at the woman.

She returned his stare coldly.

A shout from Fordus disrupted his thoughts.

He sprang to his feet, and the earth split apart beneath him.

Kneeling in a daze at the edge of the slag, Stormlight watched the creature rise out of the fissured glaze, its broad wings glittering with spark and ash.

Fordus rushed out of the smoke, Northstar and two of the bandits beside him, as the creature took shape out of fire and cloud: an enormous hook-billed bird—its shape that of a condor or vulture, its naked head blistered and ugly, its black eyes glittering like gems.

Fordus stopped in his tracks, dumbfounded, as the bird wheeled above the desert, shrieking and smoldering. Below, the bandits hurled axe and spear and imprecation, but all bounced harmlessly off the rough skin of the bird, who pivoted slowly, ponderously, as though only recently come to its own body.

With another cry, the creature swooped awkwardly. Its attack was predictable and slow, its sharp beak clattering against the shield of one of the bandit spearmen, a young man from Kharolis named Ingaard. Ingaard feinted and laughed, and the bird staggered back, preparing to lunge again.

With a defiant cry, Ingaard braced himself to hurl his weapon, but suddenly, as though the whole desert had fallen under a terrible, malign enchantment, the lad's feet slipped in the tumbling sand, and he fell on his back, loosing the grip on his spear. The condor's beak crashed against his uplifted shield, again and again until the tough hide tore and the great bird snatched Ingaard into the air, rending his flesh and hurling him into the molten slag.

The other bandits turned and fled, screaming.

Slowly the creature pivoted toward Tanila, its eyes glowing red and smoke rising from its dark, angular feathers. Again, it fanned its wings, and the hot fetid air swirled like a hurricane around the Plainsmen.

Tanila, enraged, lost her balance in the eddying sand, but Stormlight alertly stepped between her and the monster, raising the bronze buckler of one of the fallen bandits. With a shriek, the condor lunged toward Stormlight, lightning blazing from its black, depthless eyes.

The bolts flickered and danced around the elf, who braced himself as the smoldering bird struck him, stopping the searching claws with the little shield and pushing the monster back and away. There was a shattering sound, like porcelain or glass, and the great bird groaned and drew his head back, his long neck arched like a scorpion's tail.

For a moment the desert was silent, as though sound itself had passed through the fissures and vanished. Elf and monster faced one another in a desolation of sand and rising steam.

"Kill him!" Tanila hissed.

And then, with a cry that was no doubt heard at the gates of Istar, the condor lurched after Stormlight. The elf stepped back, then lost his balance as the great beast cleared the edge of the slag, for a moment grotesquely in flight above the desert. With another deafening cry the condor swooped, falling upon Stormlight and driving him to the ground amid a gauntlet of slashing talons.

Larken whistled for her hawk and snatched her drumhammer from her belt. Deftly stepping over a widening fissure, she raced toward higher, more solid ground, rifling her memory for a powerful music.

Stormlight fell to his knees, bent backward by the weight of the creature. The condor hovered triumphantly over the struggling elf, its claws digging at his rib cage, its neck arched for a final, fatal strike.

Stormlight cried out and glanced beseechingly toward Fordus . . .

Who was about other business entirely.

* * * * *

Fordus stood on a narrow natural bridge of rock and dried earth left by the lake of molten sand that bubbled and swirled on the desert plain. It was a thin strip of solid ground, untouched by the fire and magma, and narrowing slowly as the hot current ate against its foundations.

It was the country of his dreams: the fire, the lava, the dark bird.

He stood breathless, abstracted, until the shouts of his men awakened him.

Fordus was faced with a choice. Stormlight lay in the pocked and bubbling field, the condor over him, batting its burning wings, while Northstar, only a dozen feet away, stared desperately into the glowing liquid, calling plaintively for help.

Stormlight was in peril, it was plain to see.

But the condor . . .

Was Fordus's old friend, his dream-summoner.

And Stormlight . . . was dissident. A troublesome lieutenant. Whatever happened to him was in the lap of the gods.

Fordus rushed toward Northstar, pulling the lad from the lip of the widening chasm.

"My medallion!" Northstar cried. "The disk!"

Fordus knew what he meant at once. The religious pendant, given to Northstar on his naming night, was a bronze replica of one of the fabled Disks of Mishakal. Worthless to anyone but the devoted lad, it now hung by its broken chain from an outcropping of rock scarcely a foot above the widening crevasse.

"Walk carefully toward the high ground!" Fordus shouted, leaning over the burning lake, his lean, muscular arm stretching toward the medallion, his fingers spread and extended. "Save yourself, Northstar!"

It sounded heroic, like the stuff of Larken's poetry. It would make for a good song in the evening's Telling.

* * * * *

On his back in the middle of the steaming field, Stormlight pushed the bird away yet again.

His arms were seared by the hot metal buckler he carried, and the smell of sulfur and burnt rock singed his nostrils, rushed down his throat and into his lungs.

Once again, he tried to cry out, but the pain was unbearable, smothering.

So this is the way it ends, he thought, strangely calm, the smoke gusting into his eyes and the hoarse cry of the condor on all sides of him.

The dull, dry shriek of the bird was answered by a call more shrill, and suddenly, miraculously, the sky cleared over Stormlight. He blinked painfully, scrambled to his feet.

Lucas swooped toward the Red Plateau, the condor glowing and smoldering in pursuit.

Swiftly, gracefully, the little hawk banked in the air, dodging the heavier, clumsier bird with a grace born of a thousand hunts, of a year's reconnaissance in the desert sky. Blindly, furiously the condor followed, the ground beneath the path of its flight blistering and blazing at its passage.

The hawk flew a wide, looping circle and returned toward the field and Stormlight, the condor picking up speed, swiftly closing the gap until it seemed that Lucas would be caught, ignited, consumed by the fiery monster.

Then Larken, standing on a sloping rise, seeing the danger to her companion, battered her drum loudly, slowly, in the stately Matherian rhythms of high magic. The song began in an incandescence of words, an elvish tralyta that trailed off into a hidden language, into the words that bards speak only in whispers, and only to the gods.

But the little bard gave her song full voice, and at the margins of the lava flow, the red glaze darkened and crusted, cooling so rapidly that the sound of its shattering echoed over the desert.

Still the bard's song rose above the chaos and noise, the words completely unintelligible now, trailing into birdsong, into distant thunder and the rush of water, into the sound of the wind through the nearby crystals.

The crystals themselves, at the edge of the Tears of Mishakal, were breaking to shards, crumbling silently to powder.

Lucas soared high above the cooling earth, then dropped five hundred feet through the smoky air, landing roughly on the sand and mantling, his wings spread over him like a tent, a canopy. The condor followed, a trail of flame in its wake, stretching its glowing talons to strike.

Then, fifty feet above the floor of the desert, the monster collided with the power of the bard's song.

Tanila whirled and shrieked and covered her ears.

For a moment, out of the corner of her eye, Larken saw the dark woman hobble toward the Tears of Mishakal, trailing black dust like a cloud of billowing smoke.

Then suddenly, spectacularly, the air went incandescent.

The condor splintered into a thousand sparks, slowly raining deadly flame over the parched landscape, the igneous rock, the cowering bird.

Just before the fire shower reached Lucas, Stormlight, racing over the hot ground, snatched up the hawk and hurled him free of the deadly rain. Lucas tumbled through the air, regained his balance and wings, and soared clear of the fire as Stormlight sprang free of the burning earth, rolling, his clothing on fire. Larken rushed to the elf, but by the time she reached him, the fire was smothered and he lay, dazed and breathless, in the shadow of a huge cactus.

Shimmering steam rose from the condor's ashes and spread angrily across the fire-ravaged plains.

The bard crouched over the elf-warrior, singing a brief song of healing and gratitude. Groggily, leaning on Larken's shoulder, Stormlight rose to his feet, looked her level in the eyes, as though he saw her for the first time, past the roughness and dirt, the weathering and the matted, neglected white hair.

Suddenly, Fordus shouted in triumph across the smoldering plain.

The War Prophet stood on the narrow strand of earth, holding aloft a brightly shimmering object, red and golden as the afternoon sun. He danced a victory dance, and Northstar, safely on the other end of the strand, danced with him.

"He's mad!" Stormlight whispered. "Fordus is completely and red-mooned mad!"

Larken remained silent, her hands occupied in gently supporting the injured elf.

Fordus lifted aloft the medallion again, laughing and whistling. But suddenly the dark smoke bundled and rushed toward him at a blinding speed. Trapped on the narrow bridge, he could not elude it, could not outrun it. In an instant it engulfed him, swirled about him like a whirlpool, like a maelstrom, then dissolved into the clear desert daylight, leaving him lifeless on the scored and barren rock.

Stormlight never remembered what happened after that.

He thought he heard Larken singing once, maybe twice, and Northstar shouting, and the distant cry of the bard's hawk. He felt himself being moved, carried . . .

And then there was torchlight, and shamans, and medicine women dancing attendance over him, and he felt the pain lift from his arm and legs.

Fordus, he told himself, Fordus is dead.

His sorrow was not pure. In the midst of the mourning, of the weeping, he felt something heavy lifted from him. *At last it is over*, a voice said or seemed to say, and he felt a strange upsurge of joy, even in the midst of his bereavement.

Later, when he awoke at the foot of the Red Plateau, drenched in rainwater and wrapped in cool hides, he tried to forget that traitorous delight. Northstar stood over him, watching him intently.

"Northstar."

"The commander is alive, Stormlight. Thank the gods he is alive! Twice he has asked for you. Can you stand? Can you walk?"

"I . . . I think so," the Plainsman replied, pulling himself painfully to a sitting position. "He's . . . he's still . . ." Something tugged at the edge of his memory—something he should remember but could not, given the fire and smoke and the great raging bird.

"His spirit stands at the edge of this life, where the dusk surrounds him and the shadows stalk. But he is strong, and we hope for his recovery."

Stormlight leaned hard against the younger man, his eyes on the fire, the assembly atop the Red Plateau where Fordus lay injured, perhaps dying. Slowly, with great exertion, he matched pace with Northstar, as the two of them crossed the deserted campground and began the gentle, roundabout ascent to the top of the plateau, where a throng had gathered and the drum beat a mournful rhythm.

The Branchalan mode. The mode of remembrance.

Perhaps he was already too late.

"Hurry, Northstar," he muttered through clenched teeth, and the young man quickened their pace.

"Five sentries are dead," Northstar explained, as the sound of the drum grew louder. "Gormion survived, and Larken, and three of the bandits."

The drum droned on, and a clear voice rose on the rhythm, the melody doleful and lonely.

"Poor Larken," Northstar murmured. "A widow's weeds though never wed."

Stormlight stood upright, stepped away from the young man's support. The memory, elusive in fire and battle.

Tanila.

"The woman, Northstar!" he shouted, his strong hands grasping the guide's shoulders. "What happened to Tanila?"

Northstar shook his head.

"Vanished. No sign of her at the dunes or amid the slag. There's a chance the eruption swallowed her, or . . ."

"Or?" Stormlight was insistent, shrill.

"I stepped to the edge of the salt flats, where she was headed when Larken's song began, when the monster descended. There was nothing there but the faint outline of a woman's body, already half-vanished in the shifted sand."

"An *outline*? No tracks leading away?"

"None. Nothing but a smaller pile of rubble . . . a heap of black crystal and salt."

Chapter 12

They had been forest at one time, these ranging caverns beneath the city of Istar. A hundred thousand years ago, or two hundred, the volcanoes, now dormant and lying beneath the great Istarian lake, erupted in the last of the great geologic disasters, before the All Saints War of the ancient Age of Dreams. It had buried this landscape beneath lava and ash, and the caverns had formed slowly, inexorably, beneath the rise and fall of a hundred civilizations. The five races stepped forth onto the face of the planet, the House of Silvanos rose in the young forest to the south, the gnomes were born, and the Graystone formed in the

divine forges of Reorx. It was then that the strange
process of opalescence began in the petrified trunks
and limbs of the buried trees, and water from the
new lake hollowed passages through the porous
volcanic rock.

Now, after thousands of years, living eyes marveled at the immemorial forest, and twenty years of
pick and shovel had not yet spoiled its eerie,
unearthly beauty. In the smokeless torches of the
elven miners, the fossilized landscape glittered as
though touched with an ancient, frozen dew.

Three elves descended the long, narrow passage
between petrified oaks, glowing amber lamps in
their hands. They were masked against the dust, and
their green eyes flashed like stars in their ash-
blackened faces.

This night, they were not searching for opals.
Despite the Kingpriest's orders, all mining had been
set aside to search for the child.

They had imagined her dead, along with her
mother and three other elves, when this part of the
cavern collapsed two nights earlier. They had sent
out runners and scouts into the midst of the rubble,
clambering and crawling back into the darkness
until they could clamber and crawl no more, calling
the names of the five missing miners.

Tessera and Parian. Gleam. Cabuchon.

Little Taglio. Only a child, but old enough to hold
a lamp while the others worked.

Just this afternoon they had heard her crying.
Now, having combed the most accessible regions of
the mines, the Lucanesti had secretly sent several of
their strongest and best into more perilous depths,
the realm of cave-in and rockslide, and of the spirit
naga—the serpentine monsters with the tranquil
human faces, whose spellcraft dried the opalescent

bodies of the Lucanesti and left them dust and brittle
bone in the deep, forgotten corridors.

Dangerous territory indeed, and the sound of the
elf-child's crying had haunted them for hours, as the
three gaunt miners dug and scrabbled toward the
source of the sound.

The oldest of the searchers, Spinel, held the lamp
above the younger, stronger elves. Seventeen hundred years had dulled the sharpness of his eyes, the
power and resilience of his arms, but the old elf was
shrewd, tunnelwise, just as aligned to the dark shift
of corridor and passage as the dwarves he had
fought for centuries under the earth.

He held the light in hopes of finding one of his
vanishing people.

* * * * *

Once a noble, if minor, branch of the Dimernesti
elves, the Lucanesti had roamed the grasslands
south of Istar, their keen woodsense transformed by
their travels into an uncanny discernment of hidden
underground springs.

Water in rock. It called to them from its tomb in
the dry earth. The Lucanesti had become essential to
the early caravans and migrations crossing the face
of evolving Krynn. "Dowsers," the wanderers had
called them, and hired them at great expense as
guides and augurers.

Dowsers.

But they were paid well, and the insulting name
had become a badge of curious pride. Over the
years, though, water had become taken for granted
by the wood elf and high elf, native to river lands
and watery forests. The scant influence of the
Lucanesti dwindled. They were ignored at the high

council of the elves, mocked as vagabonds and ruffians.

The old names returned. "Dowsers." "Hedge elves."

In the midst of such scorn and contempt, the opals came to them like a favor from the gods.

Water and rock, it was again, for those stones were formed over thousands of years in which water and rock commingled beneath the Istarian mountains. What it was that led the Lucanesti underground had been forgotten under the tide of centuries, but the maze of cubicles in the opal caverns beneath Istar were evidence that they had mined the roots of the city for ages.

And yet they remained a people of open country, of fresh winds and the high arrangement of stars. Their sojourns underground were brief and efficient, the white *lucerna* of their eyes attuned to the water in the opals, their digging precise. The mining took its toll and changed them, their skin hardening with age and silica and water, until the old elves were translucent, shimmering, opalescent like the stones they hunted. They used the change to their advantage, masking their presence against intruder and predator, fading into the rubble where they stood breathless, indistinguishable from surrounding stone.

When they were old enough—two thousand years, or maybe less—the opalescence had its inevitable way, and they entered the stonesleep, unable to return from the dark, encrusted dream.

But while they were young, there were opals to mine and riches to gather. And the Lucanesti mined and gathered, bringing the stones back to the surface. Soon what had been a poor and marginal tribe flourished with disproportionate wealth.

A wealth that drew the attention of cities, of the Kingpriest.

Of the *venatica*, the hunters and spies in the hire of Istarian clergy.

Soon the Lucanesti were observed. Then accompanied—in what the *venatica* called "the interest of geologic science," though it was really an armed surveillance. Observation and accompaniment changed slowly, like a stone in the swim of underground water, and the elves found more and more of the red-robed Istarians as companions, advisors . . .

The "cooperative" venture turned into slavery one day when Spinel and a party of followers made for the surface, for fresh air and light, but were stopped by a squadron of Istarian swordsmen.

The mining Lucanesti never saw the surface again.

Still, the Kingpriest's request surprised none of them, really. After all, *relocation* had been the death sentence for a thousand innocent peoples since the dawn of the planet, and the mountains and plains around the spreading, marbled city were littered with abandoned villages, burned hamlets, and the moldering relics of swallowed civilizations.

It was the way of Istar to finish what greed had started.

* * * * *

Now, in his waning years, the opalescence spreading and constant on his pale arms, Spinel could only guide as his companions combed the rubble for the missing child.

"I never thought it would come to this," he said. "Scarcely a century under the city, and the children are dying."

Heedlessly, the two younger elves continued at

their task. They were *spela*, what the Lucanesti called the generation born and raised in the caverns under Istar. They remembered no sun, no paired moons in the starry sky. Many, fancying that their greatest enemies were the crumbling rocks and the nagas that lurked therein, had no recollection of the Istarians.

Spinel pitied them. They were as buried as the child they sought.

The older of the two *spela*, a young female named Tourmalin, held aloft a dark, shining stone.

"Glain," she said tersely, extending the gem to the older elf. "At least we will bring *something* home."

Reluctantly, almost ashamedly, Spinel took the opal from her and placed it in a pouch on his belt. Another stone to crush into powder for the Kingpriest's mysterious rituals.

"We'll find the child," the old elf asserted, his voice thin and wavering in the torchlit alcove. "By Reorx and the lamps of the eye, we shall find that poor creature!"

With pickaxe and dagger, they moved slowly and delicately through the ragged volcanic rock. The frail voice called to them faintly from somewhere behind the baffle of stone and darkness, the child begging for water, for her mother . . . finally, for Branchala and the Sleep He Brings.

When Spinel heard the hymn begin, the low birdlike keening that heralds the stonesleep of the Lucanesti, his orders became urgent. Intently, his hand on Tourmalin's shoulder, he guided the three diggers through convoluted layers of rock.

Steady, he told himself. Do not lose faith or judgment or the faint sound coming from somewhere beyond that wall of stone.

Barely audible, the stonesong continued. For a moment, Tourmalin seemed to gather strength. Muttering a mild oath, she redoubled the speed of her digging, and her companions followed her example, the corridor ringing with the sound of metal on stone, the shallow breathing of the four miners.

Yes, we are breaking through, Spinel thought as the sound of the pick took on a new resonance. Only a matter of minutes now, and if the child survives, if we can bring the poor innocent to air and light . . .

"Faster!" he commanded through clenched teeth.

And then, Tourmalin's hammer crashed through the last layer of rock. Exultantly, Spinel surged by his younger companions, reached for the new passageway, his torch aloft . . .

But another wall of rock, not two feet behind the breakthrough, blocked his passage. He swore, scrabbled at the hard stone with his nails, pushed madly against it with his shoulder . . .

As somewhere in the deep recesses of the earth, the stonesong of the child dwindled.

Spinel rested his forehead against the cold, dividing wall and wept. The years would take the child's bones and transform them. Someday, perhaps, descendants of those who dug for the babe in vain would find the form—small, curled, and glowing, in the midst of the rock that had swallowed her and made her its own.

"Opal," Tourmalin breathed, the light of compassion fled from her eyes. Her callused, pale hand touched the new, dividing wall. "Glain opal."

So they all would come to glittering dust, in the heart of this indifferent place.

* * * * *

Above the rocks and the rubble and the sorrows of elves, miles away in the city of Istar, the Kingpriest's armies watched and waited in boredom and uneasy readiness.

The Shinarion approached—the great festival of gaming, industry, and trade, the great time of commerce and coincidence. Istar and all its tributaries came together to celebrate the glory of the goddess who, it was said, watched over the vast, interwoven economies of the region. As usual, the city was adorned with silk and gold leaf, the inns were swept and strewn with fresh rushes, and throughout the narrow streets of Istar, everyone—from the gray-robed, exclusive diamond merchants to the painted bawds and nimble pickpockets—readied their wares and skills for the coming week.

Even the Temple of the Kingpriest prepared special ceremonies in honor of Shinare. Jasmine incense billowed in the great square, and the tower bells chimed in the dawn carillon that dedicated each morning to the goddess.

It seemed that nothing was amiss in Istar—that the great business of ritual and trade continued gracefully and quietly, as though there were no nasty, ill-starred wars erupting in the desert. The mourning banners had come down in the noble houses, and the black cloth on the doors of the poorer dwellings had been replaced by the bright reds and yellows of Shinarion. The fallen soldiers, buried scarcely a week ago, were forgotten.

But the guards on the walls still watched nervously, the cavalry stopped and inspected all of the caravans, and in the high temple towers a thousand eyes turned regularly and apprehensively south. There were rumors that the rebel commander, the Water Prophet, stalked the city like a wounded lion.

He was coming, the rumors said. In a month's time, if not sooner. Fordus Firesoul was headed

north, torch in hand and wading ankle-deep in Istarian blood. His goal was the city and the temple itself,
its ornate walls to be ransacked and stained with
still more Istarian blood.

For the first time in memory, the city was humming with the threat of invasion.

Yet the Shinarion would take place as it always
had. So the Kingpriest had decreed. Daily life would
not give way to panic; the city would not become an
armed camp.

And the city would profit, above all. Most importantly, the metal from Thoradin, the silks from
Ergoth, the grain from the Solamnic plains, would
not have to go elsewhere to be sold.

Already the caravans had embarked for Istar,
laden with expensive and exotic goods, and as the
time approached, the first of the merchants arrived
and the first booths and bazaars went up in the
rapidly filling city. By the end of the week the numbers would be greater still. Balandar claimed that the
population of Istar doubled during the Shinarion.

Hidden by a carved screen, Vincus watched the
arrivals from his master's library window. As wine
steward for the Kingpriest's Tower, Balandar was
busy all the time now, and Vincus was often left to
his own devices. He divided his time between
secretly reading obscure manuscripts and nosing
through the crowded Marketplace, watching the
preparations for the festival.

In most years, the arrivals were exotic—almost
enough to make the young servant believe that the
city did *not* go on forever—that the legendary lands
that travelers described were actual and true.

The acrobats had come, and the fortune-tellers
and dancers. A band of dwarven musicians was
expected on the festival eve, and rumors even had it

that Shardos, the fabled blind juggler, would attend and entertain.

But this year the first arrivals were somehow disturbing. Vincus wandered the Marketplace, seemingly casual, but totally observant. The acrobats, huge and hulking, practiced their stunts badly, the dancers seemed surly, and the fortune-tellers tight-lipped and private. The dwarves and the juggler were long overdue and the young servant began to suspect that the more famous, legitimate acts would not perform this year.

He saw few rehearsals, and the fortune-tellers' predictions, when they came, were tentative and vague:

Today is your lucky day.
You are more insightful than ordinary folk.
Your future is bright.

Not legitimate. That was it, Vincus was sure. The arrivals were impostors.

At first, Vincus was hesitant to bring up the matter to the druid. Vaananen, preoccupied with his rena garden, had little love for acrobats and dancers—they did not suit his austere western ways.

But finally, two nights before the festival was scheduled to begin, Vincus slipped through the druid's window. Vaananen did not stir. He crouched, as usual, in the rena garden, drawing a rain glyph.

The rena garden had grown, Vincus noted. Vaananen had dismantled one of the wooden walls that kept the sand in place, and now it sprawled onto the floor, spreading like a creature with volition of its own. The druid had added another stone and a squat green barrel cactus to the stark, mysterious arrangement of objects in the sand, and two new glyphs adorned the far walled edge of the garden.

Then Vaananen noticed him, rose and turned, his

meditations over.

"What have you brought me, Vincus?" he asked with a weary smile.

Vincus's dark hands flashed the first of four elaborate signs.

Vaananen laughed. "Impostors? Why, Vincus, *all* fortune-tellers are impostors."

Vincus shook his head, his fingers a blur.

Vaananen turned back to the garden. "You have tried hard," he announced. "Thank you."

Vincus shrugged, scratched beneath his silver collar. Perhaps he was wrong after all. He rose and turned toward the window, stepped to the sill . . .

And climbed out into the close Istarian night, leaving the druid to contemplate the cactus, the stone, the shifting shapes in the sand.

* * * * *

Vaananen might dismiss the suspicion, might laugh it away in his quiet meditation. But there *was* something different about the city—something strange and curiously out of line. Vincus was accustomed to watching the streets, to sensing with eye and ear and an insight more subtle than the senses when something had shifted, when something was not right.

And it was that feeling, that insight, that took him back to Balandar's library.

Always before, the library had been a place of peace for Vincus—a maze of sanctuary amid towering shelves, with its powerful smells of mildew and old leather emanating from the long-neglected volumes. As a slave boy, illiterate at first, sold to the tower to repay his father's debts, he had taken books down from the high, obscure shelves to pore over at night after his master was abed. Slowly, his intelligence had matched the illuminated drawings in the margins of the ancient texts with the shapes of letters. It was like reading glyphs, this long process that had translated indecipherable scrawls into meaning, into things and ideas.

It had taken all of a year, but he had taught himself to read in the shadowy, candlelit room.

Each time he returned he felt the same absorbing calm and quietude. This time he came as an intruder, a spy, gathering intelligence.

Silently, he thumbed through old Balandar's records. In a shabby old book the priest had kept account of the temple wineries for years, since before the Siege of Sorcery and long before Vincus himself had been born. He had dwelt upon this very book learning his letters and numbers: "claret" and "malmsey" were among the first words he could read.

Looking at the most recent records, those of the last several months, Vincus quickly tallied the number of wine barrels brought from the warm north into the Kingpriest's cellar.

The expensive claret was the Kingpriest's favorite, reserved for only the highest clergy. One barrel a month sufficed, and Vincus noted no change in the order. Nor in the malmsey, which the lesser clerics and the officers drank with a certain . . . license. Seven barrels this month, six the month before, and six before that.

Vincus nodded. A slight increase in the malmsey. Festival time.

The port, however, was the soldiers' wine. Rationed to the Istarian men at arms, it was issued in the barracks and taken afield. The Istarian soldier was naked without his wineskin.

Vincus smiled, adding the numbers.

Ten barrels, then eleven, and this month . . . twenty-two.

Vincus absently fingered his silver collar. There was a marked increase in the port wine, far beyond festival allowances, beyond common sense. It definitely supported his suspicion.

Someone new was in the city. Unannounced, unaccounted for.

And port was the wine of soldiers.

Chapter 13

The first night of the Shinarion spangled the city with a gaudy light. In the quiet, less-traveled pockets of the city, marbled squares and opal windows shone with the borrowed glow of Lunitari, red and darkly brilliant like candlelight on wine. But the lamps and the torches drowned the busy commons and thoroughfares with the flashy light of commerce, and like a respected matron who has drained the glass once too often, the elegant city burgeoned with a loud, inelegant life.

Yet those who had been here before knew otherwise—knew that this year was unlike any that had come before. This time the celebration was fevered, almost desperate, and the promised thousands of pilgrims, merchants, and performers had yet to arrive.

Nonetheless, the festival caroused from the center of the Marketplace, the beating heart of the trading, where jewelry, silks, and spices changed hands, to the booths by the gates of the city, where vendors and hucksters sold fireworks, knives, and the red glass bottles of godslight—the strange, everburning mixture of phosfire and salt, dangerous and volatile, that, if handled wisely and cautiously, would provide steady light for weeks.

No one, however, expected wisdom and caution from a drunken reveler. Already Peter Bomberus, commander of the city militia, had been called to extinguish three fires by the city walls.

Two had been simple wooden lean-tos—the kind of makeshift dwellings that followed the festivals from Hylo to Balifor. But the third was different: a permanent dwelling, hard by the School of the Games, the dry wooden rafters and interiors igniting almost by themselves—a careless spark from a torch, perhaps, or godslight discarded by a drunken reveler.

By the time the commander reached the building, black smoke billowed from a marble husk, and the red flames joined with the red lamps of the Istarian night to create a harsh, hellish light. Two hours of frenzied work had quenched the spreading, dangerous fire, but the building still smoldered at midnight, the woodwork inside glowing faintly as the interior slowly fell in upon itself. Reckless revelers tossed fireworks into the burst opal windows, and the racket resounded into the dark Istarian morning.

But Bomberus and his militia arrested no one. By the time the fireworks began, they were far away, bound toward the abandoned High Tower of Sorcery, where yet another fire had erupted—a metal gate ablaze with phosfire.

On the road to the burning gates, passing through the cluttered Istarian thoroughfares and alleys, Bomberus saw the sights of the Shinarion—the dreamlike arenas of commerce and deception and curious, fraudulent magic.

In a perfumer's booth near the Banquet Hall, two Kharolian merchants stood smugly behind an array of uncorked, parti-colored vials and bottles. The smell of a dozen colognes and attars and oils mingled in the smoky city air, and, reflecting in the red godslight, a thin, transparent hand snaked out of the mouth of each vessel, wavering like a desert mirage, like the blurred air at the lip of a flame.

The hands gestured and beckoned as the militiamen passed, but Bomberus had instructed his troops well. On they trudged, past the hall, toward the Welcoming Tower, where a game of chance spilled from a speculator's booth onto the cobbled street, and an odd company of gamblers crouched and knelt and sat on the thoroughfare. Dwarves from Thoradin, Ergothian merchants, and a kender from Hylo gathered around a circle scratched on the cobblestone, the kender's hands tied in front of him according to the house policy of any establishment frequented by the little folk, and the ten-sided Calantina dice flickered through torchlight according to some obscure Ergothian rules.

Bomberus stopped at this booth, peered over a dwarven shoulder. Perfume and wine held no attractions for the commander, but gaming . . .

A rough hand at his shoulder drew him away. Old Arcus, a veteran of some forty years, stared at his commander with black glittering eyes. Smiling knowingly, he pointed up the road, where the red fire glowed on the eastern horizon like a premature sunrise.

"Best be gettin' there, commander," he suggested, shouting over the dwarven racket and the carnival *come-hither* of the gamers. "Whilst some of it is standin', and the fire don't spread."

Bomberus muttered to himself and followed.

Now he found himself in an awkward spot, in the midst of his men rather than at the head of the column. All around him the militia sheared off from the avenue toward the dozen temptations that littered the lamplit center of the city, and together Bomberus and Arcus collared the younger soldiers, scolded them, and set them aright on the eastern road toward the tower.

At first, ashamed at his own wayward behavior near the gambler's booth, the commander was hard on the unruly and gullible boys, planting his foot firmly in the backside of one who crouched beneath a beer barrel, openmouthed, to receive the cascading beer from the opened bunghole. Swearing angrily at the young man, Bomberus prepared to kick him again, but a cautionary wink from Arcus brought him to his senses.

It was bad as the dice, this anger.

Bomberus took a deep breath, helped the beer-soaked novice to his feet, and shoved the young man up the thoroughfare, where the light from the distant burning suddenly vanished in the stronger glow from the central Marketplace.

Wisely, cautiously, Bomberus steered the militia around the well-lit square. From a distance, in the faceted lamplight he could see the booths of the jewelers, the shimmering silks draped over awning and counter. The expensive booths, heavily guarded by the private soldiers of a dozen merchants.

To stray into the Marketplace in armed company would be to invite disaster. At Shinarion, the merchants governed themselves with little regard for Kingpriest or clergy.

No wonder that Istar had hidden a legion in town.

Oh, no one had *told* him of the hidden legion. Indeed, he had not spoken of it either—not even to the trusted Arcus. Bomberus knew of the army's whereabouts only through instinct, through the inspired guess of a veteran constable who notices subtle changes on familiar streets: new hands with the calluses of crossbowmen, the unmistakable shape of a pike wrapped in canvas in a wagon bed, swords carried with quiet, respectful wisdom.

Standard security, to be sure. But more than that. He had never seen concealed troops in these numbers, not even at the great festivals of five years past, whose opulence and magnitude dwarfed the sorry excuse for a Shinarion unfolding this first, unpromising night.

What could they be planning in the Tower?

He shook his head, continued up the wide street, past the smithy and the Slave Market, to where the spellcraft flourished and the illusions stalked.

* * * * *

Translucent and flitting they were, like ghosts in search of solid flesh.

Slowly, in an almost stately dance, they cavorted on the battlements of the abandoned tower like corposants on a stormy mast, and the night air rumbled in accompaniment with the sound of fireworks and thunder, of the last combats in the raucous arena. Above the slack-jawed guardsmen the air crackled as the watery smell of lightning reached them through the smoke and powder and incense of the Shinarion.

Peter Bomberus reached for his sword, then laughed quietly, grimly. As if edged steel would fend off these mirages.

In the fitful firelight behind the burning gate, there at the base of the tower, the illusionists gathered for duels and enchantments. Artificial stars glittered above them, spangling the minarets of the tower with borrowed light.

It was a show, the best of the Shinarion. A second heaven formed around the deserted tower, and languidly the constellations, drawn from the memories of the participating illusionists, wheeled about the spire of the tower as though a year were passing in little more than a minute, a century in two hours. Meanwhile, at the shadowy base of the tower a chorus of incantations rose on the air, a great choir in all the known languages of Ansalon, from the watery vowels of Lemish to the harsh Kernian brogue and the suave accents of Balifor.

As the guardsmen covered the burning gate with doused canvas, with earth, with ashes, smothering the strange flames of phosfire, Peter Bomberus watched the spectacle in the western sky. In unison, as a hundred languages choired below them, the imaginary stars and planets lifted into the higher regions of air, sputtering and fading as they caught a sudden wind and scattered, in a babble of fire and voices, over the bay of Istar.

They were always good, these illusionists, with their false light and treacherous mirrors. But this year, their flashy, empty show seemed to suit the city and its festival.

Peter Bomberus stood before the smoldering gate and watched the smoke trail into the heavy sky.

The festival was a showy failure. This year was the worst of them all—as many fires as pilgrims, it seemed. And beneath the smoke and incense and the smell of new wine, the pungent, unsavory odor of decay and death.

* * * * *

The Kingpriest himself watched the illusions sail out and crumble over the water.

Like dust, he reminded himself.

Like bright and magical dust.

Turning from the window, he closed the thin shades behind him and, oil lamp in hand, hastened to the table where he kept the long work of his dreams.

He was almost through with the gathering. The opal dust filled two large vials already, and the third and final receptacle was three-quarters full. But the mining was laborious, even under the skillful labors of the Lucanesti, and the great day of the ritual might still be months away.

Time enough for that mad Prophet to storm the city. To ruin everything.

His pale hand trembled as he touched the last vial. Oh, might the gods speed the harvest! But the Prophet . . . the Plainsmen and rebels . . .

"They will not be enough to harm you," a dark voice breathed from somewhere in his chamber.

The Kingpriest was suddenly tense and alert. He had heard this voice before—in the clerestory of the great encircling corridor, in the glossy dome of the council hall, and finally, most intimately, in his own private chambers. Yet it never ceased to surprise him, insinuating itself into the depths of his dreams, coming upon him always in solitary and unguarded moments like a thief to an unprotected house.

"T-To harm me?" he stammered, mining for a false bravery. "What have I to fear from . . . *petty bandits?*"

"But there is one who is *more* than a bandit," the voice teased.

The Kingpriest glanced to the window he had just closed. A dark heart at the center of the opal sheet contracted eerily, like the eye of a reptile, and the voice trailed through the brilliant translucent pane, filling the room with melody and dread.

"This one is close to you, my friend, and it would not be well for you to see him . . . face to face and eye to eye. It would be a hall of mirrors, in which you might well become ensnared."

The Kingpriest frowned at the obscure threat. Then, dropping all pretense of courage and confidence, he faced the window and asked the question that had kept him sleepless for most of the week.

"If I cannot face him, who can? If five generals have failed, then who will stop him?"

"Your commander is coming," the voice soothed, a strange opaque flatness in its tone. "Rest easy, my friend. I shall let no rebellion touch you."

In the answering silence, the Kingpriest waited, attentive and expectant. What did it mean—this dark, ambiguous promise?

Soon it was apparent that the voice had left the window, that its last sentence had been these odd words of assurance.

Assurance, indeed. It would protect him, deliver him.

Then why did his hand still shake?

* * * * *

It was an odd officer who made his way into the quartermaster's offices on the following morning.

His uniform was a ragtag assemblage, mixing rank, regiment and legion with almost a clownish abandon. The lieutenant's tunic from the Istarian Twelfth Legion contrasted strangely with the violet cavalry cape left over from the Ninth Legion, which had been disbanded by the Kingpriest two years before. The green leggings the officer wore had come from the Ergothian infantry and the helmet, fashioned of ornate boiled leather, was a relic from some other time.

A mercenary, the quartermaster deduced, glancing over his shoulder as the motley man entered the offices. No man to reckon with. Or cheat.

The quartermaster might have been more curious had he seen the officer emerge from a nearby alley not minutes earlier, rolling the end of the cape around his silver slave collar, effectively hiding it from curious eyes. He might have wondered who the man was, what was his business. And why he wore the mark of a slave in the first place.

Busy with his inventory, the quartermaster noticed nothing more about the man—not even that he spoke not a word to the other soldiers milling through the assembled supplies, but that his hands flashed secretly with ancient Ergothian numerical signs as he counted, tallied, and took his own inventory of the provisions gathered in the military offices.

The quartermaster scarcely took heed when the officer left, busy as he was with an order for a thousand pairs of legionnaires' boots and as many water-skins.

Nor did the armorer in the shop three streets away pause to notice when an acrobat entered his establishment, dressed in the black tunic of tumblers and fire-dancers. After all, festival performers often came to the armory, searching for old throwing knives, older darts, and other dramatic blunt weapons to lend a certain edge of danger to the torchlit midnight productions. Bent over a used sword he was hammering into shape for a sergeant in the Twelfth Legion, the stocky craftsman did not notice the acrobat's eye stray to the spearheads, arrowheads, and the new short swords requisitioned by the garrisons of the city.

Had he looked closer at the acrobat, the armorer might have noticed the metal band peeking through the violet ruffle at the performer's neck.

The silver collar was the sign of a Temple slave, and would have caused suspicion and alarm.

The barracks keeper, four streets away, also did not think to be suspicious. He noticed the fortune-teller stroll by the barracks, his conical hat tilted comically, his long red robe unable to cover the fact that he was barefoot, no doubt penniless and desperate to augur and forecast his way to a festival meal. When the man stopped in front of the barracks and weaved drunkenly, he appeared to be talking to himself, and the keeper snickered and shook his head, assured by the sighting of his first drunken wizard that the Shinarion was about to begin.

Had he been closer to the fortune-teller, he might have seen the man counting quietly, estimating the beds freshly set in the vacant barracks. And had he watched intently and followed the augurer, he no doubt would have seen the man slip into a shadowy alcove and hoist a large sack, bulging with well-worn clothing, then make his way along half-deserted streets west through the city, past the Banquet Hall and the Welcoming Tower toward the sound of the roaring crowd as the first gladiatorial contest of the festival began.

Had these three servants of the city—quartermaster, armorer, and barracks keeper—met in a tavern that first festival night, had they compared notes and curious observations over the last several days, they might well have placed together that all three passersby—mercenary, acrobat, and fortune-teller—were exactly the same height, age, and coloring.

Indeed, the Shinarion was a time of commerce and coincidence.

There was one other similar visit in the central city—the last of the four—in a large stable not far from the School of the Games. In the shadowy, musty-smelling barn, a solitary groom mucked out a stall amid the whicker of horses and the buzz of bottle flies. He scarcely noticed when a slave appeared—a dark young man, wearing the white tunic of the Inner Temple.

Balandar's servant, the groom observed dimly, his mind neither on nor off his work.

No doubt the old priest was set to buy another mare.

The young slave nodded to the drowsy man and passed between stalls quietly, as though shopping for horses. The groom left him alone, no more interested in his business than the quartermaster, armorer, or barracks keeper had been earlier in the day. Finally, the groom fell asleep over his broom, dreaming of winning a hefty wager at the First Games of Josef Monoculus, and spending it . . . spending it . . .

All on beer.

Vincus, meanwhile, moved from stall to stall, looking for anything odd or out of place. Most of the animals were familiar to him—the roan that belonged to young Trincera, a priestess of Mishakal, the two mares that his master Balandar owned, and the Kingpriest's half-dozen stallions.

There were others, however, less familiar. Vincus approached one, then another. The great beasts were calm and steady beneath his confident hand, as the young slave quickly checked ears and flanks and teeth.

The brands on the flanks of two geldings clearly indicated that they were the property of merchants from Balifor. Nothing surprising there.

The braided mane of the pony indicated its Thoradin origins. Vincus smiled to imagine a dwarf riding the creature, unsteady in the saddle, cursing and muttering and pulling at his beard.

It was the fourth mount that caught and held the young man's eye. A strong, spirited gray mare, weathered but well tended, stood in the far stall, eyeing Vincus defiantly. An old, long scar creased her withers, and her right flank was pocked with four arrow wounds, healed years ago as well.

As Vincus approached, the mare lowered her head and snorted once, menacingly.

Vincus slowly extended his hand. The slice of apple, an offering of truce, settled the animal's temper. A bit skittishly, the mare let him stroke her long dark mane, let him examine her flanks and hooves for identifying markings.

Nothing. The horse was unmarked.

Making a soothing, clicking sound, Vincus reached up and opened the mare's mouth. There, on the pink of her inner lip, was the blue tattoo.

The hexagon. Glyph of the Sixth Legion.

Vincus sucked in his breath. The Sixth Legion was the stuff of legends. Istar's finest, a tough, relentless group of veterans trained by Solamnics and schooled in the Siege on Sorcery and in innumerable raids against the ogres. They were noted for their swiftness and endurance . . .

And utter lack of mercy.

Now they camped on the borders of Kern. At least that was what he had heard in the taverns and the School of the Games—the information he had brought back to Vaananen in their weekly visits.

His thoughts racing, Vincus examined the lip of the black gelding in the adjoining stall, and the chestnut mare near the entrance to the stables. The blue hexagon marked them both.

The Sixth Legion was in Istar.

Quickly the young man's mind rushed over the gatherings of the day. New provisions, new weaponry, and now a horse that named the stranger. The Sixth Legion, under cover of darkness and disguised as acrobat, dancer, and merchant, had been recalled to Istar.

The Kingpriest was preparing for the rebels.

Chapter 14

For ten days he stood at the border between worlds, as the shamans despaired for his life. Larken sang healing songs over him, and the music and words trickled into his long, dry sleep like a dream of water.

Fordus would rise toward the surface then, toward light and waking, but there was another voice inhabiting his sleep—a voice deep and tranquil and alluring.

Lie down, be at peace now, you have fought long and hard and done your best, let someone else do the hard work henceforth and come to me, come to me in the sweet darkness.

I will teach you everything of prophecy.

On the third day after his wounding, he gave in to the voice, to its soothing and promises and to his own curiosity, and his dreams revealed wonderful things.

It was always the desert he traveled, a featureless desert with neither rock nor salt flat nor arroyo to mark it, to distinguish one path from innumerable others. And always in this dream, he came upon the kanaji pit by surprise—an old wide well swallowed by sand, rising from the heart of nowhere.

He entered the pit, the darkness, and his hands began to glow with unexpected light—a light that seemed to rise from his own veins, filling the high circle of limestone wall.

But instead of the expected glyphs, the accustomed marks in the sand, the woman Tanila sat before him, her dark eyes glittering and wild.

The words came to her readily, easily, like the words of Larken's songs. *You have opened the rift of the world*, she began, as he extended his glowing hands toward her. *Let the new world arise from rift and confusion. Let it change in the flame of your hand.*

Then the light in his veins would extinguish, the blackness would surround him, and he would sleep heavily, darkly, until the voices returned, Larken's first, then the deep soft voice in pursuit. The dream would happen again and again. And each time, before complete and oblivious darkness, he would hear the other voice, melodious and solitary, blending with his memories of Tanila's voice. And it would tell him the last thing, the thing his heart remembered as he slept.

Your studies are over, Prophet. Now the world will shake. You no longer need glyphs to prophesy, nor the customary second tongue. You will speak to the multitudes on your own, needing neither interpreter nor bard.

In the depths of his sleep Fordus tried to argue, tried to say no, I have not done this before, have not prophesied and interpreted as well. It is not permitted. The ancient way of prophecy is twofold.

But the voice was insistent.

You are a city unto yourself, a wondrous city, Fordus Firesoul. Istar will pay you tribute, will be subject to your command. The rival you have longed for awaits you in Istar: the Kingpriest, your match in valor and worthiness. But you will triumph.

And this I promise: In the heart of Istar you will find out who you are.

Who I am? he asked, with the same insistent yearning he had felt upon first learning of his strange adoption.

Hurry. You must hurry to know. You must storm Istar now.

Do not delay.

But we are too few.

Do not delay.

* * * * *

On the plateau the rebels held hopeless vigil over their wounded leader. Northstar knelt at his feet and Stormlight at his head, praying the deep prayers to Mishakal. Larken stood above the three of them, beating the drum slowly and singing the Three Songs of Healing, over and over. They stopped only for an hour's fitful sleep.

On the second night, Gormion took her followers back to the red tents of the bandits. It was enough, she concluded. The man was dead, and all that remained was to name Stormlight as his successor.

The Que-Nara were more faithful. Many of them

stayed through four, five nights, but on the sixth day the number of watchers began to dwindle. Women led the children to their tents, and some of the older warriors and the shamans returned to camp on the seventh day.

The grumbling began. Stormlight heard it first from Gormion, when he returned after the seventh night's vigil, headed for his tent and three hours' sleep before sunrise.

All responsibility had fallen on Stormlight. In the seven days that Fordus had lain silent atop the Red Plateau, he had come to see how unwieldy the sole command of this irregular army could be.

It was sleep, however, that he thought of now, and when he heard the rattle and ring of jewelry approaching from behind, for a moment Stormlight envied Fordus his coma. He turned to face the dark-haired bandit, his expression level and impassive.

"It is time to decide, Stormlight," the bandit captain declared, her eyes flashing with impatience and anger.

"What would you have me decide, Gormion?" His voice remained calm, he believed—no hint of the rising irritation he felt as the woman drew near him and raised a solitary, thin finger, pointing and jabbing at him like she wielded a dagger.

"The fate of the rebellion, Stormlight. I would have you decide what is next. Instead of waiting for the . . . *visionary* to die."

Stormlight remained impassive.

"While we crouch on our haunches," the bandit continued, "and await the passing, Istar is moving troops to the north."

"You know this for a fact, Gormion?"

He knew that she didn't.

"What would *you* do if you were Kingpriest,

Stormlight?"

"I am not Kingpriest, Gormion."

"You could be. You are resourceful and brave."

Stormlight laughed wearily. Seven days had worn thin his patience, but this was the most ridiculous of Gormion's proddings. Was she foolish enough to believe that an elf whose greatest enemy sat on the Istarian throne . . .

"And you command these armies."

Tanila had spoken the same words a week ago when he first met her at the fireside.

Astonished, Stormlight stared at the bandit leader. Gormion's face, once beautiful, had wrinkled and lined over the years with scheming and anger. Not yet thirty, she looked twice her age.

"What did you say, Gormion?"

With a sniff of disgust, the woman backed away from Stormlight, who continued to stare at her, his dark eyes intent and wide. "I said what I said, elf," she decreed, the menace in her voice brittle and thin.

She wheeled about in a chiming of bracelets and a rattle of beads. "I said what I said," she repeated, calling the words over her shoulder as she fled to the darkness of her tent, to safety and concealment.

"And you, Stormlight of the Lucanesti, had better listen. Or be lost like the rest of your people!"

* * * * *

Back in the Abyss, her female crystalline body abandoned in the fires and eruptions, Takhisis banked in the windless air and laughed exultantly.

Gormion would be easy, when the time came. Hers was a spirit primed for hatred and strife.

Takhisis beat her wings, her laughter settling to a low, contented rumble.

For wherever strife and hatred abounded . . . there was confusion . . . and confusion was an inroad for her every evil work.

Her defeat was only a temporary one, and not without some satisfaction. For Sargonnas's glowing condor also had crumbled in the air, the bard's song changing the vaunting god into a harmless shower of sparks.

It had been rather beautiful. A bright show of fireworks in the desert sun. It had given Takhisis an image as well . . . an idea how to punish her insolent consort.

When they returned to the abyss, she had set upon him like a hawk on a sparrow, swooping through the bottomless darkness, folding her wings in a searing dive through the nothingness, sensing him somewhere below her.

Her thoughts called out to Sargonnas in the blackness, and he answered. Penitently. Fearfully.

He told her of Fordus's weakness—of the man's great desire to discover his origins, his parentage.

Then suddenly she found herself above him, and dove, and he was there, turning his ruddy face, his lidless eyes wide in astonishment and terror as she crashed into him like a merciless black comet.

He exploded from the power of her assault, shattering into a hundred thousand shards and fragments, which squeaked and twittered as they scattered in aimless flight through the void.

It would take him a century to reassemble.

Now, as she remembered the moment, her rage subsided. Or rather, it turned back to the world, to the Plainsmen who ranged the fringes of the desert in clear defiance of her Istar, her Kingpriest, her plans for the Cataclysm.

This Fordus had shown himself well nigh indestructible. Neither the desert nor its creatures, the Istarians nor Sargonnas's fire and clumsiness had had enough power to bring down this man.

Yet, he was suggestible. His ancestry weakened him. Which was why Takhisis had come to the man in his dreams, breathing lies and nonsense about his great and far-reaching destiny.

He was ambitious enough to believe anything.

Takhisis purred contentedly.

She had lingered awhile in the Plainsman's dreams, burrowing deeper and deeper into the recesses of his memory, past the layers of adolescence, of childhood, past the time he was brought to the desert's edge, in secrecy and in night.

His mother was a slave girl, an attendant in the Kingpriest's Tower. She learned that, easily.

Now, more importantly, Takhisis knew his father. And there is great power in knowledge, great freedom. She would use that knowledge to destroy him.

Now the Prophet was rising from sleep. Fordus lay in a pool of sweat, his breathing easy and his fever broken. But his spiked golden torc tightened ever so slightly upon his wasted neck. The ends then welded in a silent, seamless joining, symbol of a new alliance that could never be broken.

Fordus would waken with an altered heart.

She would leave the final, brutal work to her earthly minions, when time and opportunity converged.

When the moment came, the Prophet would beg for oblivion.

* * * * *

In the evening of the tenth day, when the Water Prophet opened his eyes, only a handful of the faithful were left on the plateau. Kneeling beside him, Northstar offered him water.

"I have dreamt strangely," Fordus announced after a long drink, a new sound in his voice. His eyes were bright and sunk deeply into their sockets from the ten-day fast of his sleep.

Northstar and Stormlight bent over him, and Larken, jubilant, ceased her drumming.

"And I have seen signs and wonders in my dream," he concluded, sitting up painfully. "Assemble the people for a new word."

Larken sounded the gathering call on her drum. Its message echoed from the heights of the Red Plateau, borne on the shouts and calls of the sentries, passed from encampment to encampment, from the white tents of the Que-Nara to the red of Gormion's bandits. They came in throngs, from the battle leaders and shamans and Namers down to the youngest child, for Larken's drum was a powerful summons.

When the gathering drum sounded, the gods were ready to speak.

Stormlight waited with the rest of the company as Fordus stood weakly in the midst of the jostling crowd. Fathers lifted children onto their shoulders to better see the Prophet, and the rumor circulated among the awestruck Que-Nara that Fordus had passed through the land of the dead and come back with the deepest prophecy of all. Leaning on Northstar's shoulder, the blood on his mending side caked and dried as though he might brush away the wound, Fordus trained his sea-blue eyes toward the horizon.

"My dream has spoken to me," the Prophet proclaimed. "Istar is burning. The fire has come, and the world has opened."

A murmur spread through the crowd, and a thousand eyes turned to Stormlight, who stepped aside, waiting for the lightning to strike as it always struck, for Fordus's obscure poetry to become clear.

Quickly, with the confidence born of long experience, he isolated the symbols from the Prophet's speech.

Fire. A burning city. The crack in the world.

As he felt the words stirring, felt them rise from that mysterious source in the depths of his spirit, suddenly he heard an excited rumble from the crowd.

Stormlight's unspoken words froze in his throat.

"Hear the word of the Prophet!" Fordus proclaimed, blue eyes scanning the encircling faces. "The meaning of my dream has come to me, and to me alone. No longer do I need interpreter!"

Stormlight shivered with a sharp intake of breath. His power, his position, had been usurped.

"For I have passed through the fire and the fever," Fordus continued, his hands raised aloft, "and I have walked on the margins of shadows and looked over into the places from which no man returns."

Uncertainly, with a sidelong glance at Stormlight, Larken beat the drum once, twice.

"My dream has told me that Istar is burning. The fire that will destroy the city has not yet been kindled, but we are the ones who will light it."

Slowly, the circle of people surrounding Stormlight widened and dispersed, as the Plainsmen turned in rapt attention toward Fordus. Dumbstruck, the elf watched in befuddlement as Larken, too, turned toward the Water Prophet, storing his words for a song.

"Rest tonight," Fordus said softly, his eyes turned north, to where the red moon and the white sat low on the horizon. The Namers and shamans who circled him strained to hear his words, caught them, and passed them to the Plainsmen and bandits who waited behind them, so that the message spread like brushfire over the listening crowd. "Rest tonight, for tomorrow we march. We march on Istar, and there will not be peace until the city is mine."

Chapter 15

Stormlight decided to speak against Fordus's prophecy. Standing before the assembled camps, his voice rang loud and true and assured, as it had on a hundred occasions before, when he had helped to guide the Que-Nara through long, waterless stretches of the desert in search of oases, of underground pools, of arroyos suddenly and strangely filled by an outburst of subterranean springs.

In the years of drought his voice had been rain, so the people were inclined to listen.

"I have heard the prophecy of Fordus Firesoul," he began, "and I believe his dream has misguided him. Where before have we found the water, and looked in the sand for the approach of Istar, for other dangers and for enemies? Speak, if you know."

The sea of faces was still and quiet. They knew, of course, of the kanaji pit—that there was a magic within the crumbling, sand-swallowed walls that had lasted an age or more. They knew that Fordus entered the pit to seek visions and wisdom. They knew something of the glyphs, and all believed that the gods sent messages through them to the Prophet.

But they did not know how.

"In all those times," Stormlight continued, "I have stood beside the Water Prophet. I have seen the birth of the visions, and when he has spoken, I have spoken after him. His words were cloudy, but I have made them plain so that you may understand them. Always we have worked together—the Storm of Prophecy and the Stormlight. We have found water, and when we needed to elude the slavers, they went home with their collars empty. In these wars of liberation, we have found Istar and the unprotected flanks of the Kingpriest's army."

"Why did the wars start, Stormlight?" Fordus asked softly, and all eyes turned to the Prophet, all ears awaited his answer. "Was it in the kanaji that the gods told me to move against Istar? No, I tell you. This vision came to me in a dream. I alone was its Prophet and interpreter. The Namers and the shamans all know that I speak the truth."

A dozen gray heads in the first circle of watchers—heads covered in beads and oils, locks caked with penitential and meditative mud—nodded in fierce agreement.

The Prophet was a dreamer. And Stormlight? Perhaps he was jealous. Perhaps the gods had moved him aside.

Stormlight himself wavered with a moment's doubt. *Was* he jealous, as no doubt they must believe? Had the words of Tanila and Gormion struck him so because they were the same words, spoken on the same day, or because they had touched the secret desires of his own heart?

Yet he knew it was foolish—these doubts, these suspicions—because most foolish of all was Fordus's reckless haste. If they moved in accordance with Fordus this time, all of them, Plainsman and bandit alike, would surely fall in the grasslands north of the desert, where Istar's might was ready. There were fifty thousand of them, to the rebels' five hundred.

He could not let that happen.

Stormlight gathered himself for an answer. "It was your dream that began this war, Fordus. I cannot deny that. But did you dream the thousands of slaves, both Plainsman and elf, who wear the Istarian collars, laboring in their households and markets on their swarming docks and in their lampless mines? Did you dream the legion after legion that Istar has set before us, and did you dream the great mountains south of the city, and the lake we need to encircle, and then more plains, and, finally, the great Istarian walls, twenty feet thick, of solid stone?

"There *will* be a time for great victory, a time to march through the streets of Istar in celebration, with thousands more following us, thousands more at our side. And we *will* set them free, and forever break the bondage Istar has put upon our people. We *will* leave the desert and have warm homes and restored families. But it is too soon. Istar will crush us like shells."

He looked out over the armies. Some of the leaders—Breeze and Messenger among the Plainsmen,

Gormion and Rann among the bandits—nodded in agreement with his words.

They were war leaders, skilled soldiers all.

A fleeting cloud of distaste moved over Fordus's face, but almost at once he converted it to a limpid sweetness. He lifted his hands—the Prophet's gesture of inspiration and blessing—and he turned with a smile toward Larken.

"In the time of glyphs and of defense," he said, "*Three* of us guided you, not two. I call on Larken in this new age. I call on her song to lift us out of questioning and debate."

Stormlight's hopes sank as the girl stood and walked slowly to her drum. Larken was Fordus's bard; he was her true love. She had followed him for years, exalting him, adoring him.

There was no question whose story she would tell. How could it be otherwise?

"Let her sing," Stormlight proclaimed quietly. "She will surely sing for *you*. Once before you led us out of the desert's fastness, and the Kingpriest's army followed us back. There are orphans and widows who remember that day sadly, and there are grieving ancient ones who did not expect to outlive their sons.

"And now you lead us forth once again, and again we will follow. I will come behind you—not *follow*, but *come behind*—because the Que-Nara are my people as well, and will need someone to defend them from your great foolhardiness. Still, I cannot blame those who choose to stay behind.

"But know this: If your ambitions outstrip your love for your people, if you venture into country that promises death like the death that swept down on us beneath the Red Plateau . . . why, I shall be the first to turn against you. I will kill you myself"

With a silent prayer that his words had found listeners, Stormlight stalked from the council. The crowd parted like high grass in his passage, but he did not look back until he reached the steep, inclining trail that led down from the plateau.

Northstar had stayed.

And Larken . . . immoveable in her uncertainty.

Nonetheless, ninety warriors came behind him. Gormion and Rann and their henchmen, Messenger and Breeze and their followers and families descended the trail in a long, uncertain line.

He looked toward the camp, where the muted fires, left untended, had lapsed into darkness.

"May the gods and the god beyond them hear me," he whispered. "And may Fordus and Larken someday understand."

* * * * *

"You are a dead man if you leave me, Stormlight," Fordus shouted to the backs of the departing rebels. "*All* of you are dead. Without me you will have no water, no defense. Istar will take you at its leisure, or you will go to the Kingpriest and beg for his mercy!" Without so much as a good breath between, he turned to the loyal and continued in an even conversational tone.

"The gods alone send dreams, and the Prophets alone can divine them."

He clambered atop a stand of stones and looked down upon the sizeable crowd that remained. Four hundred Plainsmen and barbarians sat on the hard, rocky ground and watched him expectantly.

"Stormlight did not remind you that his words interpreted mine when we emerged from the kanaji. It was *he* who told you that the water was north of the desert, the moon and wind were on our side, and that Istar was waiting."

Larken looked up at him sharply.

Some of the barbarians stirred and murmured among themselves.

"If any prophecy failed," Fordus continued, "it failed when the interpreter brought you the words."

Larken set aside the drum. The only music Fordus wanted was that of his own voice. He stood above his company, waving and gesticulating, his movements swift and frenzied and sinuous. His argument was as shimmering and elusive as a mirage. She could not piece the logic of it, and yet those who remained were listening, were nodding, were agreeing.

As Fordus spoke, preparing his followers for the morning's march into the lands of Istar, the bard fingered her drum hammer absently, uncertainly.

Perhaps, she thought guiltily, her music for Fordus had fled along with her love.

Confidently and ardently, after the speech of the Water Prophet, her cousin Northstar stood in the midst of the seated multitude.

"Hear the word of the Prophet!" Northstar cried exultantly, lifting his salvaged bronze medallion into the cool desert night. "Fordus Firesoul is the War Prophet, the man who needs no translator, no interpreter of broken words! I, for one, have kept my eyes to the heavens for forty turning seasons. I have steered you by planet and star, and I have steered by my heart and mind as well.

"For those years, the gods have told me to guide. And now my heart tells me to follow.

"To follow Fordus Firesoul, the War Prophet, the Liberator! On to Istar, warriors of the Que-Nara! To the walled city, friends and brothers!"

A roar arose from the seated multitude, a rumble and shout like the roll of an enormous drum. Lucas soared away from the loud and menacing sound, circling dolefully in the silence of the upper night air until he seemed like a swiftly moving planet, a meteor in the dark vault of the heavens. Below him, the torches converged and filed toward the camp, the council doomed and concluded.

* * * * *

The next morning the rebels departed from the camp at the base of the Red Plateau.

The War Prophet was steady now, firm of footfall and strong in his stride. His pain had vanished, replaced by a fierce and jubilant sense of his own destiny.

He set off on foot at the head of his army. Waves of the Que-Nara danced in their white robes behind him, and the motley garb of bandit and barbarian decorated the bleak desert with color.

It was the morning of the Shinarion, and they formed the last of the caravans headed for Istar.

If the gods willed it, Fordus Firesoul would be in the city within a week, celebrating the close of the holy days on the throne of the Kingpriest.

Stormlight watched their departure from the edge of the salt flats. Fordus, his eyes straight ahead toward the beckoning north, did not acknowledge his old companion, nor did the others who flocked around the War Prophet, watching each gesture and listening to each word, certain they were present at the making of history.

Wearily, Larken set out in the middle of the column. Almost as an afterthought, she wrapped the lyre, carrying it in a knapsack over her shoulder.

Dreamlike, she touched the instrument in the dark cloth, and it seemed to quiver in her weary hand.

By the jostling of totem standards and bandit banners milling in the company ahead of her, she could locate Fordus, though she could neither see nor hear him. All around her a river of robed bodies surged and pushed, and she felt as though she were being washed away to the north, borne on an irresistible tide.

Once she looked back. At the edge of the Tears of Mishakal, framed in the glittering black of the crystals, a solitary figure watched the passing of the army, at last signaling his forces to follow, his gestures tired and heavy. He was distant, his features lost in the sandy wind and the liquid shimmer that rose from the hot desert surface, but she recognized him at once.

Stormlight.

She wanted to wave, to signal to him something about peace and friendship. But a banner, waved by an enthusiastic barbarian boy, flashed green and golden through her line of sight, and the babble of a foreign tongue distracted her. When she looked to the flats again, Stormlight was gone.

She looked to where the banners encircled Fordus. Energized by the sun, by the adulation of his followers, the Prophet was moving more quickly. Already the colors danced at the edge of her sight, moving resolutely into the distance, where the cloudless sky seemed to open and swallow them.

* * * * *

At midday, deep in the Tears of Mishakal, a funnel of black sand swirled skyward, propelled on an unnatural desert wind. Weaving between the crystals like a dark, intangible river, the sand brushed and chimed against the ancient, gleaming stones until the whole salt flat seemed to wail and whistle like a thousand lost souls.

Out into the desert the black wind rushed, over the site of the Plainsmen's recent battle with the condor, scattering sagebrush and ash in its path as it hastened north. It passed about a mile to the east of Fordus's marching legions, and the scouts and outrunners took shelter on the leeward side of the dunes, convinced that the wind was the herald of a great approaching rain.

In its wake, the desert lay calm again. Brush tumbled from dune to dune in sedate, everyday winds, and the sun beat relentlessly over the shifting browns and reds of the arid landscape. The Plainsmen soon forgot about the storm as they scanned the horizons for signs of the Kingpriest's army.

But high above them, a solitary bird soared after the dark wind.

The bard's hawk, Lucas, his wings extended, watched the curious cloud from a distance as it raced from the desert into the plains. Skimming low over the dry terrain, the bird watched the ripple of the high grasses and followed the path of the wind through that wide and deceptive country.

Soon the grasslands gave way to rocky slopes, to foothills, as the dark wind hurried over farmlands and villages, headed toward mountains and the daunting walls of Istar beyond. Soaring at hunting speed, Lucas at last overtook it as it skimmed across the great expanse of Lake Istar, and from his high vantage, the bird looked down upon the gritty, undulating spine of the wind.

It seemed to the bird that he flew above a huge serpent or above the thrashing tail of an even greater beast. Cautiously, he kept his distance and continued to follow and watch.

As the wind neared the city seawalls, its writhing form condensed and compressed. The wind became liquid, then solid, darkening and coalescing until, to the hawk's acute eyes, it looked like a watersnake, glittering like crystal in the harsh sunlight, wriggling swiftly over the lakeside to the city walls, winding and thrashing across the steep, rocky incline.

Now, his confusion over, Lucas swooped for the snake, gliding low over the water behind it, extending and flexing his fierce talons. He narrowed the gap in seconds, caught a glimpse of faceted edges in the skin of his quarry, the smell of salt, and the smell of something older than salt, brilliant and sinister. He shrieked, struck out with his talons, but the snake was swift, elusive. Slipping through a small crevice at the base of the great wall, it vanished, the tip of its tale flickering tauntingly against the gray stone.

Lucas landed hard by the city walls and ruffled himself in frustration. Then he climbed steeply on a thermal close to the Istarian walls and, turning above the Kingpriest's Tower, made for the south and Fordus's approaching forces. He would not forget the snake and its strange transformations.

And somewhere in the dark beneath Istar, the long, serpentine form altered and grew.

Chapter 16

Shinare's festival was doomed from the outset.

From the abandoned Tower of High Sorcery, its gates draped in drooping golden ribbons in honor of the goddess, all the way across the central city to the School of the Games, where tarnished bronze griffin wings hung as a reminder of earlier, more vibrant festivals, the city stiffened under a turgid pall. The few paltry booths, decked with the ribbons of the goddess, looked muddy and stained in the hot, windless afternoons. The goods sold in the Marketplace seemed tawdry and cheap: shoddy earthenware statuary from Thoradin replaced the customary carved stone, the scrimshaw from Balifor seemed abstract and rushed, and the scaleless fish from northern Karthay was the worst of all failures.

This fish, brought to the markets in thousands of pounds and kept on ice from the Karthayan mountains, was intended as the principal delicacy of this year's Shinarion. But the heat of the city grew suddenly unbearable, and the catch had spoiled by the second day, leaving the air of the city tainted, almost unbreatheable.

The visitors could not help but notice. Despite the fuming incense on the windowsills of houses, despite the cloves hung by the thresholds and the attars of roses and violets let run in rivulets through the gutters of the streets, the city stank.

By the second evening of the Shinarion, those who were leaving the festival outnumbered the arrivals. Into the adjoining towns about the bay they retreated, past the monastery or through the Karthayan forest, rushing on horseback, in carts, on foot toward the fresh, cool air, shaking the odors of incense and dead fish from their clothing.

The few among them who looked back, nostalgic, no doubt, for the merriment of earlier festivals, saw the lights of Istar flickering and dim across the dark water. The Shinarion candles, once used to mark the festival time in such profusion that the light was visible ten miles away, had dwindled to a few sad thousand, barely producing light to steer by.

It was not long before the travelers lost the city behind them in the rising dusk.

* * * * *

Alone on the Temple battlements, gazing out over the putrid city, Vaananen marveled at the quiet and darkness of this most unusual festival time.

The city looked besieged.

Of course, the rumors had spread through Istar more quickly than the smell of the rotten fish.

A rebel force had come out of the desert again, headed toward the city, its numbers unknown. At its helm was the same man—the Water Prophet—who had burst into the grasslands less than a month before, inflicted great casualties on the Twelfth and Seventh Istarian legions, then hastened back into that godless country of rock and sand, where he had vanished like a dying wind.

Vaananen shook his head. It was too soon.

No matter the powers of this Fordus Firesoul, he and his rebels were not ready. The forces arrayed against them were more than formidable, the road ahead of them perilous and long.

With Fordus away from the kanaji, there was no chance to warn him. Vaananen leaned against the cooling stone wall and stared out over the city. In the distance, the School of the Games blazed with gaudy purple light, and a roar erupted from a crowd accustomed to gladiatorial slaughter and reckless horse races.

Now was the most dangerous time—for his own mission in the city, and for Fordus's rebellion in the outlands.

For the Sixth Legion had indeed arrived in Istar. Of that much Vaananen was certain.

After his trip to the stables and the other discoveries, Vincus had rushed back to the druid's quarters, scrambled through the window in a net of torn vines and brambles, and gesticulated so wildly that it took Vaananen the goodly part of an hour to calm the young man down.

By now, the druid believed the servant's story, but

he accompanied him back to the stables anyway, and the horse's tattooed lip had confirmed the unpleasant truth.

Not even three legions of Solamnic Knights could hope for victory against Istar's garrison of over five thousand veteran soldiers.

He had warned the Prophet accordingly, drawn the glyphs in the rena garden, four symbols bold in the dark sand.

But who would be there to read it?

Vaananen pulled his cloak tightly about his shoulders. It always seemed to happen during the Shinarion: the last days of summer blended unaccountably into the first of autumn, and sometime, usually in midfestival, one cool, unforeseen night would signal a change in the season.

Vaananen descended the battlements. The sun had drifted behind the delicate white spires and domes of the western city, staining the luminous buildings with an ominous red.

He had one desperate hope. The Kingpriest, for all his skill in ritual and politics, was not known for his perfect choice of generals. Each successive commander had been worse than the last, culminating in the abysmal Josef Monoculus. To find a good leader had become next to impossible when the Solamnic Order, disgusted with Istar's policy of oppression, had ceased to support the Kingpriest's sterner measures.

And a good thing that was, Vaananen concluded, because the Istarian army with a real general at its head would be matchless.

Shivering at the thought, the druid pulled up his hood and entered the great Council Hall of the Temple, where, in his guise as a loyal follower of the Kingpriest, he would join a handful of other chosen clerics in receiving the next, no doubt, in a sorry line of military leaders.

"The fool of the season," Brother Alban had called the new commander.

None of the priests had met the new man.

Always an occasion for curiosity, the moment arrived, and Vaananen was somewhat shocked when, entering the torchlit hall, he saw the clergy crowded around the impressive figure of a black-robed man. The man stood next to the Kingpriest himself.

For the first time in years, perhaps the Kingpriest had chosen wisely. Vaananen could tell by the cut of the man: sturdy and strong, his pale body chiseled, almost translucent, as though an able sculptor had carved him of marble. The black silk tunic he wore was simple and elegant, a striking contrast to the billowing, ornate robes of his clerical hosts, and he wore a battered sword at his side—a weapon that had seen years of action, the druid guessed, unlike the ornamental baubles banging around on the belts of the last three generals.

This man was dark-haired, handsome in a feminine, almost reptilian fashion, and he held the gaze of the Istarian priests impassively, with neither respect nor condescension. He refused the wine offered him by Brother Burgon and remained standing when most of the clergy chose to sit, his pale arms crossed over his broad chest.

Beside him, the Kingpriest displayed his gentlest features. He was a lean, balding scholar with bright sky-blue—no, sea-blue—eyes. If the power of Istar had not resided in the little man, he might have been mistaken for the new general's obsessively proper secretary.

The two dignitaries spoke quietly to one another, as the priests and monks leaned into the conversation.

The Kingpriest looked tired, harried; what remained of his auburn hair had thinned even more since Vaananen had seen him last, and for a moment the druid wondered if the monarch was ill.

But when the blue eyes turned toward him, they were bright and hectic.

And afraid.

How odd.

Vaananen edged closer through the crowd, hearing the stranger's name bandied excitedly by the murmuring clerics.

Tadec? Tanik? The whispering was insistent, distracting, the words blending together so that the druid could not make out the name in question. But whoever the man was, Tadec or Tanik, he continued to charm his hosts: a low, melodious comment from the man drew animated laughter and, with an icy smile, he scanned the room, his eyes locking at once with Vaananen's.

The eyes of the new general were amber, depthless, and slitted. He stared at the druid, and the black core of his gaze opened malignly. Looking into the heart of those eyes, Vaananen saw an image of a dark void, a huge winged shape spiraling in the windless nothingness, its webbed, extended wings flexing and shimmering.

I know you, a dark voice seemed to say, rising from nowhere but registering inside the shaking druid's head.

Then, as suddenly as it struck, the feeling subsided. Vaananen blinked, the general turned away, and the image vanished. But in that moment's communion Vaananen knew both what the man called himself, and who he really was.

"*Takhisis,*" Vaananen whispered to himself, as the clergy around him slipped past on their way to meet and admire and adore this new, mysterious leader. "*Takhisis* commands the armies of Istar. Now I know.

"And now she knows, too."

* * * * *

The corridors of the tower were drafty and dank as the druid made his way back to his quarters. The hour was still early, his priestly brothers either at prayers or the festival . . . or adoring the general, breathless and rapt like vermin mesmerized before a sewer snake.

There was still time to warn the rebels, if Fordus returned to the kanaji.

Vaananen knew that the days to come would be dangerous for all of them. Now he would have to lock his doors, board his windows against the suddenly hostile night. The goddess had recognized him—he was almost sure of it. And since that was true, his life was forfeit.

A faint light wavered and approached from a side corridor. *Not even an hour, and it has already begun,* Vaananen thought, wrestling down a rising fear. He stepped into a dark threshold, pressed himself against the polished wood of the door . . . and watched as a sleepy acolyte passed, bearing a torch to the last prayers of the night.

Vaananen moved out from the darkness, laughed softly and sadly. It would not do. He would not hide and hole away in the temple, waiting for Takhisis to strike. He would not lie trembling in bed, awaiting a footfall outside his locked doors.

And yet, despite his brave thoughts, Vaananen sighed in relief when his own door was behind him, when it was locked and double-locked against the night and his own fearful imaginings. At once the druid moved to the rena garden, to see if the four glyphs he had drawn that morning lay untouched in the shadowy sand.

Yes, they were still there. Fordus had not received them.

Vaananen sat on the black stone. It was time for a fifth symbol. The druids had taught him that a powerful magic lay in the crafting of this extraordinary glyph—a magic to be used only when circumstances were dire. The message of the fifth symbol was always loud: sometimes a warning of famine or sudden flood, often, during the Age of Dreams, a token that a dragon approached. It was distinct from the other glyphs, for it beckoned with an impulse as strong as hunger or weariness.

Now the message would call out to Fordus from the landscape itself—from the rocks in the foothills to the mud along Lake Istar, wherever his army marched. The fifth rune would summon him back to the desert, to the kanaji.

Carefully, shaking ever so slightly, Vaananen drew the glyph beneath the other four. It was an ancient symbol, used last, the druid believed, in the time of Huma—in the Third Dragon War that had driven the goddess from the face of Krynn.

The markings were twofold, overlapping. The image of a woman upon that of a man.

Beware Takhisis! the glyph read. *Beware the dark man!*

* * * * *

Tamex greeted the last of the clergy, two balding old men who bowed and scraped before him as though he were the Kingpriest himself. They babbled their amenities, their little phrases of flattery and adoration, never noticing that the new commander's amber eyes had strayed from them.

Quick, ruthless, and efficient, she had come to Istar for business. Crawling through the city as a snake had been a pleasing reconnaissance. No one noticed another serpent in Istar, anyway. And there had been no one to bar entry to the arena, no one to disturb her next transformation.

Out of the sands she had assembled Tamex, and it had been easy for this embodiment, this creature of crystal and lies, to win over the Kingpriest and his company—indeed, to win over all of them.

All of them, that is, except that druid.

Oh, yes. She had seen the druid for the first time in a vision, exultant at Fordus's victory, raising his bared arms. It had to be him. She had seen the red oak leaf tattooed on the inside of his left arm.

That information alone, in the proper hands, would be enough to silence him.

Yet, at times the court of Istar moved with exasperating slowness. Misdemeanors could take years to try and judge, and a capital crime such as this—high treason against the empire—could take so long the druid might die of old age before he was sentenced.

No, his silencing would come by older, more traditional means.

Tamex moved through the dispersing crowd, taking care not to brush against priest or acolyte. The cold, stony feel of the adopted body would surely arouse suspicion. Moving the heavy limbs without overmuch noise or breakage was difficult enough.

Watch your windows, druid, the crystals in Tamex's blood whined and whispered. *Watch your doors, and watch your back in the corridors.*

And, oh, yes, count the sunrises and the sunsets, and bless each one of them. For you, there are few remaining.

Chapter 17

A third day had passed, and a fourth, while the glyphs lay unchanged in the rena garden. Always before, they had vanished on their own, a sign that their message had been received by the rebels.

But now Fordus was far afield, and Vaananen's concern deepened with the passing hours. Had the fifth sign not called him back? Perhaps the Prophet refused to return to the kanaji, to the intelligence that might save him and his small army.

Vaananen's own time had run out. He knew Takhisis was coming for him. It was only a matter of when and how.

As he sat on the red stone in the rena garden,
Vaananen composed his last message. He picked
gingerly at a black silken hair caught on the inch-
long needles of the large barrel cactus near his foot.
The strand caught on a ripple of his breath and
settled back upon the spines, this time well entan-
gled. Vaananen stared abstractedly at it for a
moment, and then caught a tiny, odd vibration from
the life-current in the plant. He noticed the cactus
had also swelled somewhat over the last few hours,
as if there had been a sudden rain the afternoon
before.

"Just like the new commander's power," he muttered. "Swelled full-blown overnight."

The priests of Istar had reveled as the new commander assumed the reins of the army. The scattered
Twelfth and Ninth Legions recombined within a day
and were renamed the Fifteenth, joining the First,
Second, Fourth and Eighth in the defense of the city.

With the current size of the city's garrison, three
legions could at any time march out the gates and
still leave a sizeable guard at home. The town now
knew that the fabled Sixth had arrived—the hexa-
gons drawn in charcoal on the stone walls of alleys,
scratched on doors and hung on tattered banners
from the windows of abandoned houses, bore ominous witness that at last the legion was showing
itself.

Soon they would all join together. Tamex would
have his army, and the goddess within him would
have her foothold in the world.

Vaananen shifted on the red stone. "But it isn't
over yet," he said firmly, quietly.

Outside the window, almost in mockery, the distant sounds of the shabby festival reached him from
the Marketplace, and the druid stood, stepped away

from the garden, and walked to the lectern, where he scrawled a hasty note on a scrap of parchment. He stepped into the corridor, handed the note to a passing linkboy, and ordered the child to the library.

"I want this book from the dark young man, the silent one," he whispered, and the linkboy hurried off.

Of course, it was no book Vaananen awaited.

Vincus arrived minutes later, his hands ink stained and sandy from Balandar's copying tasks. He found Vaananen somber and crouched above the rena garden as usual, but this time circled by lanterns as though he awaited a deeper darkness, as though all of that light was meant to ward him from something deadly and close.

Instantly, Vincus knew that this time was different. This time was special.

Vaananen beckoned him, and cautiously Vincus approached. He knew there was a magic in this garden, but it was quiet and meditative magic—far from the fire and thunder of the festival illusionists.

And yet, best be alert.

Solemnly, the druid showed him four symbols drawn in the sand. "You're a copyist, Vincus," he whispered, "and a good one, I hear. How is your memory?"

Vincus stared at the symbols in puzzlement. His memory was sharp and searching. Though he had seen them just once, he could have told of each booth in the Marketplace, the merchant's name and his wares, his home country and the color of the pennants on his tents.

No, there were no clouds in Vincus's recollection.

But the druid was asking for more than memory. And what he was asking for . . .

Well, Vincus was not sure.

So he shrugged, his right hand flickering with three tentative signs.

I remember as well as some, he told the druid.

Vaananen raised an eyebrow and smiled grimly. "You'll have to do better than that," he whispered. "You're the only one I can trust."

Vincus averted his eyes.

"No, look!" Vaananen urged, clutching the young servant's arm, pointing at the row of glyphs. "Could you remember these?"

Vincus looked. The lines were simple, bold. He already knew them. And yet . . .

Slowly, reluctantly, Vincus nodded.

Vaananen erased the glyphs. "Show me," he said.

Vincus drew again the four simple signs: Desert's Edge, Sixth Day of Lunitari, No Wind, the Leopard. And then the fifth symbol—the elaborate interlacing of two ancient letters.

"The last is the most important one," Vaananen said quietly. "The one that must reach Fordus Firesoul—and he is far away, beyond the city walls, in the desert. Go."

Vincus looked up sharply in disbelief. The mythical rebel commander!

"Yes, you must go to him," Vaananen said, smiling, trying to ease the young man's mind.

I will, Vincus signed. His gestures were confident, perhaps a little too bold. He would go. But he would never come back. Vincus did not believe in Fordus, nor in the world outside the city, for that matter.

Vincus stepped to the windowsill, searching the dark expanses of vallenwood below, the walls and the city beyond. Vaananen moved to him and touched his silver collar. A sharp blaze of blue crackled in the air at Vincus's ear, and he jerked away, dazed.

Vaananen looked him in the eye and said, "For years I have been striving to pay your debt—your *father's* debt—legitimately and legally. I have wrestled the Kingpriest, losing under his self-serving rules. But all the rules are broken now. Go in peace. Your collar will tell Fordus who you are."

The druid produced two books from beneath his cot. He handed them to Vincus, who turned the volumes over in his hands, then opened one.

On the frail, brittle pages was a story in the elusive Lucanesti script, of gods and goddesses, of Istar and inheritances and the rightful ruler. Vincus could read little of it. The other was a copy, but still written in Lucanesti.

"The one is too fragile to travel," the druid observed. "Here is a copy. Old words upon new parchment, as much as is legible. Take it with you. One will ask for it soon, and you will know it is right to give the book to that person."

Vaananen placed the book and some food, along with a dagger and some odd seeds, in a small hide bag, and pressed it into Vincus's hand.

"You have served well, Vincus," the druid concluded, as Vincus moved away, still puzzled. An odd note of finality crept into Vaananen's voice. "Well done."

Vincus descended through the spreading branches, climbing away from the words.

* * * * *

He stood at the edge of the Marketplace as the festival closed for the night. One of the merchants—an enormous wine seller from Balifor—walked wearily from lantern to lantern, slowly darkening his brightly lit booth.

Vincus stepped into the shadows as the merchant passed. Uneasily, he fingered his silver collar. The druid's magic still stung.

It was too much, this task Vaananen had set before him. Until now, his work for the druid had been easy and intriguing—find this, listen to that, carry rumor and gossip and the whispers of officers back to Vaananen's quarters. And in return, Vaananen made sure Vincus received the best food and lightest duties.

What the druid did with the information could be anything, and it could be nothing. Whatever happened had been none of Vincus's business or care, until now. This thing fretted at him.

He leaned against a marble wall that formed the southernmost edge of the Slave Market. On the day the Temple had bought him—a lone boy of eleven, he had stood in the square between two auctioned Que-Kiri warriors and been sold for the debts of a larcenous father—nobody had supposed him a spy in the making.

If they had only known! The strange, bright-eyed boy in their midst, inexplicably mute, had come to be trusted with the keys to a dozen chambers, to the library and the upper room of the Tower, where the Kingpriest spoke to his counsel. They had given him books and scrolls to carry and sort and store.

They never knew when he had learned to read.

Vincus's smile was veiled by the dark of the alley. They had always underestimated him—all except Vaananen, that is, whose bidding he had followed over the last year. He scooped up a fistful of sand from the base of the wall, scattered it into the shadows, covering his tracks. Out in the lamplit square, the vintner stored the last of the wine barrels in his rickety oxcart and, with a soft, guttural command to the huge animal, steered the vehicle into the dark.

Vincus rose slowly. The square was empty now. But tomorrow the vendors would return, and the day after, and for five days after that, unless the impossible actually happened. Unless the mythical rebels, who were scarcely more than a fleeting, unpleasant dream amid the chanting and ritual of the Tower nights, stepped into the waking world, closed down the festival, captured the Tower, and *liberated* Istar.

Liberate. It made Vincus smile again—that confident, foolish word. Oh, he had heard talk from the other servants that, if Fordus seized the city, there would be freedom for many who now were enslaved. Each would receive a handful of silver, a cart, or a tun of ale—depending on the version of the rumor.

But the elder slaves, the ones who remembered the old Kingpriest and the times before the Siege on Sorcery, said that freedom talk always arose, drifting like smoke into the corners of the city, when a new leader threatened old power. The grayheads did not believe in Fordus, did not believe in a coming freedom.

After all, they had seen the years, seen Kingpriest and liberator come and go. And they still wore the collars—brass, copper, or silver—and the slave trade continued to boom in Istar.

Now the square was empty, the lanterns shut and darkened. With a cautious glance toward the torchlit Tower, the young man crossed the open Marketplace, headed toward the School of the Games and the ramshackle houses that lay in the western slums of the city.

There he had grown up, his friends and companions the child thieves and pickpockets of Istar. They would receive him back, and he could lose himself in the narrow streets and alleys, where neither Istarian Guard nor clergy nor the Kingpriest himself would bother to look.

It would be like it was before.

Vincus slipped past the Welcoming Tower, past the great Banquet Hall to where the streets narrowed and darkened, the older wooden buildings leaning in on each other like wind-felled trees, the faint scent of the harbor lost in the sharp stink of tannery and midden.

Pale faces peered out of the darkened windows. An old woman in an upper story lifted her hand in a warding sign. Someone in the mouth of an alley, cloaked and bent, hissed at him as he passed.

He knew better than to stop or even look back. This was a part of the city untouched by the festival, by the priests or the merchants or the guards.

These were the ones whom Fordus would *liberate*.

Vincus quickened his steps. He was south of the arena now, somewhere south of the School of the Games. At a decent hour, he could have located himself by the sound of the crowd at the gladiatorial combats, could have told the street name and the nearest alley by the echoing roar. But it was far past a decent hour now, and dark.

He was not exactly sure where he was. It had been longer than he remembered. Things had changed.

He found himself on a commercial street—a shabby line of storefronts on the slum's edge. A dozen or so darkened buildings, boarded and barred, lined a road that led to a small, circular court, in the center of which stood a broken fountain, littered with ashes and refuse and crawling with rats. No doubt the night had turned toward morning, for every shop hung in uneasy quiet except a small pub, the Sign of the Basilisk, outside of which three torches sputtered and popped, casting a blood-red light on the fountain square and streaking the storefronts with long shadows.

A solitary watchman, lantern in hand, passed from storefront to storefront. Vincus slipped back into the shadows until the lantern weaved into the darkness and vanished. Laughter from the Basilisk broke uneasily in the close, humid air, and from somewhere in the vaulted shadows of the buildings there came the unmistakable sound of wingbeat, the harsh cry of a bird.

Cautiously, Vincus stepped into the torchlight. The Basilisk was as good a place as any to start—a run-down pub, not far from his childhood haunts. There might be someone here who would remember him—certainly someone would remember his father. And once he had made the connection, had touched on old friendships and older memories . . .

There would be a safe place for him somewhere in the city's intricate, anonymous alleys. This was his big chance.

As he watched the door of the pub, it swung open. Four young men walked out of the smoky light and into the square. One of them, a lean, wiry type dressed in a tattered gray tunic, shielded his eyes against the torchlight and returned Vincus's stare.

"Y'got an eyeful, pup?" he shouted. He was well into his cups, and the wine blurred his thick street accent.

Vincus was not sure what the man said next. Something about "feast" and "come on over," but his gestures were large and violent—waving his arms and beckoning dramatically—and it could have been greeting or challenge. The other three brushed by the drunkard, headed up the street between the storefronts, and when Vincus stepped uncertainly toward the gesturing man, one of them turned and regarded him.

"Vincus?" the man asked, his tight face breaking into a grin. " 'Tis you, old post? Old cat-tongued barnacle?"

He recognized the taunts, the pet names. Pugio, who used to tease him when the gang of boys stole loaves from the bakery by the Welcoming Tower. Vincus walked toward the young man, smiling sheepishly.

Sure enough, it was Pugio.

Vincus gestured. *It has been a long time*, his hands said.

Pugio laughed and shrugged. "I don't remember none of that hand-jabber. No use for it in Bywall."

Bywall. Vincus had forgotten the name.

The worn, crowded settlement pitched in the shadow of Istar's original fortifications was known as Bywall. When the city had expanded beyond its original boundaries, wealthy Istarians had moved north of the Tower, or south into outlying country villas, leaving the older buildings to the itinerant, the unhoused, the poor.

The buildings had collapsed and burned in a fire two years before Vincus was born. In the midst of the rubble and ashes, the destitute survivors had built a city of tents and lean-tos, of capsized wagons and abandoned vendors' booths, carried from the festival grounds and the Marketplace to the filthy, shadowy strip at the foot of the ancient walls. While Vincus was growing up, he and his friends had avoided that part of the city where the plentiful and average dangers turned large and unmanageable.

Vincus approached reluctantly, already misgiving his hopes of renewing old friendships.

Pugio was hard, almost stringy, and there was an ashy sallowness about his skin. He was scarcely a year older than Vincus, yet his hair was wispy and matted, and a long purple scar laced jaggedly across his right forearm. No more than twenty, Pugio looked three times his age, and the men with him were even worse for wear—toothless and scarred, but not past menace and danger. Vincus watched warily as the three men spread out, walking slowly toward him across the torch-haunted square.

"Y'member Anguis," Pugio said, nodding at the man to his left. "And Ultion. Ultion done the games at the School under Angard."

Vincus nodded and lifted his hand to both men. He remembered neither of them, though Anguis looked faintly familiar—a face recalled in the red light of Lunitari . . . something about knives.

"Y'member us all, don'ya, Vincus?" Pugio asked, his street talk thickening the nearer he drew to Vincus. "Y'member us well enough for the handlin'?"

The handling. Vincus raced through his memory for the word.

He remembered, shook his head.

"Livin' high put you out o' thievin', Vincus?" Ultion drew back mockingly and asked with a faint, pleasant smile. "I hear of it happenin' when you got three square an' all. Nice clothes they give ya."

Pugio and Anguis murmured in assent. "A one-timer?" Pugio asked. "Just an old-times handle on the rug merchant over to the Marketplace?"

Vincus shook his head. The three drew nearer.

"No?" Pugio asked, his voice filling with a steely coldness. "Then you'll be givin' us your food, I'm certain. You don't starve an old friend, Vincus."

Suddenly chilled, Vincus looked into their eyes. They returned his gaze steadily, calmly, almost innocently, and then, when his guard descended slowly, when he thought that perhaps his suspicions had all been wrong, that they had been the good and loyal friends he remembered . . .

Anguis glanced over Vincus's shoulder, a quick, flickering movement to his narrow eyes. Vincus saw it, and spun about . . .

In time to catch the drunkard's club, as it descended with swift ferocity.

For a moment Vincus stared his attacker face-to-face, saw the man's eyes widen, smelled the stale wine . . .

Then, with a strength born of life and health, of steady sleep and three squares, he pushed the man aside and, spinning with a fierce, desperate lunge, brought his fist crashing into the face of Ultion.

Ultion fell back with a cry, but the others leapt greedily onto Vincus. Strong fingers probed his throat, and a blinding punch, hurtling out of nowhere, struck him firmly on the side of the head.

He turned toward Anguis, but the air itself seemed to resist him, and one man hit him, and then another. The silver collar snapped and dropped from his neck, and Vincus fell to his knees on the cobbled square, the drunkard stalking toward him, club raised.

Suddenly, his assailants scattered. Shouts followed them from an alley, a rushing column of torches.

The Istarian Guard, Vincus thought. I am safe.

He looked down at the collar, the heavy silver broken in two neat crescents at his knees. If the Guard caught him here even Vaananen could not help him.

* * * * *

Vincus crouched on the roof of the building, peering down like a bruised gargoyle onto the milling soldiers.

He had snatched up the collar and run, only steps ahead of the torches and shouting into the nearest alley. The window into the adjoining brewer's shop was boarded, but not well. In less than a minute, his strength doubled in the desire to escape, Vincus had pulled down the boards and scrambled into the darkened brewery. Dropping into a stack of empty barrels, he clattered and rolled into the warm, yeast-smelling darkness, lying still until the torches and shouting passed.

Then he ascended the stairs to the attic, and, stacking barrel on barrel, he clambered through cobweb and rafter to the trapdoor in the ceiling, firmly bolted from the inside against acrobatic trespassers. Vincus threw back the rusty bolt and climbed to the roof, where he could see by starlight the dark maze of streets beyond the receding torchlight of the guardsmen, as far as the Old Wall, the settlements on the shore of a great lake, and on into the black foothills of a distant mountain range.

He had never ventured outside the walls, not even in thought or imagination.

Gaping, marveling, still shaking, Vincus lay down upon the roof and looked into the wheeling constellations.

There *was* a place where the city ended. Vaananen had told him so, talked about the way past those far-away mountains and into the desert. In the towers, all you could see was the city, and Vincus had always believed that Istar extended to the end of sight, and that the end of sight was the end of the world.

The collar, now two slivers of silver moon, lay cold in his dark hand. The breaks were clean, like they had been cut. Right through the letters of his name.

Dabbing at the cut over his right eye, Vincus held

the pieces up before the lightening sky, so that his name was whole again upon them. The metal was deeply notched but for a hair-thin edge at both breaks. Let alone, the collar would have dropped off by morning, long before he could have made his way to the gates. Now he understood the druid's parting words.

"The rules are broken. . . . You have served well, Vincus. Well done."

Vincus smiled slowly and looked through the silver circle to the wide country beyond the city. Here was a freedom and a country greater than any of his imaginings.

He would see if Fordus was real, too.

Chapter 18

The Old Wall faded into the darkness behind him as the first of the lakeside camps came into view.

For a moment Vincus stopped in the shadows, baffled.

The camp looked like Bywall, or Westedge, or Pierside—one of the sprawling communities of paupers that dotted the shimmering marble of the inner city. The tents were there, and the lean-tos, the banked fires, and the barrels set on their sides to house the poorest of the huddled poor.

For a brief, disorienting second he imagined he had somehow turned himself about in the city, retracing his steps unknowingly.

But no. Behind him was the Old Wall. If he stepped back from the camp and looked carefully, he could see the outline of the ancient battlements, the crenels jagged and crumbling like the rotten teeth of an ancient animal.

Through the camp the ragged people moved, dodging in and out of the firelight. Perhaps what he had seen from the brewery roof was illusion.

Perhaps the world *was* all city, all Istar.

All of a sudden the country ahead of him, glimpsed only fleetingly from the starlit brewery roof, seemed like a murky maze again, its whorls and corridors leading nowhere. And yet the memory of the lake, the dark waters and the vaulting horizon beyond rose foremost in Vincus's mind as he passed from camp's edge to camp's edge on his way toward the shore.

It is only an hour's journey, he told himself. I will reach the lake in an hour.

* * * * *

But it was longer than that.

Twice in the early morning, when the campfires behind had settled to ashes and the road before him lay at its darkest, he had slipped behind tents to conceal himself from a passing squadron of the Istarian Guard.

"Rebels," they muttered. "Fordus."

Once in the rumble of voices and rattle of armor, he thought he heard the druid's name. He leaned forward, wrapping himself in musty canvas, and listened intently for more, but the name and the noise and the squadron passed on into the night, and scarcely three breaths later, Vincus leapt from behind the tent, running to keep himself awake and alert, his hands silently saying an ancient protective prayer.

It must have been prayer that protected him on the last occasion, scarcely an hour before dawn, when a company of Istarian cavalry rode by, their commander so lost in thought that he never looked above, to the branches of a blasted vallenwood, where Vincus perched like some huge, outrageous bird, newly flown from its cage.

Finally, in the purple dawn, the tents and ruins gave way to the cemeteries, the great funerary grounds that bordered the south of Istar. Now, beyond the scattered white monuments burnished by the rising sun, Vincus saw shimmering blue rising out of the darkness and smelled the waters of Lake Istar—the lake of his rooftop vision.

It is true, he told himself, leaning against a marble stone. There is a lake out here, and there are mountains, beyond the buildings.

And Fordus is somewhere beyond the edge of sight. I am glad I kept believing.

And he rested, free from fear and Istar, for the first time in years.

* * * * *

At nightfall, Vincus found the coracle Vaananen had left tied to a willow by the lakeside. Slowly and clumsily, for it was his first time in a boat of any sort, he steered the craft into midlake, where he circled aimlessly, rowing ever more frantically as a distant bell tolled and the night turned.

He could not be found here in the morning. He had to get across the water.

Now Istar and the mountains seemed equidistant—

dark, looming forms against the darker shores. Worn out with rowing, with spinning, with trying to steer by stars that ducked in and out of the clouds, Vincus lay down in the coracle.

Just a few minutes, he promised himself. An hour at most.

When he awoke, it was nearly noon. The craft had drifted to the far side of the lake, and the foothills lay in front of him, inviting and solid and wonderfully, delightfully dry.

Vincus thanked whatever gods had taken charge of the water and the fools who ventured onto it, and, giving the craft a kick he hoped would send it on its way back to the Istarian shore, he scrambled up a narrow path and, by midafternoon, found himself at a great height—at the mouth of the Western Pass with a distant view of the city.

* * * * *

Of the three passes leading through the Istarian range, only the Western Pass was free of the *sterim*—the harsh winds off the desert that seemed to gain force as they climbed. Had Vincus traveled through either the Eastern or the Central Pass, his chance of survival would have been slim.

Vaananen had known, Vincus thought. Those hundreds of times he rattled on about it—they were all for this. For by the time he had wakened on the southern shores of the lake, Vincus was so turned around, so disoriented, that he was not quite sure if the path he followed led to the Western or the Central Pass.

Then he saw gentian and edelweiss—hardy mountain flowers, but not stormfast—at the mouth of the pass. It had to be the Western Pass, Vincus concluded, and he set out through the treacherous mountains by the lone safe route, congratulating himself on his new-found mountaineering skills.

Three days later, he emerged on the southern side of the mountains. Thinking that the hard part of his journey was over, he trudged merrily southward, his last day's food his only baggage besides the precious book.

As sunset overtook him, he crested a rise and looked down into a quiet, shadowy valley, where felled and stunted trees littered a gray basin in the midst of the plains. To Vincus's city eyes, it seemed like the area had been touched by fire or high wind in a distant time; the dried boles of trees, already crusted with sand and salt and a shimmering opalescence, were a pleasant change from the grasslands' monotony.

Vincus lay down amid the sheared remains of a vallenwood grove. Branches of elm and willow littered his campsite, and he gathered some of them to build a small fire in the twilight.

He would travel by night from now on, he decided. It was easier, he had seen, to steer by the stars and to avoid discovery.

With a smile of contentment, he rested his head against the blackened trunk of a willow. All of a sudden he was weary, and his thoughts strayed over the road behind him and back to the city.

What was it called?

Istar. That was it.

For a moment it seemed to Vincus that something was not right, that he should have remembered the name quickly, more easily. But his mind drifted from this brief, pointless worry, and he began to drowse.

It seemed as though the collar was back around his neck.

Vincus stirred uneasily.

The collar tightened, and tightened again, and the young man sprang into wakefulness.

The dead branches of the willow had closed around his neck, gripping, clutching, and strangling.

A rare carnivorous plant, the black willow masked itself as log or tree and preyed on hapless creatures it lulled to sleep beneath its spreading, branchlike tentacles.

A child of the city, Vincus had never seen such a monster, and when the willow grabbed him, he struggled vainly against its grip and his own growing drowsiness. The plant seemed to sing to him, an eerie and menacing lullaby, and despite his fright, the young man found himself listening.

No. From his robe he drew half of his silver collar, a ragged crescent that glittered in the moonlight. Desperately, his strength and senses failing, Vincus sawed at the largest branch with the sharp metal edge until black sap, sticky and cold like the blood of a reptile, dripped over the tendril and onto his chest.

The willow let out a shrill, hissing scream and, for a brief moment, released him. But a moment was all Vincus needed. He rolled away from the monster, snapping two thinner branches that remained around his shoulder. Springing clear of the grove, he crouched in the dry grass for a moment and gathered his breath, rubbing the long, fresh lashes on his arm where the pliant wood had whipped and cut him.

He had seen everything now, he thought.

The country itself could kill you.

Forewarned and wary, he slipped the silver crescent—an excellent weapon, he had discovered—back into his robe. He would make good on his plans tonight, traveling sleepless by moonlight.

Surely he would be safe as the desert slept.

* * * * *

Many months ago, at Vaananen's insistence, Vincus had scanned a map of the plains. Meticulously, the druid had moved the small meditative stones in the rena garden—red Lunitari representing the mountains, white Solinari the plains beyond. Slowly, precisely, Vaananen had traced the safest route with his finger, and then, standing over Vincus, had urged the young man to mind it all.

Now, Vincus wished he had minded more closely. Was the army southwest of the city, or had Vaananen said *go south-southwest?* Was the camp five miles from the desert's edge or six miles?

He could not remember.

Vincus scrambled to a little rise, a high point in the featureless landscape. Prairie stretched all about him, endlessly and shapelessly, the warm wind rustling and rattling through the dry grass. Even from this vantage he saw nothing but plains.

Unless it was the floating shadow on the farthest southwest horizon—a cloud, perhaps, or a mirage, but at least *something* amid the sea of grass. Vincus shielded his eyes and stared long and hard, but he could see nothing more than the shifting, formless gray.

* * * * *

When the night came, it was cloudy. Solinari and Lunitari darted in and out of the clouds, the only luminaries in a slate-gray sky.

Vincus knew that the tail of the constellation Sargonnas was his guiding star, that it would point him due into the heart of the desert. But glimpsed fitfully in the early hours of the morning, the constellations seemed different, almost alien. Vaananen's neatly plotted drawings of the heavenly maps were gone now, and in their place was a chaos of faint and wavering light.

The morning's red sky restored the east, and Vincus found that he had turned in the night, had wandered due west on the indefinite plains. His hands flickering a mild oath, he sat down on a small cluster of rocks and, chin cupped despondently in his hands, watched the horizon shimmer and recede as another day of uncertainty began.

He felt famished. He breakfasted on the provisions he had brought from Istar, and the grimness of his situation dawned on him.

Soon he would have to forage for his food, for meat and roots and water in this inhospitable country. Armed only with a dagger and a schoolboy's knowledge of edible plants, he faced even greater hunger in the days to come.

That is, unless the Istarians caught him.

Vincus drew his new dagger slowly, scratching idle designs on the dry earth. Istar and slavery almost seemed better now. A sudden anger at Vaananen fluttered briefly through his thoughts—at that druid with his intrigues and fond ideas.

Fordus, indeed! Vaananen had conjured the rebels out of sand and stone. They were no more real than . . .

Than Vincus's freedom.

He looked down at his feet. Absently, numbly, he had sketched Vaananen's five glyphs on the hard, grassy ground.

No. He had come this far.

It was then that the hawk shrieked overhead, and Vincus looked up.

* * * * *

Lucas had been circling for an hour, aloft on the morning thermals. His red feathers glowed in the sunrise, and his angular wings tilted smoothly as he circled.

His mistress had loosed him to forage and scout in the early hours, whispering a song of return in his ear. Over the plateau he had arced, then east over the Tears of Mishakal, gliding swiftly in a low flight before gaining altitude and sailing into the grasslands, where the hunting was good and the Istarian army ranged uneasily.

The solitary man seated in the midst of the grasslands was something new. For a while Lucas watched him curiously.

Not enemy. Not a soldier.

When the man took a small scrap of meat from his pocket, Lucas noticed immediately.

Noticed as well the jagged pieces of silver in his hand as they caught the sunlight.

It was something more than instinct that made the bird circle and call, made him skim the high grass and pass not five yards from the seated man, his hooked wings banking gracefully as he rose again, turning and returning, circling and calling, through all of his actions urging the man to follow.

* * * * *

Once in his motioning, the bird had swooped near enough for Vincus to hear the bells on its jesses.

Vincus stood and followed.

The bird had surprised him with its circling and cries. South and north it sailed, south and north, shrieking as though in signal and warning.

Vincus had laughed at the thought. Too long in the wilderness, he told himself, when a bird becomes your messenger.

And yet the bird would know where to find water and game.

For a morning he followed, the hawk never lost from his sight. Turning and returning, its circles narrowing, the bird seemed attentive, almost protective. Far to the west a column of smoke hovered on the horizon—the gray shadow that Vincus had seen the day before, now obviously no mirage, but the watch-fires surrounding an armed encampment.

Istarians. Had he been slightly wiser, and hadn't needed to follow the hawk, he might have walked right into their camp. Vincus shuddered to think what might have happened.

He quickened his step, searching the sky for the hawk that had become his omen and guide.

* * * * *

Seated on his horse, shielding his eyes against the sunset, the sergeant watched the man trudge out of the foothills and onto the dry, waving margins of the grasslands.

A solitary wanderer. On foot.

The sergeant nodded to his three companions—troopers, skilled swordsmen, and even more skillful riders. Dressed in the light brown cotton robes and red kaffiyeh of the Istarian desert fighters, mounted on roan horses, they blended with the brown landscape until, with the blinding sun around them, they were almost invisible—mirage warriors on the high ridge.

In tight formation, the four cavalrymen descended from the high ground toward the trespasser, their horses breasting the tall brown grass in long surges, overtaking him quickly when the grass gave way to rocky flatland.

The war horses' hooves clattered over the ground, kicking up stones and dust. Nearly engulfed, the traveler turned, raised his hands, began an elaborate series of gestures and signals.

Mage! the sergeant's instincts cried. *Somatic preparations!* Since the strange death of his lieutenant—the one dissolved by the spells of a dark enchanter—a month ago, he was wary of encounters with solitary men in the desert.

With the quick reflexes practiced over a dozen years of horse-soldiering, the sergeant leaned back in the saddle, reined his horse to a skidding halt. One of the troopers, a young man named Parcus, weaved and nearly fell as he fumbled to draw forth his short bow.

"Move your hands no more, sir!" the sergeant shouted. "Upon your life, be still!"

Abruptly, the fellow buried his hands in the folds of his tunic. Two of the troopers dismounted and approached him.

Parcus stared at the trespasser over the shaft of a nocked arrow.

* * * * *

Vincus clenched his fists hard in his tunic as the Istarian troopers drew near, tightening his grip on the silver crescents hidden in his robes.

The plains were no city street. Here were no shadows, no alleys, no dark thresholds. Here in flat bare country and relentless sunlight, there was no place to hide.

He had begun to pray at the sound of hoofbeats, praying ceaselessly until the bowman menaced and the sergeant shouted his warning.

They would find the broken collar. They would . . .

"Who are you?" the sergeant asked coldly, standing up in the saddle.

Vincus did not, could not answer. His great golden eyes never blinked.

"Bring him to me, Crotalus," the sergeant ordered.

The trooper dismounted and seized Vincus roughly by the shoulders.

Aloft in a swirl of wind, his sharp eye scanning the edge of the desert, Lucas saw the riders surround the man. Saw them dismount, approach him, and drag him toward the horses.

Something in the bird—an old instruction from his mistress, perhaps, or something embedded and patterned since his time in the egg—stirred him to action.

Folding his wings, the hawk plunged from the sky a hundred, two hundred, five hundred feet. The bird dove gracefully, its talons extended like deadly, curved knives, the falconer's jesses and bells trailing.

In a shimmer of ringing music, Lucas struck the sergeant in the back of the neck just as the man leaned over to question Vincus. The sergeant fell headlong, neck broken in a heap of spattered robes, his horse bolting away with a terrified whinny.

The bird jerked to free himself from the kill, the awkward jesses tangling and knotting in the fabric of the sergeant's robes.

He flies bound. Enslaved, too! Vincus thought. Somehow the thought inspired him.

With a fierce, powerful surge, he shook loose the astonished troopers. Crotalus spun about, his sword ringing as it fell to the hard ground. The other man, quicker and more resourceful, had already lifted his spear.

Rolling away from the flashing pont, Vincus drew forth the slivers of his collar, the edges forming deadly hooks on each side of each hand. They glittered in the dying sun like scimitars, like the talons of the hawk. Before the spearman could recover, the broken collar's sharp edges whipped cleanly and fatally into his throat. Vincus pushed him aside in a fierce, pantherlike rush toward Crotalus, who had managed to find and draw his crossbow from its place on the saddle of his skittish horse, just as Lucas hopped free of his tangles.

A piercing cry and the flap of wings about his head forced Crotalus's point-blank aim high, and the bolt whizzed over Vincus's shoulder, skidding long and hollowly over the cracked earth behind him. With a lunging leap, Vincus wrestled Crotalus to the ground, and the two men scuffled briefly, until the other collar half flashed high in the sunlight and plunged downward.

Moving away from Crotalus, who had breathed his last foul breath, Vincus covered his head, still expecting a rain of arrows from the last trooper's direction. But he heard the soldier cry out weakly, and looked up to see him already borne far away atop his rampaging horse, the two remaining steeds following close behind.

In high pursuit of them, Lucas swooped and glided and dodged, all the while crying shrilly until they were dwindling specks on the horizon.

Vincus stood up painfully, more bruised than he first had realized by the struggle with the outriders.

The hawk, unruffled and fresh, sailed back to him through the climbing dusk. With a cry it circled overhead, then soared toward the southwest, its flight now framed by Lunitari low in the sky.

His heart rejoicing for the bird—for its mastery and bravery—Vincus threw his hands up and followed eagerly. They had fought together. The hawk would not betray him.

When darkness had fallen and the stars spangled the clear sky, a comforting light seemed to rise from the looming shadows.

Vincus laughed and quickened his pace. He called to mind again the druid's patterns in the sand of the rena garden, the arranged stones, and the instructions.

At last Vincus knew where he was.

The camp of the rebels lay ahead in a soft, wavering firelight.

Chapter 19

Silently, moving through the tall grass like he moved through Istarian alleys, Vincus made his way to the edge of the rebel encampment.

He was not sure, actually, why he chose such secrecy. After all, he had come this far, through dangerous country and Istarian patrols, and finally, with the aid of the mysterious hawk, had reached his destination. But all of his instincts—born, perhaps, of his years in slavery and his childhood on the fringes of Bywall—urged him to be cautious, not to drop his guard just yet.

So he approached the camp stealthily, crouched

low to make his movements small and quick through the grass.

The camp was laid out in three concentric circles. The outermost contained the outposts and fires of the sentries, the first warning line against assault or raid.

The men here were young: sharp-eyed, but also inexperienced. If an army had approached, they would have surely given warning, but Vincus was a solitary traveler, and a slippery, streetwise one at that.

Folding his tattered cloak and the bag Vaananen had given him close to his side, Vincus moved easily between two sentries—sallow-faced bandit boys from Thoradin, part of Gormion's following. He crept around the shadowy side of the first tent he came to, then waited until a cloud passed over the red moon, and raced through an open dry expanse until he reached another tent, another shadow, the second circle of the camp.

Instantly, Vincus knew he was among more seasoned and watchful troops. These were men and women who had fought the year's war in the service of Fordus Firesoul, and had probably come to the Water Prophet battle-scarred and ready.

As Vincus crouched in the tent shadow, he suddenly heard a low growling behind him. Slowly he turned to face a snarling midsized dog, its teeth bared and its fur bristling with aggression.

Vincus extended his hand. With the last scrap of his Istarian traveling rations, he bribed the dog to silence. He sat in the darkness, rubbing the willow-wounds that scored his shoulders, feeding bread to his newfound friend, mulling over a dozen ways—all unsatisfactory—to try to reach the center of the camp.

Something rattled against the book in the bottom of the bag. Reaching into the dark folds, gently brushing away the curious, snuffling dog, Vincus drew forth something hard and oblong, smelling green and citric, like the soft, thick husk of a freshly fallen walnut.

A zizyphus fruit. It could be nothing else.

Vincus wrinkled his nose. The zizyphus was inedible, good only for a soporific—to induce the sleep that banished pain. Clerics and druids made infusions from the fruit that their patients would inhale, and, within a matter of minutes . . .

Vincus smiled, tight-lipped.

Tossing the very last crust of bread into the shadows, he waited until the dog vanished after it, then crept around the side of the tent.

He approached another tight circle of tents and fires, perhaps a hundred yards away, that marked the command post of the rebel army. Vincus fell to his belly at the sight of two sentries standing watch by a fire in the open ground.

* * * * *

Raindiver and Bittern, the Plainsman sentries, stood faithfully at their posts, exchanging few words and staring out into the darkness. The banked fire between them was dim but warm, and while they watched, their thoughts slipped in and out of vigilance like the moon slipped in and out of the scattered clouds above the plains.

It was a night like any other, until something whistled by Raindiver's ear and skittered into the ashes, scattering sparks and filling the air with a thick, acrid smoke.

Bittern bent toward the fire and saw the small,

oblong seed aflame in its very heart. Suddenly, the seed and the fire began to waver and double and blur, and he looked up to call to Raindiver, to warn him that something . . . something . . .

But Raindiver was already facedown in the grass, snoring contentedly.

Bittern dropped to his knees and tried to call out to the other sentries, to Fordus or Northstar, but another cloud seemed to pass over the moon and the sky and the fire went dark, and he felt himself falling.

Someone brushed by him, running. Bittern tried to shout again—a cry of alarm, of warning. But a pleasant dreamless sleep rushed over him, and he remembered nothing more.

* * * * *

The man had the look of a Prophet.

Vincus, belly-down in the dark grass like some enormous lizard, watched the auburn-haired Plainsman from a distance.

It was Fordus, he was certain. The slight blond woman who stood beside him in the firelight spoke in sign language—a strangely inflected version, but easy enough to interpret.

And there was the hawk, perched on a ring near her!

She had called the man "Commander." Called him "Prophet."

Vincus rose to his knees, peering through the last stretch of darkness toward the firelight. Not yet, he told himself. I will wait here for a while. For there is something more I am supposed to know.

"Bring me water!" Fordus commanded, his voice deep and melodious and a little too loud. "Bring meat, and a cup of wine as well."

A young man leapt at his command and rushed off into the darkness.

"Where is that boy? Where is the wine?" Fordus asked, much too soon. His followers stood about him uncomfortably, averting their eyes as he stared at each of them.

Finally, Fordus turned in Vincus's direction.

Though Vincus was well out of sight, hidden by tall grass and shadow, the firelight showed him the full face of the Prophet—the handsome, windburnt features and the auburn beard.

Unusual for a Plainsman. As were the eyes.

Vincus had seen that color before. Sky-blue? Sea-blue? Had seen it in Istar . . .

At the School of the Games? No. It must have been at the Kingpriest's Tower.

Barely had the name crossed through his thoughts than Vincus remembered. The hushed room of the great Council Hall, the man almost swallowed by a globe of brilliant white light, reflected off the polished marble and the luminous pellidryn stones that spangled the Imperial Throne.

The Kingpriest. The Kingpriest had eyes like that.

And the other features. The thin aristocratic nose, the high cheekbones, and even the auburn hair. The resemblance was uncanny. Fordus might have been the Kingpriest's brother. Or . . .

Vincus's thoughts recoiled from the prospect. The priesthood of Istar was austere and proper. Suppose the Kingpriest . . .

It was a thought he could not even finish.

For a moment he lay silent in the darkness, his thoughts far away—on Vaananen, on those in service to the Tower and the city. He had come a long way with a single message of great importance.

But now, having seen what he had seen, would he deliver that message?

He would think on this a while, find a sheltered place in a greater darkness. He would have the night, at least, perhaps until sunrise. Then he would decide whether to approach the Water Prophet, or go.

He started to back away from the firelight, intent on losing himself somewhere outside the encircled tents. But suddenly, rough hands seized him by the shoulders and jerked him to his feet. Vincus spun around, but his attacker caught his arm and, with a flawless wrestler's maneuver, twisted it behind his back.

Hot pain shot through Vincus's shoulder, and he looked into the face of his assailant.

A Lucanesti elf, his arms encrusted with the first bejewellings of middle age, regarded Vincus calmly.

"I am not sure whether your intentions are good or ill," the elf whispered. "But perhaps by other fires and among other people, we can find out just who you are, and why you spy on Fordus Firesoul."

*　*　*　*　*

The elf's name was Stormlight. He was a lieutenant of the War Prophet, but had fallen from favor in some recent dispute of policy.

After he seized Vincus near Fordus's fire and tents, Stormlight had taken his captive to the other side of the encampment entirely—to quiet quarters, where a half dozen veteran Plainsmen waited in silence.

Stormlight had questioned Vincus, and when he failed to understand the sign language, had reluctantly sent for the woman, the one with the yellow hair, whose name was Larken. With her odd, alien gestures, she translated Vincus's signs in her own silence.

"What proof have you that you were a slave in Istar?" Stormlight asked finally, regarding Vincus with a stare that was melancholy but not unkind.

Vincus showed him the collar, how the pieces fit together, how they spelled his name. Stormlight nodded, placed the pieces around Vincus's neck, and was satisfied they fit. He started to ask another question, then fell silent.

"How did you find us?" he asked finally, and Vincus told of his journey, of the pass through the mountains and his guidance by the benevolent hawk.

It was a god, he signed. *I am sure it was a god taking the bird's form to guide me. He camps with you? I saw him perched by your fire.*

Larken smiled as she translated his gestures for Stormlight.

The elf's expression softened.

"And *why* have you found us?" he asked. "What do you ask of us? Or what do you bring us?"

Vincus gestured excitedly, knelt on the ground. Stormlight dropped beside him, and the Plainsmen, Larken, and Gormion stood above them, watching curiously and intently.

Though he had mistrusted Fordus from the start, Vincus felt surprisingly safe in the company of the elf. He knew that Vaananen's glyphs were meant for this man, for Stormlight was one who asked instead of commanded.

To Vincus, that was a sign of wisdom and discernment. He had heard enough of command in his servitude.

Confidently, he drew the five glyphs on the

ground before Stormlight. After he was finished, he looked up.

Stormlight stared at the glyphs intently.

"Desert's Edge," he said. "Sixth Day of Lunitari. No Wind."

It seemed to be nothing new to him until he reached the fourth glyph.

"The Leopard? And . . . there is a *fifth* one that follows. Something dreadfully important here."

I shall bring Fordus, Larken signed, but Stormlight waved the thought away.

"Not this time."

Larken frowned, a question forming in her thoughts.

Stormlight stared at Vincus, and a long moment passed in which the camp lay silent.

"Is the Sixth Legion in Istar, Vincus?" Stormlight asked.

Elatedly, Vincus nodded, gesturing excitedly as Larken struggled to translate his account of his own discoveries, of conveying the news to Vaananen, of the whole series of events that boded danger for Fordus and the rebels.

Stormlight leaned back, his face lost for a moment in the shadow. Then, craning toward the fifth glyph, he read it and proclaimed: "Beware the dark man."

He looked up at Vincus, then at Larken. A crooked, bemused smile played at the corner of his mouth.

"Hear the word of the Prophet," he whispered, with a laugh.

"Beware the lady," he said flatly. For a while he knelt before the fifth glyph, tracing its outline with a callused finger.

"I see," he murmured. "I should have known by the amber eyes. Tamex . . . Tanila . . . They looked alike. *Reptilian*.

"And then . . . the dragon tracks through the Tears of Mishakal!"

* * * * *

"One will ask for it soon," Vaananen had said. "And you will know it is right to give the book to that person."

So Vincus gave the book to Stormlight, trusting the same instinct that had guided him through the desert and steered him from Fordus at the last moment.

After all, the book was written in Lucanesti. What other sign could a man expect?

Together, the elf and the bard puzzled over the ancient text, Larken frowning at the complexities of the scattered, angular script, but Stormlight nodding, reading . . .

Until he came to the lost passages. Gray dust eddied in the hands of the elf as he knelt at the campsite, spreading the opened book before him.

Stormlight bowed over the page and inspected it for a long time. "Perhaps," he murmured, "it is in my language, and it is prophecy as well."

"The Anlage . . ." he murmured. "The oldest seeing."

* * * * *

Long before the first migrations of the Lucanesti across the Istarian desert, before the first discoveries of glain opal, and perhaps even before the time when the elders of that dwindling people had discovered the powers of the *lucerna*, another deeper way of seeing had been encoded in their thoughts and memory.

The Anlage. The great mine of elventhought. The shared memory of the race.

In its depths lay the earliest recollections of the mining elves: their wanderings, their departure from Silvanesti. Some even said that, in the hands of a wise and anointed elf, the Anlage could reveal the earliest days—in the Age of Dreams, when the First-born of the world opened their eyes to moonlight upon a newly awakened planet.

It was all there. All memory and all imagining.

So the elders had told Stormlight in his childhood and youth, in the long years of wandering before the ambush, his wounding, and his adoption by the Plainsmen. The elders had told him how to draw upon that power as well, and of the danger therein— the risk that the visionary might not return to the waking world, but sleep and sleep until the opalescence of age covered and swallowed him entirely.

Yet without fear or misgiving, Stormlight sank into these meditations, tunneling deeper and deeper until he reached a level where he knew the thoughts and recollections were no longer his own, and he sank into a cloudy vein of mutual remembrance.

Around him, his Plainsmen companions, Larken, and Vincus watched helplessly, expectantly, as though they stood on the shores of a great ocean, waiting for a distant sail.

But Stormlight was calm, preternaturally alert. No fear, he told himself. No fear is very good.

Mindfully, he explored the shadowy dream, a shifting landscape bedazzled with the light of both . . . no, of *three* moons. The five elements enfolded him: the fire of the stars, the water in the heart of the earth, the desert and stone, the parched and wandering air.

And memory. The fifth of the ancient elements.

Dancing, as the elders said it did, as a gray absorbent light on the margins of vision. Stormlight directed his thought toward that grayness, and it parted before him.

For a moment there were grasslands, the pale face of someone he neither remembered nor knew . . .

Then forest.

The book, he told himself. Keep your mind on the book.

Briefly, a great darkness yawned to his left, full of flashing color and a strange, seductive beckoning. For a while he stood at the borders of that darkness, which seemed to call to him, promising sleep, an easeful rest.

But that way was dangerous. He would be lost if he entered it.

The book, he told himself. Nothing but the book.

And then it appeared before him, its pages crisp and sharp and entirely intact. Eagerly, he opened the pages with his mind.

He read and remembered.

Finally, Stormlight looked up, and Vincus saw the transformation.

For a moment the elf looked blind, his pale eyes milky and unfocused. Vincus started, believing the book had struck Stormlight sightless, but then the eyes of the elf changed again, a white shell or a pale film dropping out of his gaze and receding beneath his eyelids.

"Come with me, Larken," Stormlight urged. He shot to his feet as though at a call for battle. Grabbing the bard by the arm, he ushered her into the night, whispering a warning or strategy that reached Vincus only in snatches, in fragments.

"Against us" he heard.

"Incarnate. Opals."

"Takhisis."

And "opals" again, the last word swallowed by the rising night.

*   *   *   *   *

So the stones that protect us will enable her to enter the world? Larken asked.

Stormlight nodded. "And if we deny her the stones, if we destroy them or hide them, we relinquish our protection."

Together they stood in the twilight not a hundred yards from the fire. Overhead, scarlet Lunitari reeled through the night sky, and the landscape, rock and rubble and distant tent, seemed bathed suddenly in dark blood.

What shall we do, Stormlight?

Her hands did not shake, Stormlight noticed. She was awaiting *his* command, and was not afraid.

His face softened, and for a long time the elf stood silent. "I am not sure, Larken. Nor were the elves who wrote the manuscript. But the text is clear on one thing. Whatever it takes to stop a goddess will demand our utmost. Something perilous and altogether new.

"Despite our quarrel, Fordus must know of it. I shall warn him this night." Without further word, the elf stalked off into the darkness, his destination the level plain to the east, the largest circle of campfires.

Larken watched as Stormlight receded into the night.

"Something perilous," he had said. "And altogether new."

She was ready. She had changed. She felt it now, with a slow certainty. Danger and novelty no longer frightened her. Out of a strange solitude, she awaited the approaching change calmly and with a new eagerness.

* * * * *

Stormlight came back at dawn, a great heaviness in his cold eyes.

He had talked to Fordus, the rumors said. He had told the Prophet the news of the discovered text.

But Fordus had stared beyond him, into the nothingness of desert and night. Had called Stormlight a dead man, said that his words no longer had life.

Fordus had rejected him, and it was Stormlight now who stood at the edge of the sea, a powerless observer.

By midmorning of the next day, Fordus's group had resumed the march, and by late afternoon, they had reached the foothills of the Istarian Mountains. Stormlight's troops still followed at a distance.

Vincus leaned gratefully against an outcropping of rock, making certain that the ground around him was free of willow branches. It was the best of times to camp, he thought, before darkness fell in the midst of rough and treacherous terrain.

A courier came back from the ranks to Fordus's rear guard, to where Vincus waited with Stormlight and two older Plainsmen, Breeze and Messenger.

It was a man Vincus had never met—a young man named Northstar—who brought the word.

"The Prophet Fordus," Northstar said, speaking the name in quiet and reverent tones, "had a dream in which a dead man visited him with a warning."

Stormlight turned away at these words.

"The dead man told him," Northstar continued, "that Takhisis herself—She of the Many Faces—has arrayed her dark powers against the rebellion, against the Prophet Fordus."

"And what else did the . . . *dead man* say, Northstar?" Stormlight asked bitterly, his back to the messenger.

"All the rest was lies, says the Prophet Fordus. For Takhisis sends her minions to deceive, to waylay and destroy. Her army is the living and the dead, and none are to be believed. So says the Prophet Fordus.

"But the goddess is afraid now. Her warnings and threats are the words of a beast in flight. For if she thought she could defeat the Prophet Fordus . . .

"She would not let him know of her presence. She would wait, and hide, waylaying him when he least expected, when he stood at the edge of his greatest victory, rather than now, before the war has even begun."

Stormlight shook his head.

Vincus tried to follow the reasoning of the Water Prophet. Perhaps Northstar had not remembered it right, for it seemed cloudy and formless, a poor and shoddy logic.

Yet Northstar was ardent, rapt, fresh from the presence of his hero, his lord.

"We shall continue the assault on Istar," the messenger proclaimed. "Her threats are the banner of the Kingpriest's fear. So says the Prophet Fordus.

"We shall march through the night, for speed and surprise are our allies, and the mountains will be ours by morning. Through the Central Pass we will go, and let those who dispute the word of the Prophet Fordus stay in their camps and cower.

"We are bound for Istar, and to us will the city belong!"

Having spoken, Northstar wheeled about and

raced back up the column, his long strides eager and jubilant. Stormlight turned, an overwhelming sadness on his face, and stared at Vincus.

" 'Tis the wrong pass, is it not?"

Vincus nodded, started to gesture, to explain that it was the *Western* Pass that was free of the *sterim*, free of rockslide and shearing and the terrible destructive wind.

But Stormlight rested his hands on Vincus's shoulders and regarded him openly, honestly.

" 'Tis what I told him last night, when I spoke to him and warned him. Told him that I had a man in my camp who could guide him safely through the mountains if he chose to continue, but that it would be far wiser to return, to go back to the desert. And it was no dream. But he is no longer listening to me. He pulls phrases from the air, words out of their places, and distorts them into what he wants to hear—into what he says those damnable dreams and visions are telling him."

Stormlight turned away. Far ahead, Fordus's banners flew aloft in the dying air, red in the sunset light. Already his columns were starting to move again, and somewhere far up in Fordus's ranks, a solitary drum began a slow, stumbling cadence.

The new drummer was no match for Larken.

"He is completely, utterly mad," Stormlight said. "And I have no choice but to go behind him and to fight his enemies. For the time is coming when he will take my people into more than the weather, more than the death of a few in a narrow, storm-swept pass.

"The walls of Istar are coming. And the Sixth Legion. And Takhisis herself. And before Fordus rides out to meet them, someone will have to stop him."

Chapter 20

The Central Pass through the Istarian mountains was wide and moonlit, littered with fallen branches, with stones, with smaller, uprooted alder and fir.

Despite Solinari and the clear sky, the rubble in the pass was an ominous prospect to Stormlight.

Vincus had warned Stormlight, who, in turn, had tried to warn the War Prophet. Follow the Western Pass, they had urged. But Fordus had not listened, had stared through Stormlight as if he were water, all the while toying with the enormous golden circle that enclosed his neck. It bristled with spikes that seemed to grow daily with his madness.

Now Fordus marched through the Central Pass at the head of his exhausted troops. Seven hundred had followed him before the Battle of the Plains, and scarcely five hundred survived it. Seventy had fallen to the Istarian ambush, and a dozen to the desert eruptions.

What do you want, old friend, dear madman? Stormlight thought bitterly as Fordus's banner danced out of view. *Your forces have been wrecked, and yet you march. You cannot arm a legion with promises.*

* * * * *

By sunrise they were midway through the Central Pass, climbing through boulders and downed pine and aeterna. Fordus's new drummer had struck up a song for courage and endurance.

But the going grew slower and slower as dawn crept into midmorning, and by noon, their hands blistered and their limbs bruised and scratched, the trailblazers stopped to rest, and noticed to their astonishment that they had traveled only a hundred yards in the last two hours.

There was no magic, as there had been in Larken's songs, to help.

Aeleth, his leather armor soggy with sweat, wiped his brow and scrambled to the top of a stone out-cropping, glaring over the rubblestrewn wasteland.

"What do you see, Aeleth?" Fordus called up to him.

Aeleth thought before he answered. Suffering from shortness of breath, muttering at the thin mountainous air and the countless obstructions in the path, the War Prophet had become an impossible commander, short with his lieutenants and merciless in his quest to reach the other side of the pass by the evening.

Two men had fallen over dead from exertion, and despite the urgings of the Namers, Fordus had left the bodies where they lay.

"It's . . . it's downhill from here, sir!" Aeleth called down.

Heartened, Fordus turned to face his followers.

"Another vision has come to me!" he proclaimed, his bony hands clutching his golden collar, fingering the dark glain opals. "If we march through the night, we cover ourselves with the mantle of surprise. When we reach the shore of Lake Istar, there will be nothing the Kingpriest can do to stop our advances!"

* * * * *

The storm charged upon them suddenly, rolling out of the south in a rumbling chaos like a herd of horses.

For a moment the air was still, and the hardy mountain birds—raptor and thrush, the loud purple jays of northern Ansalon—fell quiet in anticipation of the rising wind.

Then it surged through the pass behind them like a flash flood through a dry arroyo, the wind picking up velocity and force as it barreled over the felled trees, over the rocks and boulders, scattering sand and gravel and branches as it shrieked through the pass.

Stormlight turned around in astonishment as the wind roared past and over him, knocking him to the ground and thundering through the back of his followers.

Children were swept up and dashed against the rockface. Terrified, their mothers screamed for them, their words lost and useless. Stormlight covered his ears in the fierce, deafening wail, and a wave of sand broke over them, stinging and abrading.

Up ahead, a felled vallenwood launched into the air and crashed into Gormion and a handful of her followers. The bandit captain shrieked and rolled from the path of the hurtling limbs, scattering earrings and bracelets as the wind took her up, buoyed her, and hurled her, alive, into a stand of aeterna.

The rest of the bandits fared even less well. The vallenwood branches exploded with screams as the heavy tree crushed the hapless men against the rocks.

Clinging to Stormlight and Breeze, Vincus rode out the storm with his head in his hood. The pass vanished in a whirl of sand, and from the murky cyclone ahead he could hear wail and outcry. Occasionally a dark, unrecognizable shape rocketed past, and from somewhere back up the pass came the skidding, too-human sound of frightened horses.

Then, as suddenly as it had rushed over them, the storm was gone. The sand settled lazily over the mountain rocks—the desert transported by the fierce and merciless weather—and slowly, almost imperceptibly, a few moving shapes emerged from rock and sand and thicket.

When they all had gathered, they were sixty less.

A new wailing began, the ancient funerary call of the Que-Nara rising like another wind, echoing from the mountainsides. Plaintively, eerily, the cry spread through the Central Pass, until even the returning birds began to sing in response—thrush and jay in full cry from the ravaged, wind-blasted trees.

But Fordus scrambled up the rockface, clinging like a grotesque spider, and waved his hand for silence.

It was a long time coming. The rebels were grieving, swept away by the dark river of their own sorrow.

"It is the vengeance of Takhisis," Fordus rasped, his breath shallow and panting. But nobody was listening.

"Hear the word of the Prophet!" he cried. A hundred pairs of eyes looked up at him, new fear flickering alongside their old devotion. The rest of the survivors milled aimlessly, combing the rubble for the injured and the dead.

"There are a thousand roads to Istar," Fordus proclaimed, his voice gaining power and authority as the words rushed from him. "Each of those roads is guarded, with torment and danger and hardship.

"But we have passed through the first of these hardships, my people. And though there are some we must leave behind . . ."

His gesture toward the gathered bodies of the dead was quick and casual, as though he brushed away a fly.

"Let them be remembered, and let their names be sung, at the time when we will remember all the fallen, commemorate all those who spilled their blood in my glorious cause."

Still clinging to the rockface, Fordus pointed north, the collar at his neck afire in the reflected light of the sunset.

"Their names will be sung around the throne of Istar, when I ascend to the lordship of the great Imperial City. We will sing them in glory when I am Kingpriest, set to the music of drum and passing bell. For the glyphs and the signs and my own dreams have told me that the rule of Istar is mine.

"You have followed my dream through four hard seasons. We have sown seed in the bitter ground of the desert, in obscurity and distance and sand, where all ambition was water. We have watered the plains with our blood, and tilled in the storm-furrowed mountain passes. Now Istar stands open to bandit and Plainsmen. My worthy rival—the kindred warrior and prophet in the Kingpriest's Tower—has met his adversary in the southern fields! The season has come! Set your hand to the harvest!"

For a moment the rebels fell into complete, astonished silence. All eyes were riveted on the Water Prophet, all ears turned to his feverish, wild pronouncements.

"Hear the word of the Prophet!" Northstar shouted.

A pathetic *tap-tap*, late and halfhearted, accompanied his cry.

"The word of the Prophet King!" the young man continued, unfazed and triumphant, and to the surprise of the elders and the Namers, a voice deep in the milling rebels took up the call—a dark voice, neither masculine nor feminine, but a voice that seemed to rise up within the hearts of all assembled. Another cried in response, and another, and soon the young men, chanting "The Prophet King! The Prophet King!" lifted Fordus atop their shoulders and bore him through the wreckage, through the wide path that the wind had cut over rock and rubble and undergrowth.

At the mouth of the pass, Larken, Vincus, and a score of Que-Nara remained, as Fordus's companions hastened toward the lakeside road and the plains and city beyond. Her dark eyes distant and mournful, Larken watched as the Prophet's banner was hoisted into the air, and the walls of the mountain pass resounded with this new and alien cheer.

"The Prophet King!"

As the cry carried down the column, Fordus's rebels picked up their pace. The weary trudge became a brisk, revitalized march, as a strange, perfumed wind rolled through the pass, bearing upon it the smell of jasmine and juniper, of attar of roses and spice and old wine.

Istar the temptress was calling them. Soft and feminine, conniving and poisonous, at sunset she cast her nets of beguilement.

*   *   *   *   *

As Fordus and his followers ranged through the treacherous passes, the seeds of another insurrection were being sown in the depths of the mines.

Deep below the city, their dead mourned and placed reverently in porous pockets of volcanic rock, the elves resumed their digging.

Exhausted, the sounds of little Taglio's cries still echoing in his thoughts, Spinel guided his work-numbed crew into the dark recesses beneath the shores of Lake Istar.

These were the newest mines. No sooner had the mourning ceased than word came down from the Kingpriest's tower to open them. Obviously, some event above had changed the nature of the labor, brought a new urgency to this mysterious need for the glain opals.

By lamplight, Spinel examined the most recently discovered stones. Judging from the veins of opal the diggers had found, the glain themselves were young—younger by far than any he had mined in his thousand years of subterranean labor.

The stones looked oddly familiar—as though in a shape—a formation—the old elf should recognize.

He knelt, examined more closely.

There was something deep and important he was forgetting.

It was time for the Anlage.

The *lucerna* closed over the old elf's eyes as he entered the deep recollection of his people. Abstractly, he fingered the gems.

He remembered the years of mining beneath the city. The bright eyes of the Kingpriest's guards, the serpentine, human-faced nagas, with their enchantments that dried and paralyzed the Lucanesti, the wanderings in the Age of Might.

Remembered the Age of Light, of Dreams, his thoughts tunneling back into Starbirth, into the God-time . . .

Then he looked at the stones in his hands, and cried out in horror.

* * * * *

"Bones," Spinel told the assembled miners. "The glain opals, the special black ones the Kingpriest covets, are the bones of our deepest ancestors."

Tourmalin frowned in disbelief, but her gaze faltered under the withering stare of the ancient elf.

"No, neither your fathers nor your grandfathers, nor the bones of any in five generations of Lucanesti. But the eldest of the race—those who entered the company of Branchala in the years before the ward and the wanderings. How could we have been so blinded?"

He extended his pale, encrusted hands.

"Istar has blinded us!" someone shouted from the borders of the torchlight, but Spinel shook his head.

"Istar has used our blindness," he insisted. "Used our greed and our cowardice for its own dark strategies. All the while, the Anlage was there for us, bearing this terrible secret. Why did we never consult it?"

His words tumbled into a long silence. Spinel leaned against the rock and gazed out over the torches and lamps, over the glittering eyes of his people.

"Blame and punishment are not the answer," he insisted, and others—the oldest of the company—nodded in eager assent. "For years we have complied, have knelt in submission to the Kingpriest and his minions. Now we must redress our wrongdoing. Regardless of the guards and *venatica*, one road remains for our people. We must reclaim and rebury our ancient dead."

* * * * *

The rebels reached the shores of the lake at midnight.

Barely three hundred of Fordus's followers remained. In early evening, Larken and Stormlight, who had been following at an unfriendly distance, had taken a sloping path into the sunset, headed for the Western Pass and a safe route back to the desert.

Fordus did not acknowledge them. With Northstar and three of the younger bandits, he approached the lapping waters of Lake Istar, dark and spangled with the reflections of a thousand stars. He knelt, recovered his breath, and stirred the waters with his hand.

The surface of the lake glittered with starlight and torchlight, for the bandits had brought fire with them, the better to burn the city.

"With neither glyph nor interpreter, he finds the greatest of all waters," Fordus pronounced, an eerie laughter underscoring his voice. Resolutely, he stepped into the water, took another step, and waded waist-deep into the lake. Pensively he traced his finger across the glittering surface.

"I had thought to run to Istar," he murmured cryptically. "Perhaps my steps would skip over the water, or the lake itself would buoy me . . ."

"But we must travel like mortals," he conceded with a smile. "For all of *you* are my charges, my minions, my . . . celebrants. And though to cross the water would be more swift, I would have to do it alone—to leave you here to plod in your brave little paths."

He stepped forward, sank to his chest.

"I choose not to travel alone," he declared. "At least not yet."

* * * * *

The drama that played out in the mountains was small, insignificant compared to the large struggles among the pantheon of Krynn.

Deep in the Abyss, the dark gods felt the absence of the Lady. In the dark unfathomable void they waited—Zeboim and Morgion, Hiddukel and Chemosh, the dark moon Nuitari hovering over them all. It was strangely restful, this respite from her chaos and torment. Oh, there would be time to gather and turn on one another—to intrigue and rend and divide and wrestle for power. But for now they were content to recline and bask on the dark currents, to recover and regroup their failing energies.

All except one: the most devious of all the evil pantheon. Sargonnas circled the void in a thousand pieces, his fragmented thoughts on the War Prophet whose campaigns he had inspired and nurtured. He had been foolish, trying to break into the world through the sands of the desert, but the knowledge that Takhisis walked the earth and spoke to *his* minions, *his* Prophet, was too galling, too frightening for silence and inaction.

Now, fragmented and abstract, he spread through the void like a cloud of locusts, like a monstrous contagion.

There would be a time. He would watch and wait. In her desire to destroy Fordus, Takhisis's attentions would shift elsewhere, and there would be a time for him to strike.

He would precede her into the world. His clerics would build their fortresses of stone and lies. And even if they failed, he would spoil the plans of the Dark Queen.

His mind on vengeance, Sargonnas dropped a thousand miles through the chaos, glittering darkly as he fell like a fiery rain.

* * * * *

Alone in the rena garden, Vaananen stirred the sand over yet another futile message of glyphs.

The druid had done all he could. And the hope that stirred within Vaananen was now the hope of flight. Solitary and recklessly brave, the druid had remained in the city, gathering information and sending it nightly through the white, decorative sands to a distant point in a distant country—information that could save rebel lives, perhaps ensure rebel victory.

Absently Vaananen rubbed his tattooed arm. His efforts had gone unheeded. And now Fordus stood at the outskirts of Istar, and it was time for the druid to save himself.

He'd tied his belongings in a hide bag not much larger than the one he had given Vincus. Three druidic texts, as yet uncopied, took up most of the space. For the last time, in the hopes that somehow Fordus would receive the message, Vaananen scrawled the five glyphs in the sand of the garden, beside the yellowed, rapidly swelling cactus.

Desert's Edge. Sixth Day of Lunitari. No Wind.

The Leopard and the fifth and warning symbol— the sign of the Lady beneath the sign of the Dark Man.

It was all he could do.

The turgid cactus beside him trembled. The plant, usually deep green and healthy, had suffered like this for days. Three nights before, searching for rain, the druid had passed his hand just above its spiny surface and sensed a tremor, a boiling from the center of the cactus, as though it heralded a new and unnatural life.

He had ignored it at first, and now he chided himself for his negligence, searching his memory for a healing chant, for something to soothe and settle the plant.

He began slowly, whispering an old warding from Qualinesti. But a humming sound from the heart of the cactus, unlike any song or language of plants the druid had ever heard, drowned out the chant before he had really begun. Alarmed, Vaananen stepped back from the plant, which swelled more and more rapidly, like a grotesquely inflated waterskin, its shiny yellow surface mottling and browning.

Vaananen realized that the cactus was no longer just a plant, but had been transformed into something monstrous and menacing. *Run!* the druid's instincts told him.

He turned to the lectern to gather the last of his

belongings—his copying pens and inks—as the cactus sizzled and whined, the sound reaching above audibility. Mesmerized, the druid stayed one second too long—and with a shattering boom, the cactus burst open. The room filled with a hot, swarming rain of something fierce and stinging and relentlessly hungry and alive. Vaananen felt searing heat course up his legs and run down his back, and he futilely lifted his arms to shield his face.

Tiny black scorpions covered his shoulders, his neck, the hidden red oak leaf on his wrist.

The druid cried out once, briefly, but the poison that raced through his blood felled him like a crosscut oak. He sank to his knees in the midst of the white sand, with a last painful brush of his hand erasing the final glyphs he had written for Fordus, the message the War Prophet would never read.

I am again surprised, thought Vaananen, sinking into green darkness. How remarkable.

Swarming over the room, their dark mission accomplished, the scorpions turned upon one another until all of them, stung by their own poison, lay as dead as the druid.

The next day, the stunned acolytes found that the sand from the rena garden covered the floor, the bed, the lectern, the dead scorpions, and Vaananen, too, in a thin white layer like a fresh new snowfall. It was pristine, almost beautiful, except for a wide stain of sand hardened into dark volcanic glass, in the center of the garden between three standing stones.

Chapter 21

The gold and gray plains at the edge of Istar stretched out sandy and rock-littered—little more hospitable than the desert in which Fordus had wandered and prophesied and fought for most of his life. There was said to be forest somewhere farther north—a land of thick and luxurious green, dripping with soft autumn rain or the hard, thunderous downpours of an Ansalon spring.

Standing in the midst of his ragged army, for a moment Fordus let himself imagine that northern country. He had never seen a landscape of lush and resplendent green, never walked beside brooks or looked up into a vault of leaf and evergreen. His country was brown and red and ochre, its landmarks visible for miles over the level terrain.

Landmarks like the towering city of Istar, carved of marble in the Age of Dreams, the heart of an empire.

Soon to be his. City and empire alike.

What did it matter that so few warriors stood behind him now? What did it matter that his numbers were not the thousands, the hundreds of thousands, he had dreamed long ago in the Tears of Mishakal and again, a few nights ago, high up on the Red Plateau?

It was not loss, not attrition. It was a weeding out, a culling. Only the finest fighters remained, their worthiness proved by their survival.

For Northstar was still with him, and Rann and Aeleth. Somehow Gormion had wrestled down her natural cowardice, and she was beside him as well, as were threescore of the younger men and women, their sunken eyes alight with adulation, their thoughts upon the liberation of the Plainsmen enslaved in Istar.

Stormlight is dead, Fordus hallucinated. He is a forerunner, a harbinger, the vanguard of an invisible legion.

For the dead would arise and follow Fordus Firesoul. So he had read in the fissures on this cracked and graven plain.

Oh, he had not told the others yet. Not even Northstar knew. At night Fordus found himself laughing at his little surprise, at the army he *knew* was coming. For the dead army would fear nothing . . . especially not death.

He held back a high and rising laughter as he crouched among his lieutenants on the stubbled plains. Milling before the city walls, the Kingpriest's army assembled—soldiers and mercenaries called from all corners of Ansalon.

Because the Kingpriest was afraid now. Fordus's dreams had told him that as well.

It was the time of the Water Prophet, and the War Prophet, and the Prophet King. The Prophet King's army, bound for Istar, set to marching around the lake, rising to Fordus's demand yet again, tired beyond belief and helplessy enthralled. Their torches fanned the shoreline like glowing gems set in the half-circlet of a crown. Fordus would be Istar's new monarch, and their native prince. They needed no songs, no chanting of bards to dismantle the walls of Istar. With his gallant following and the huge invisible army at his back, Fordus would scale the walls himself.

Into a city promised him before the beginning of the world.

* * * * *

Stormlight watched from the encampments, as Fordus organized his few men for the assault.

Just as he had previously seen huge, destructive storms brewing and approaching, he could see this disaster in the making—less than fourscore rebels marching against the assembled might of the city. Left behind were the children and grandfathers and pregnant wives, starved and vulnerable amid smoking campfires and tattered tents.

Even if, as a last resort, he killed Fordus, the others would still attack, propelled by the martyrdom of the Prophet King and by his final prophecies—some delirious foolishness about armies of the dead.

Stormlight had known it would come to this when

he bade Larken farewell, told her to wait with his followers while he set out after Fordus's quick-marched forces. He had looked over his shoulder once, twice, and she stood as he had left her, silhouetted against the red light of Lunitari.

"Wait here," he had told her. "I shall return."

Now he was not so sure.

Miles away, on the other side of the lake, Larken stood in the Western Pass, staring across the water toward the harbors and walls of the marbled city.

Vincus stood at her shoulder, stroking Lucas, who danced back and forth eagerly upon her gloved hand. The young man believed that Lucas was his closest friend among them, the creature most worthy of his trust and reliance. Larken's sign language was soothing and familiar, as well.

Through the afternoon he had guided Larken and her hundred followers to the Western Pass. There they meant to wait—for tidings of the battle, for Stormlight and returning survivors.

All of them sensed the disaster approaching, doom riding the air as heavily, as corrosively as the wind-driven sand in the southern *sterim*.

Oddly, the bard had set aside her drum. She held the lyre now, softly fingering its bow as though reluctant to touch its strings. Lucas hopped to her shoulder, raining amber light into the moonlit shadows, his soft voice mewling, encouraging.

Vincus tugged at Larken's tunic. *How long do we wait?* he signaled.

The bard blinked, as though awakened from a light sleep.

Three days, she signaled in reply. *Longer would be dangerous, but news travels slowly across the lake.*

If we had the glyphs . . . Vincus offered hopefully.

But Larken shook her head. *Those were the old days.*

Now we have belief and waiting. Belief in Stormlight, in his skill and resourcefulness.

Larken turned again to her harp, and the young Istarian, cast back into his own thoughts, stared north over Lake Istar.

The distant walled city reflected serenely on the glassy surface of the water.

* * * * *

With a fumbling of weapons, the ranks closed behind the Prophet King. Solemnly, as though at the beginning of a great and somber ritual, the rebels marched toward the city—toward Istar, shimmering in refracted light.

In the distance, they saw the Istarian army grouping—red banners aloft and fluttering in the rising wind. The rebels had seen these flags before, had eluded them over a world of high grass and sand, striking from the flanks and the rear with the swiftness and surprise of swooping birds.

But now, they marched to meet Istar head-on. Seventy, seventy-five warriors arrayed against ten thousand. It was certain madness.

Were it not for the promise of the Prophet King.

For Fordus had sworn their deliverance in the council fires of the night before. Never trust simple numbers, he had urged them, for I have a magic that no numbers can quell.

Now, as they saw the army assembled against them, the banners and the bright, approaching standards of four legions, for a moment it crossed their minds that the magic might fail and the prophecies go dry.

Yet each man stood at the shoulder of his cohort, and pride and illusion prevailed. Having come this far, they would not run and they would not waver.

Ahead, dressed in a dirty white robe and a brown kaffiyeh, indistinguishable from his followers, his golden collar hidden under the loose robes, the Prophet King shouted and beckoned.

Past judgment and past wisdom, they lifted their shields and followed.

* * * * *

The first wave of arrows rained down upon the rebels.

The archers perched in the distance, perhaps two hundred yards away, and their efforts, spent and inaccurate, clattered against the rebels' uplifted shields and fell harmlessly on the hard ground.

Good. The Istarians were nervous. Too quick to shoot.

The pikemen in the forward ranks lowered their weapons. Men of the Fourth Legion—old foes with a score to settle—quickened their pace, breaking into a run, a shouting, shrieking charge across the level fields where the rebels, woefully outnumbered, braced to face the first assault.

"Now!" Fordus shouted as the lines collided. Rebel weaponry flashed amid the lunging pikes, and Istarian after Istarian fell to the more mobile rebels. The Fourth Legion's attack billowed and eddied around Fordus, Northstar, and Rann, then the Istarian lines broke, the pikemen withdrew, and the distant archers showered arrows once more.

Fordus looked around him. Forty Istarians dead, but twelve of his own, as well. Even more rebels wounded, though these were rising to their feet, preparing for yet another assault.

It did not matter. Reinforcements were coming soon.

* * * * *

From the Kingpriest's Tower, Tamex looked out across the city, past the walls and onto the plains, where the skirmish unfolded. There, banners tilted and nodded as Istarian troops attacked and regrouped, then attacked again, each time suffering grievous losses, it seemed, but each time whittling away at the rebel numbers.

He could not believe the easy foolishness of this War Prophet, this Prophet King. Assaulting the Istarians with less than a hundred men.

He scanned the ranks of the entrenching rebels. Plainsman and bandit had gathered the shields and armor of the fallen Istarian pikemen. The desert robes were lost in a swirl of leather cuirasses, of burnished bronze shields so bright that the glare made the rebels hard to number, their leaders hard to identify.

Surely not Fordus, Tamex thought. Surely this is a scouting party only, and the War Prophet waited behind the lines, safe in an encampment from which he could direct the battle.

With the sight of a god couched in his crystalline eyes, Tamex scanned the horizons, his gaze reaching as far as a small rebel camp, twenty more miles of plains, and then the beginning of the forests.

Nothing.

No concealed forces. No rebel reinforcements, except for that huddled handful in the mountain pass, led by the jilted bard.

Still, the dark general refused to commit his

troops. Perhaps Fordus had surprises planned, was waiting for the full assault to unleash a veiled and dangerous tactic.

The woods themselves could be bristling with rebels.

Tamex would wait. He would hurl attack after attack at the entrenching company of Plainsmen, losing ten men, twenty, even a hundred for each fallen Que-Nara.

What difference would it make? The rebels were gravely outnumbered. Eventually, the numbers would win out.

From his balcony, Tamex signaled the herald. The mounted messenger guided his horse to the foot of the tower. Scrawling a hasty message on a scroll, Tamex dropped the missive to the young man, who took it and galloped to the gates of the city, bearing orders for Celeres, the commander of the celebrated Sixth Legion, whose soldiers waited impatiently, hidden from rebel eyes inside the city gates.

Hold ranks, the message said. *Wait until further orders*.

They would hold until he found Fordus Firesoul.

* * * * *

Weary and battle-shocked, the Fourth Legion withdrew and regrouped in the milling Istarian ranks. Again the archers drew and fired, and then for a moment the battlefield stilled, as if neither side were willing to engage again.

Then slowly, not as if they had not been ordered, but prodded or pushed or cajoled, the spearmen of the Second Legion surged over the beaten plain, two companies of the finest Istarian swordsmen following.

In a ragged semicircle, their numbers reduced to

about fifty, the rebels braced for the attack. In the center of the line, Aeleth nocked his bow, and a dozen Que-Nara readied their slings. On each flank the officers waited—Rann on the left and Fordus on the right.

It was the old tactic, straight out of the Battle of the Plains. First the rebels salted the legion with arrows and stones, then Aeleth's troops turned and withdrew, the angry Istarians charging after. At the right moment, when the Second Legion was spread out and overextended, Fordus and Rann attacked, and the rebels converged on the hapless Istarians, who turned, broke ranks, and ran under a withering assault.

Fordus, eyes alight and head high, whirled across the battlefield like a deadly wind. An arrow passed inches from his head, ripping away his kaffiyeh, and bare-headed, his auburn hair blowing back and tangling, he urged his men to pursue the fleeing Second Legion.

The enlivened rebels surged around and past him, and the War Prophet whooped ecstatically. He had turned the Istarian army, and behind his charging forces, he thought he saw wavering shapes rising out of the bloodied ground.

The dead. The army of the dead had arrived.

Hear the word of the Prophet.

*　*　*　*　*

From his vantage in the Tower, Tamex saw the kaffiyeh fall from the auburn-haired warrior, saw as well the gold collar at the man's neck.

It was all he needed to see.

"Fordus!" he whispered. Then, aloud, "Messenger!"

The next courier galloped to the city gates, where

a thousand men stood ready.

Celeres and the Sixth Legion got their order:

March. Attack. Take no prisoners.

The gates of Istar opened, issuing forth the Sixth Legion, their strides quickening with the loose, confident movement of veterans. The other Istarian soldiers parted ranks as the crack troops moved into the open field. Spears raised, shields glittering, in a matter of minutes they closed with the remaining rebels.

Twenty of Fordus's troops fell before they could return a single blow. The rebels reeled back, turned, and routed, their destination the camp, the forest—anywhere.

High in her marble perch, masked by the face of Tamex, Takhisis laughed softly. She leaned against the wall, her masculine, faceted body as hard as the stone against which it rested.

* * * * *

And so it would have been over, were it not for the storm that lifted out of the sandy fields and bore down upon the armies.

For Sargonnas had not waited and brooded and plotted to let this moment pass.

When the Sixth Legion surged through the rebel lines, the landscape burst with a hundred geysers of fire. Borne on the rising wind, the glowing ash rained havoc on the Istarian rear guard. The red banners smoldered and caught fire, and the vaunted troops scattered, screaming and burning, unable to fight what they could not understand.

In the front of the little battle the Sixth Legion slowed, uncertain. The firestorm rushed at them, passing over them in a deadly wave of fire. The stark hexagonal standards erupted in flame, and Celeres himself fell in the inferno.

On the far flank of the rebel forces, Fordus and Northstar scrambled clear of the storm. Behind them, Istarian and rebel burned on the blasted battlefield—Rann and Aeleth, the vaunted Sixth Legion fell quickly, engulfed in smoke and fire.

"The Prophet King . . ." Northstar began. He blindly searched for Fordus in the rolling murk of the smoke-filled sky.

"This way," Fordus shouted, and began to run.

"But, Fordus!" Northstar coughed. "I can't see you . . ."

The Prophet vanished in a curtain of smoke.

Spiraling to the ground, the great young guide of the Que-Nara crawled the tight circle he had already passed over, then circled it again. Cries burst from the smoke, and at the edges of his awareness, Northstar could catch the dance of flames, shadows flitting back and forth through the smothering, twilight country.

"Fordus?" he called. "Fordus?"

No answer returned from the thickening smoke.

Choking, sneezing, the Plainsman fell flat on his face. Stay low in a fire, someone had told him when he was a child. So he lay in a flat, barren clearing, clutching his rescued medallion and praying for the fire to pass, for the smoke to spare him.

When three Istarians, swords drawn, stumbled into the clearing a moment later, they found him facedown on the ground—guttering, gasping, drowning in smoke. And though they, too, were seeking refuge from the fire-storm, passage through the flame and through the strangling smoke, they were veterans and merciless, stopping long enough to follow their general's orders: "Take no prisoners."

Northstar's hand at last relaxed on the medal, and he found his way to death with no trouble at all.

* * * * *

Using his extraordinary speed, Fordus burst clear of the smoke. Behind him the plains were ablaze from one horizon to the other. Istarian legionnaires raced toward the city in panic, but Fordus passed them by, his thoughts no longer on strategy and tactics.

He was bound for the city gates, for the Temple.

And for the Kingpriest.

On whose head he would rain the fire of vengeance.

* * * * *

Upon the Tower's highest balcony, reeling in disbelief from the sudden turn of the battle, Tamex saw a solitary figure spring clear of the holocaust.

"Fordus!" he breathed, alarm changing slowly to a silent exultation as the man raced toward the gates of the city.

Oh, this is better, Tamex thought, his faceted features suddenly feminine, reptilian.

Rain on, Sargonnas. Rain on, you petty fool. May the smoke of your torment ascend for ever and ever, and may you have no rest in day or night. You cannot send fire enough to burn me, storm enough to make me seek shelter.

Now, across the burning plain, Fordus comes to Istar. He will be mine, and I shall keep my promise.

I will show him who he really is.

Chapter 22

The last morning of the Shinarion was disrupted by the smoke from the battlefield.

It began as a shifting haze overhead, a sharp musty smell in the sunstruck air. But slowly it thickened, and the merchants, the drovers, the pickpockets and vendors took to the northern streets in curiosity at what could possibly overcome the lingering smell of dead fish.

Their golden ribbons, worn in honor of the goddess, fluttered soiled and frayed. Their pockets were empty, their resources drained, for the saying held true that nobody grew rich at the Shinarion. Above all, they felt weary, tired out by the revelry, by the wheeling and dealing and the thick corruption on display in the final days of the festival.

What they sought in the streets, the air above them bristling with smoke and cinder, offered diversion.

Something was afoot in the fields outside the city. The rumors were as thick as the smoke.

So, many of the celebrants, watching the sky and listening and gossiping, missed entirely the strange, quiet warrior that slipped through their midst, borne on fleet foot through the northernmost streets of the city, his head bared, his eyes smoke-stung and ravening, his heart twisted toward murder.

*   *   *   *   *

The city lay before him like a maze of crystals, the tall reflective buildings blinding him, baffling his path to the Tower.

For long, painful moments Fordus ranged through the baffling marbled streets. Smoke from the burning plain drifted over the Istarian walls, and the new, alien landscape of man-made things clouded over, hazy and indistinct.

At the edges of his sight, just out of focus, dark shapes flitted and dodged like swamplight. The Prophet could see the gold fretting on their robes, the gold ribbons drooping over their shoulders, a testament to some forgotten god. They chattered to each other in a hidden language.

He knew the army of the dead had come to help him. They had come at last, just as he prophesied. They had invaded Istar at his orders, and were waiting for him.

Heartened, the raving Prophet wound his way through the intricate streets, past tavern and booth and vendors' wagons, always moving toward the center of the city where, through the fretted purple smoke, the looming spires of the Kingpriest's Tower dodged in and out of view.

His city. His Tower. He would meet this usurping Kingpriest face-to-face. As equals, who spoke to the gods, who commanded innumerable legions.

Into the Marketplace Fordus rushed. A passing squadron of Istarian soldiers startled, dropped their weapons, and dispersed as the haunted, robed man rushed at them silently, like some dangerous wind from the desert.

It lay directly before him now: the great Tower with its ancient marble foundations, low surrounding wall . . . and bolted iron gates.

Muttering distractedly, Fordus rattled the bars across the archway. Then, like a spider, he scrambled over the wall.

And found himself in yet another maze—this time of thick foliage and lush, overgrown garden rows of evergreen and climbing vine.

Drawing his throwing axe, Fordus cut his way through the Kingpriest's private wilderness, slashing and hacking, his anger rising until his hand touched cold marble, his axe splintering with a blind, furious blow against the strong foundation of the Tower itself.

For a moment the Prophet rested his head against the cold stone, choking and gasping for air.

Had the smoke come this far?

He looked up the Tower. Faint murky tendrils encircled the spire, and its looming top was lost in a higher haze, but directly above was the dark of a window. Instantly, resolutely, using only his fingers and toes, Fordus began to climb.

* * * * *

Through the smoke and the damaged landscape, Stormlight followed.

Wading through the burning fields, he traced a long, looping path around the flames, the massacred rebels, the ignited Sixth Legion, and found his way to the damaged gates of Istar—to the same portal through which the Prophet had passed.

Istar loomed inside them, unreal and dark. Tracing a roundabout path through the concentric pentagonal walls of the inner city, he approached its epicenter, its heart: the marble tower that housed the Kingpriest.

For that was Fordus's destination. Stormlight was sure of it. And sure, from the years of affinity between Prophet and interpreter, in which their minds had virtually melded in the search for water, for victory, for hidden dangers, that his old companion was still alive.

Alive, and bound for the end of his journey.

* * * * *

At the very window toward which Fordus climbed, Takhisis waited, breathing cold life into the crystalline form of Tamex. Her hours as a warrior of salt and sand were dwindling. Already Tamex crumbled at the edges, two of his fingers broken off in the mere act of opening the door to this sparely appointed guest chamber.

Yes, the both of them waited there—the translucent warrior and his animating spirit.

But there was another as well. A blue-eyed, balding man who cowered in the corner of the chamber, nervously fraying the lace on his high priest's robes.

Tamex had wakened him from his unsettling mid-morning slumber, where he dreamt trees as things with daggers, brooks and streams thickening and darkening in the red moon. He had almost been grateful to awaken, until he saw his visitor, translucent and eroding, at the foot of his bed.

He whimpered once, most unroyally. Fumbling for the broadsword in which the druid had instructed him all these years, he clutched the pommel desperately, but it was as though his arms had failed him—the sword was heavy and his hands trembled.

Tamex had dragged the Kingpriest from his sumptuous quarters, imprisoning him in this room to wait out the last of the night, the sunrise, the first blood of the battle. Then, coming down from the walls, the crystal warrior had joined his captive in a meeting he knew would be brief.

Now Fordus climbed the last few feet toward the window. Tamex glanced once at the Kingpriest, whose sea-blue eyes widened at the sound of something scraping beneath the sill.

Good, the goddess thought, swirling slowly in her body of salt.

Good. It is time for them to meet.

* * * * *

Fordus climbed through the window.

Moving quickly, his eyes adjusting to the shadows of the room, the Prophet saw two figures at the far door. One was Tamex, the man in the salt flats—the dark and menacing warrior who had trifled with Larken in the battle's aftermath.

Fordus crouched, prepared for battle. But then he noticed the other.

The older man—the balding, robed dignitary—he

had seen somewhere, he was certain. The face lay half-shadowed, but the curious sunlight in the room illumined the man's eyes.

Sea-blue. The color of Fordus's own.

Cautiously, the Prophet approached them, drawing his dagger.

"At last," Tamex said, with a voice that resonated out of Fordus's memory—a voice he recalled from a vision, a dream.

He shrank from its sound.

"At last," Tamex repeated, raising a cracked and crumbling hand. "I have brought us all together."

With astonishment, Fordus saw that the warrior— the *creature*—before him was a thing of rock and crystal, a breathing stone with a stone's heart.

The thing gestured toward its white-robed companion. "Bow before the Kingpriest of Istar, Fordus Firesoul."

"The Prophet bows to no man," Fordus replied coldly, knuckles whitening as his grip on the dagger tightened.

"But honor is due the Kingpriest," Tamex insisted melodiously. "A natural honor that rises . . . from a forgotten time."

"You talk in riddles, false warrior," Fordus replied.

"Who is this man, Tamex?" asked the Kingpriest nervously, and the pale man turned his faceted face to the cowering ruler.

"This is the one who would have your throne, such as it is," Tamex announced. "This is Fordus, the Desert Prophet."

"Wh-What do you want of me?" the Kingpriest stammered, backing hard against the wall and the nearby door. "I intend you no harm, no slight. Stay away from my throne!" His fingers fumbled vaguely for the latch.

"You will remain!" ordered Tamex, a new, cold authority in his voice. It delighted and amused the goddess within him to humiliate the ruler of a vast empire, but the cravenness of the Kingpriest was sometimes . . . inconvenient.

In disgust and contempt, Fordus watched the robed man grovel. Why, the Kingpriest, his chosen enemy, was nothing but a coward! A thing of robes and heraldry and high renown—no more than a figurehead, an elegant glove for his general's iron hand.

"And are you any better, false Prophet?" asked Tamex, his glittering amber eyes turned toward Fordus. "You accuse me of speaking in riddles . . . *you!* The mirage of the desert, the mockery of a Prophet!"

"You dare call me a mockery?" Fordus asked menacingly, taking a long, aggressive stride toward the warrior.

"Oh, yes, Fordus Firesoul. You *are* a mockery. And many other foolish things."

With a brittle arm, Tamex seized the Kingpriest by the nape and dragged him into full light. Now Fordus and his adversary looked at one another face-to-face, and the slow light of recognition dawned in each man's eyes.

"That is correct, Your Eminence," Tamex sneered. "The son of a slave girl you wished so . . . devoutly to forget. And when the time came, you took the child—no, you had the child taken—to the desert, and there, in a lonely place where predators stalked and the sun was nigh and merciless . . ."

"No!" the Kingpriest cried, covering his ears.

In astonishment, Fordus dropped his dagger. The world seemed to rock and tumble around him, as though once again, huge cracks opened in the earth—molten crevasses, threatening to engulf and swallow him. He staggered, fell against the far wall.

"Don't you admit the . . . family resemblance?" asked Tamex, a sinister glee in his voice. "Why, the two of you are exactly alike!"

He gestured to the Kingpriest, who had fallen to his knees, moaning and shaking his head.

"You, sir," Tamex said, "are nought but a backwater king. A ruler of ghosts and little fictions. And you, Fordus Firesoul . . ."

His amber eyes fixed Fordus once again.

"You are as much a tyrant as the man you sought to overthrow. I knew you always had it in you. In all your talk of *liberation*, you have only shackled, only oppressed!

"Yes, the two of you are identical! And you are both my creatures!"

With a cry, Fordus leapt for Tamex, but the crystal warrior tumbled into dust and swirled in a blinding cloud through the room. The dust rose, glittering and eddying, and flashed suddenly, painfully, into the Prophet's eyes.

Blinded, Fordus fell to the hard stone floor, groping for his dropped dagger, for anything. Slowly the Kingpriest approached the helpless rebel.

"Forgive me," the Kingpriest murmured ironically, as delicately he touched the collar at Fordus's neck, removing the opals with a whispered spell. He stalked from the room as the golden torc around the Prophet's neck began to sparkle, tighten, compress.

Blue lightning played over the glittering metal, which contracted with a slow, inexorable motion. Fordus, writhing and gasping, clutched savagely at the strangling collar, tried to cry out. He fell face first to the floor, stirring the unswept dust with his last, desperate thrashing. Slowly, with a choking cry, he sank into a black, abiding darkness, where the army of the dead opened their ranks to receive him. His last breath eddied on the dusty floor of the Great Tower of Istar.

At the door, the Kingpriest turned, looking guiltily back into the room. He whispered a last incantation, waving his hand over the dead Prophet, and the body of his son, now unprotected, hardened, blanched, and crumbled quickly into sand.

"I could not have done otherwise," he declared, to nothing but the dust and his conscience. "He was found in the sands of the desert, the protective torc I had devised around his neck. Sand and opals were the unsteady ground of his prophecy. Now to sand he returns, but his memory . . ."

Nor will the world remember, Takhisis replied, mingling the remains of Fordus with the whirlwind that rose and vanished through the chamber window. *We will veil it all, you and I.*

We shall decide what history is. Create it . . .

Or destroy it.

The Kingpriest reeled, as relief and sorrow and secret ambition warred for mastery in his heart.

Now do my bidding.

"But . . ." began the Kingpriest, but the last wisp of dust spiraled swiftly out the window, leaving a whisper in its wake.

Prepare for the incantation. The one we planned in the first days.

"But it is too soon . . ." began the Kingpriest, and his protest died in his throat.

Be ruled by me, the window murmured, and the chamber settled into unnatural darkness.

* * * * *

The Prophet was vanquished.

In a chaotic swirl above the Kingpriest's Tower, a

faint, reptilian outline coalescing and dissolving in the whirling sand, Takhisis watched and laughed.

Now the Cataclysm was inevitable. Now the world would begin again in chaos; the gods would be readmitted.

And she would await them all.

From her stronghold she could seize them as they tried to enter the plane. Oh, yes, they would all come—good and neutral and evil alike—but her clergy would be there before them, her way established, and the blandishments of their followers would fall on deaf ears.

The age to come would be hers entirely, and last for thousands of years.

All that remained was the Kingpriest's ritual, the binding of her spirit in the glain opals, the gods-blood stones. Then her stay would be permanent.

Never again would she be driven from Krynn.

How long yet would she wait? A year, perhaps two. The elven miners brought forth an abundance of gems from the dark.

From a dark far deeper than they imagined, Takhisis thought, and chuckled as her whirlwind moved through the cloudy Istarian sky.

But thoughts of the Lucanesti brought her back to Stormlight. The last of the rebel triad.

She would see to that elf. If only out of thoroughness.

With a shriek, the whirlwind dove into the streets of the city.

*　*　*　*　*

The elf reeled and stumbled in the wind. Full of gravel and sand, it encircled him, whirling him about, smothering him in a harsh and stinging flood.

In the heart of the wind, Takhisis swirled and

laughed.

Swept along by the bizarre sandstorm, the elf gasped and choked as the salt rushed into his nostrils, down his throat, into his eyes until, blinded, he groped his way across the Tower yards, looking for shelter, for covering, for the lee side to the pummeling wind.

Takhisis laughed again, more harshly as the pitiful creature tried to raise his *lucerna* against the gritty blast.

His hands clutched stone, mortar. With great effort, he pulled himself against the Tower wall as the wind shrieked and battered.

Like a fly in a gale he was. Like a straw in a whirlwind.

So fare all who vie with the power of a god.

Takhisis watched contentedly, her low purr rumbling in the air like thunder over Istar as the elf encrusted with sand and stone.

I have vitrified him, she thought. Only a moment more . . .

Then, from somewhere far below her, imbedded in the depths of rock and water and earth, arose a murmur, a cry of a thousand voices so deep and remote that only a god's hearing could discern it.

The miners! Takhisis shrieked and hurled hysterically against the ancient stone of the tower, sand and salt rattling against the windows. Then with a strange and urgent sighing, she settled on the cobbled streets of Istar, pouring like sand through the cracks of the stones in a sudden and frantic descent to the depths of the earth. The goddess was air and fire, salt and sand and glittering dark light, and as she poured through the crevasses of the undercity, she forgot her victory, the dead rebel chieftain and his broken, abandoned bard, and the elf translated into crusted, dried stone.

* * * * *

Deep in the tunnels beneath the city, Spinel knew that something had changed—that for a moment, and perhaps only for a moment, the chains of the Lucanesti were loosened ever so slightly.

The old elf crouched in the lamplight and whispered the last of his directions to Tourmalin. The younger elf turned away, and raced with a handful of followers down the deepest incline.

They would leave the mines collapsed in their wake, burying the fabled opals under a hundred foot of rock. It would be decades before anyone—human or elf or even dwarf—could mine them again.

Tourmalin had cleared the rubble of a hundred cave-ins. She knew how the stones fell, how a slipping shelf of rock, an ill-guided pick, or a miner's spell might collapse the whole spindly arrangement of tunnel and winze and shortwall until the ground above them shuddered as the planet fell in on itself.

Jargoon, younger still, and a band of reckless younglings, would set pick and adze to the new beams supporting five of the six adits to the opal mines.

One last entrance would remain, and the Lucanesti would use it, overpower their guards by sheer number.

Then would be the fresh light of moon and stars, and breezes the likes of which Spinel barely remembered, and the smell of cedar and open water.

With a wakened resolve that bordered on hope, the old elf rose and made for the last of the adits.

* * * * *

Sifting through the layers of shivering stone, a dark sand tumbling through the porous volcanic rock, Takhisis growled and muttered.

The least likely of saboteurs. A fossil of an elf and his cringing people.

While her eyes had been elsewhere, her powers diverted.

The dark salts settled in a lightless chamber, then rose in an eddy of underground wind, rattling eerily against the porous rock, sifting and stirring through the subterranean blackness.

The opals were lost to her now, the mines caved in and closed to her slaves and minions.

There was enough of the glain dust to bring her into the world. Not in the form and the strength she would like, and perhaps not for the thousand years she had yearned for and craved.

But fifty years. Perhaps a hundred. Enough to punish all those who had foiled her.

It would be enough.

But meanwhile the Lucanesti would pay for the time she would lose. Pay dearly and in kind, with the time they had remaining.

* * * * *

Gasping for air in the collapsing tunnels, Spinel led a handful of the Lucanesti, mainly children, toward a wavering light—the last of the entrances, supported and protected by the young elf Jargoon.

The amber torchlight was soft, almost silky through his lowered *lucerna*, and the children danced at the edge of his vision, their dark robes flickering like blades of translucent fire.

Somewhere below, Spinel prayed, Tourmalin was guiding the rest of the elves—the most skillful sappers and miners—toward the same entrance, the same faint source of light and air. Breathing a last hopeful petition to Branchala, the old elf followed the dodging, visionary light through the winding and crumbling corridors.

Sabotage had been easy. The Kingpriest had little regard for safety, and the whole network tumbled in upon itself in a vast, subterranean chain reaction. Already dust was rising from the lower corridors, and Spinel urged the younglings on, lifting a frail little elf-maid to his crusted shoulders and carrying her toward the entrance and freedom.

"Where are we going?" she asked, and asked again as the corridor snaked up through thick, glassy layers of obsidian.

Spinel soothed her with a faint, musical cooing, reached up and stroked her shoulder with a knobby hand.

He must protect these children. The fate of the Lucanesti lay in their futures.

Spinel calmed the children, stepped over the body of a battered Istarian sentry sprawled at the intersection of two collapsed tunnels. It was apparent that Jargoon had been hard at work, and judging from the face of the poor Istarian, the elves had been enthusiastically merciless.

Holding his breath, the old elf rushed up the corridor, past another felled sentry, and another. Now the entrance to the mine was fully visible, a bright arch in the receding gloom some hundred yards away.

Spinel quickened his steps.

But where was Jargoon and his company? Spinel looked to the side tunnels, all collapsed and filled with rubble.

There was no sign of the other elves.

* * * * *

Long before the Lucanesti were brought to the caverns below Istar, before the long line of Kingpriests and the city itself, a race of creatures ruled the intricate underworld of obsidian and brittle pumice and ages of dark volcanic gems.

The spirit naga had guarded these recesses diligently, jealously, hoarding the jewels, the precious metals—any stone that caught their depthless, glittering eyes—and guarding their riches out of sheer and aimless greed.

When the elves had come, the naga had fought against their invasion, and the nightmares of Lucanesti children were soon peopled with these monsters. Enormous serpents with passionless, blank human faces became the villains of a thousand elven legends, and every catastrophe from famine to collapsed tunnels was seen as the doing of the naga. Most importantly, the beasts practiced a rough and villainous magic, armed with an array of spells that blinded and stunned their unfortunate victims, so that the creatures might approach them and, using a magic more ancient and despicable still, drain their prey of all moisture, leaving the elves a mocking heap of opalescent bone.

Sinister and marginal, the spirit naga were a mystery to the Lucanesti, to the Istarians, to dwarf and druid as well.

But not to Takhisis.

Long ago the goddess had found them and made them her minions.

The time had come to deploy them.

Now, an ancient naga crouched in the shadows beside the last clear entrance to the Istarian mines, hissing with hungry anticipation. The sinuous, scaled form flashed once in the rubble.

It was answered by another movement in the darkness on the other side of the entrance.

Which was enough for the old elf to understand.

Two of them. And no sign of Jargoon.

The monsters would make short work of the children, here at the edge of freedom, unless . . .

How did the words of the chanting go? It had been a hundred years since he used the spell, four hundred seasons with his thoughts on tunnels and corridors and hidden veins of opal.

Yet it was there, if he mined his memory wisely.

Slowly, Spinel lowered the elf-child to the tunnel floor. A faint rumbling from the rocks let him know the naga awaited them, had begun their long and treacherous incantations.

"Culet," he whispered to the little elf-maid. "When I tell you to run toward the light, you will do so. It is a game we can play, you and I, but remember to keep running when you reach the light and the wind. The rest of the people will follow."

Two of the older elf-children exchanged troubled glances, and the corridor filled with the sound of a dry rustle, like something crawling over a century of leaves.

"Do not concern yourselves with me," Spinel assured them, affecting bravery, confidence, hoping his voice did not betray him. "You will follow Culet on my signal, and I shall join you later."

May the gods *grant* that reunion, he thought, his gaze flickering over the stirring darkness, the deep muttering in the rocks.

Slowly his arm encircled the elf-maid. Spinel guided her to the forefront of the company and, with a last, quick embrace, pushed her forward and away from him.

"Now!" he commanded, and the girl ran dutifully toward the light, the others following. Spinel ran with them, his old, stony bones creaking with sudden movement, and there, at the entrance to the mines, he turned to face the waiting creatures.

Mouthing an old elven incantation, Spinel stood in the opening, and a globe of amber light formed around him. As each child, each youngling passed through the glow, it was as though they were cleansed and delivered. Shielding their eyes, they burst into sunlight and fresh air and a new, unexpected life.

The nagas, unable to penetrate the amber glow of magic, groaned angrily in the darkness.

Finally, the last of the elf children leapt free of the mine. The light around him fading, Spinel prepared to follow, but the incantations, faint during his own swelling magic, grew louder and louder still.

Blocking out thought, and will, and memory.

Wearily, he took a last step toward the light, and his unveiled eyes looked longingly at the rockface, a patch of green and a spray of wildflowers in the midst of the black obsidian.

Gentian, he thought. And I had almost forgotten.

The monsters slithered into the light, blocking the entrance. Rising and arching, their pale, human faces expressionless, they chanted the last of the spell to the humped, opalescent pillar at the edge of the cavernous dark.

Spinel became one with his ancestors and the earth that covered them.

* * * * *

The Dark Queen hovered in the upper chambers of the opal mines. A black dust whirling in the stagnant passages, she heard the rumbling deep in the ground and rejoiced.

What difference did it make that the mines collapsed? That the elven younglings had escaped?

Most of the Lucanesti were far underground, easy prey for rockslides and spirit naga. As for the rest . . .

They would suffer the most in her impending return.

For now was the hour, when the Kingpriest chanted and the glain dust, the godsblood, filled with her fierce and abysmal life.

This did not go according to her schedule. Had it not been for that impudent ancient elf—the one who lay stony dead at the very edge of light and freedom—she could have planned all things in her own time.

But now, the remaining opals darkly glittering in the depths of the earth, far from the grasp of her minions, it was as good a time as any. And a time to demolish the twenty or so remaining Plainsmen in the southern passes, the fool of a slave, the bard—the lot of them.

As though a wind rose from the deepest recesses of the planet, the dark dust rose and sifted through the cracks in the earth, merging into a hulking black cloud, sprouting tail and talon and tattered wings in its headlong flight for the lofty parapets of the Kingpriest's Tower.

*　*　*　*　*

When the windows spoke to him, clouded in smoke and approaching evening, their message was urgent, angered.

Now is the time, they told the Kingpriest. *Your bride awaits you in the collected dust.*

But he no longer believed the voices. It was fear that prompted his magic, rather than hope and desire. Sifting the glain dust through his trembling hands, he began the first of the incantations, his breath enkindling the dust, spangling it with a harsh, artificial light.

I must not fail, he thought. Bride or no bride, I must do the bidding of the voice.

He did not notice the cloud of smoke and sand until it surrounded him, pouring through the stained opalescent windows and filling his chamber with a thick, choking haze.

Then the dust in his hands rose and mingled with the blinding air.

You have done your part, the voices proclaimed. *I will let you live for now.*

He knew better than to ask for the woman, the bride—the beautiful girl crafted of dust opalescent and promised him years ago by the dark voice in the clerestory. She would not come. He knew that he had been deceived. Duped and humiliated, weaker than he had ever imagined himself to be, the King-priest watched helplessly as the cloud darkened and solidified and poured out the opened windows.

* * * * *

Emerging from the temporary stonesleep that had saved him from Takhisis's anger, Stormlight watched from the foot of the Tower as a new whirlwind stirred on the balcony.

Dark sand eddied and rose, and within it the flat, opaque dust of the glain opals. The elf saw three shapes intertwined in the heart of the cloud: Tamex and Tanila, their amber eyes glittering with a strange, reptilian identity . . .

And the other one, bearded and long-haired . . .

The one with sea-blue eyes.

The shapes were insubstantial, ever shifting, sometimes indistinguishable from each other, sometimes individual and distinct. He watched, horror-stricken, and he knew, as the sand and opal dust rose into an enormous, boiling cloud above the tower, that his old friend was no more and that the fabled city they had sought together was nothing but glittering, hollow marble.

"Beware, Istar," he whispered, retreating through the streets toward the gate, the burning fields, and the people beyond who were his care and charge.

"Beware in the years to come. For the ground is unsteady."

* * * * *

Larken watched in alarm as the storm rose over the city.

A deep, brooding shadow settled on the tallest of Istar's towers, and above the marbled horizon swirled a shapeless cloud, shot through with wind and lightning.

Suddenly, the cloud took form and settled on the spire, dark wings emerging from the whirling chaos. Now a tail, now a thick, muscular neck and a strong reptilian jaw.

With a cry, Lucas vaulted into the air. Wheeling once above the mouth of the pass, he shot south ahead of the building storm. In dismay, Larken watched him fly—watched her people scatter in fear and panic.

Now a dragon perched atop the Kingpriest's Tower—a dragon of cloud and spinning sand. Slowly the wings began to flutter and fan, and Istar Lake buckled and rolled as a fierce wind passed over it. The clouds above the stormy image wheeled about it like indignant desert birds, and the air itself buckled in sheets of violet lightning, in a hundred whirlwinds racing throughout the northern sky.

What is it? Vincus signed to the bard.

Nothing. Nothing but a storm.

But the shape, Vincus insisted, his dark hands emphatic. *It looks like . . .*

Nothing, Larken signed. *Nothing more than sand and old malice.*

Then the raging wind rushed over them all.

Far worse than the *sterim* in the central pass, Takhisis's vengeance was swift and powerful. The alder trees were torn from their roots and hurled against the walls of the pass. Their crash and splinter and the cracking of rocks was deafening: all around Larken, the Plainsmen sought cover, as the wind tunneled through the Western Pass, whipping down into the plains and the desert beyond.

Now, in the ear-splitting racket of wind, in the breaking of nature, Larken took up her lyre.

The wind buffeted her frail song back to her, and, breathless, she stood in the mountain pass as the world uprooted around her.

In the midst of chaos, she found herself peculiarly calm. There was a passage—a way past the shrieking wind and the devastation. And she knew that the answer lay somewhere in her memory.

"Something perilous," Stormlight had told her. "And altogether new."

She touched the lyre's strings, gathered her last shreds of courage and hope, faced the stormy dragon and began to sing.

Fierce, driving sand clawed at her throat, and the wind took away her breath. Her voice flowed through the lyre, inaudible above the clamor, and yet she continued, singing despite the fact that no one could hear her, not even Vincus, who stood clinging to her, holding them both down, his face averted from the driving wind.

She could not even hear herself.

My song will not abandon me, she thought. It is the last thing I have against this chaos. And I will sing it until the world breaks in two.

So the song of the bard warred against the shriek of the wind for a long hour, while a dozen Plainsmen huddled in alarm and forks of lightning flickered through the distant wings of the dragon. Twice Larken lost her footing—once she even fell, but Vincus's sinewy arms hung on to her, his dark head bent above her trembling shoulder as he stood in the wind like a strong rock in the *sterim*.

Through it all Larken kept singing, sending all the verses and music she knew into the relentless assault of the wind, composing new melodies with a wild and reckless invention.

Then, slowly, the cloudy dragon drew itself up and sailed high above the Kingpriest's Tower.

As it took to the air, a wave of immeasurable silence—a last calm before the final, strangling tempest—rolled forth over the lake. The cloudy dragon followed, a swirling figure of sand, its broad wings beating slowly over the dark waters.

In that sudden silence, Larken, still singing, discovered that no sound came from her throat—none but a faint, exhausted rasping.

It is over, she thought, still trying to sing, opening her eyes and cradling the lyre like a sleeping child. I have done I can all to stand against the beast.

Then, in the flash of a second before her last frail note slipped into fear and despair, as she held to her song with her ruined voice, the cry of a hawk fractured the expectant silence.

Like a herald, Lucas flew north, out of the pass, in the fore of a great rumbling. Then the Istarian Mountains gave back Larken's lost song. It powered forth, strong, clear, and sweet, resounding with magic she had never known she possessed, of a love that sheltered her adopted people. Larken heard her own voice surge over her, echoing off the facets of a thousand rocks, a chorus magnified and deepened, echo upon echo, until the ground shook under her feet.

At the edge of the lake, the shape of the dragon began to crumble and fall, harmlessly sifting into the water. The lake hissed as it received the fiery sand, and great columns of steam rose from the boiling surface. A horrendous shriek of anger and futility drowned swiftly in the rising song, and the steam hovered in the air, molding itself into the form of a bearded Plainsman warrior, a spiked torc about his neck and a celestial sadness in his countenance.

Then a soft rain fell from the steaming clouds, and the last image of the Prophet vanished into the Istarian skies.

Neither sand nor salt would ever be the same: every crystalline structure changed to the core, all geology translated, no mineral of Krynn would ever again harbor a god.

For a moment the Kingpriest's Temple looked like a shining spire in the afternoon sun, pristine and washed.

Larken's song—her *last* song—had done this.

"So be it," she whispered, softly, absently, her thoughts on old memories, on private, inexpressible things. "Things will change after this. Things will have to change."

Beside her, to her great surprise, Vincus nodded in

agreement.

The bard had spoken, and for the first time in a long time, her people had heard her voice.

* * * * *

Another voice thundered in the depths of the Abyss.

In black fire Takhisis rolled and raged, stirring a hot and lethal wind. The godlings scattered before her, twittering like bats.

Defeated! By a squeaking bard and her attendant elves!

The darkness whirled in disarray, the Abyss spangling with bright stars, white and violet and crimson.

Slowly, the goddess enfolded herself in the leathery sheath of her enormous batwings. She soothed herself in the permeating darkness, turning and calming her anger.

Perhaps *this* time they had won.

Perhaps these petty weaklings, in their great good fortune, had postponed her entry into Krynn for a few, paltry hours.

But Fordus was dead, his insurrection crushed. She had seen to that.

Now, her thoughts burst in flames on the tough, leathery surface of her inner wings. As though she watched a mural of light take form and evolve, Takhisis guided the images, shaped them and gave them purpose.

The fire from her anger and magic splashed violet and crimson and white in the leathery cocoon of her folded wings. It shone upon a burning, collapsing city, the fall of great towers and the rending of the earth.

It shone upon the Kingpriest's Tower, where the most powerful of her minions sat amid the dust of a hundred opals, chanting the last of a hundred spells she would begin to teach him today.

Oh, it was not the inalterable future. Not yet. But in dream and insinuation, through his guilt and through the darker promptings of his heart, she would bring the Kingpriest to this spell, this moment, this pass.

Her time would still come, was still coming.

The Kingpriest would see to it all.

Epilogue

It is fitting that I, who am voiceless, should have the last word.

The druids have kept me well for a hundred years. Even in the Rending—the time that others call the Cataclysm—they sheltered me and nurtured me through the long night of this Age of Darkness.

For Takhisis won after all. She stopped the rebellion, turned us all back to the deserts south of Istar, and though the bravery of the elves prevented her early entry into the vulnerable world, she came later and more violently, when the city of Istar was torn asunder by her return, and millions died as the continent split in her fury.

In all this enveloping darkness, it has not been so dark for me.

Here in the north of Silvanost, in the last years of a long and happy life, I write in the final pages of the book Vaananen gave me in his chambers a century ago.

"One will ask for it soon," he told me. "And you will know it is right."

How was I to know that the one who would ask for it would be the one to whom it was already given? One who would return it mysteriously, giving it to me so that I might finish what had been written there?

In the aftermath of the storm and the singing, we tended to the injured and gathered the dead. Five more perished in Takhisis's rage over the mountains.

For a day we lingered, offering prayer and song. When we started our trek back through the desert, picking our way through rubble and wreckage, Larken chose as our rear guard one of the Que-Nara, a man named Raindiver, whom the others had jibed and ridiculed when, aided by the zizyphus seed, I slipped past him into Fordus's camp.

This time he was more vigilant. We had not gone a mile when word reached us up the column that Stormlight was approaching, and with him twoscore survivors—perhaps a dozen of the freed Lucanesti— all bent for the safety of the desert fastness.

They were good reunions. Plainsmen and bandit embraced and traveled south in harmony, caring for the elf-children like adopted sons and daughters. Shaken by what had just come to pass, all of them forgot the bickering and strife of the months and years in the Prophet's rebellion. They saw each other clearly for the first time since Fordus had moved on Istar.

All except Gormion. Unchanged, the bandit captain whined and menaced, lied and inveigled, but her words had lost their power to wound and divide. Now, Stormlight's followers ignored her. It was as though the curse under which Larken had labored fell on Gormion's conniving head.

She lived the rest of her short life in the desert, finally falling victim to a guardsman's arrow in an ill-advised attack on a caravan. She had always said something like that would probably happen to her.

I do not know what became of the druid Vaananen, except that he was no more after the Battle of Istar. I have since thought many times on the things he did for me. To honor him, I have taken his name as my patronym.

So his name begins this story and ends it.

Stormlight and Larken, on the other hand, created a different story.

When they met again, neither spoke of Fordus. Once Stormlight tried to tell Larken what had happened, tried to put words around what he had seen pass through the Tower window to join the whirlwind dragon in the hushed Istarian sky. But a resounding chord from Larken's rediscovered harp silenced him.

He was gone long ago, she told him.

Neither, in my hearing, brought up the subject again.

I knew by the time our company reached the plains that a new, quiet understanding had passed between Fordus's bard and his interpreter. The enmity between them had dissolved, and the distance as well. They conversed in whispers—Stormlight was delighted to hear, for the first time, Larken's speaking voice—and they spoke also with their eyes on long walks in the high, wind-torn grass as we traveled south toward the desert's edge.

Lucas the hawk, still Larken's loyal companion, kept a greater distance now, his circles expanding to surround two people instead of one.

It did not surprise me, two years later, to hear that they had wed.

I left the forest for the last time at the birth of their child—a golden-haired girl who resembled her mother, and with the strange, distant cast of her father's eyes. But by then, the Que-Nara had abandoned their fear of the *imilus* and joined in the parents' joyous celebration.

At which Larken sang.

Her voice, it is true, had been ruined according to all bardic standards. The wind and the scarring sand had taken from her a singular and famous gift.

Yet she made something new from that damaged instrument. From that tattered voice arose a depth of phrasing, a power of celebration and creativity that her clear, exalting, and sometimes mimicking voice had never owned. No, the sands never again altered or melted at her singing, nor did water rise from the desert nor storms subside. Instead, the hearts of listeners transformed. Accompanied by her harp, the new songs turned fear into faith, and sorrow into resolution and joy.

Songs of her own composing, all.

* * * * *

False prophecies passed for truth in Fordus's time. Now, a century later, Takhisis has returned. She stalks like a lion across Ansalon, and it is time for new prophecy—true words to stand against her in the continuing darkness.

I am no prophet, but this I write, in the ninety-seventh year since the Rending.

The half-elven child I saw in the desert, held by her mother as gracefully, as lovingly, as that mother once held the shallow drum of her calling . . .

That girl will be a mother as well, and a grandmother, and a great-grandmother.

For Larken and Stormlight peopled my vision, and from their line, two centuries from now, a child will be born under a gilded orb, and the Namer's task will be easy that night.

Goldmoon, they will call her.

Priestess of Mishakal. She will dry the tears and commence the healing. And she will not travel alone, but gather others to her.

And their deeds will echo like the lost song in the mountains.

Hear the word of the prophet.

Vincus Uth Vaananen
Silvanesti
97 A.C.

313